THE MINDWALKER

E J Lyle

Copyright © 2015 E J. Lyle
All rights reserved.

ISBN: 1514721511
ISBN 13: 9781514721513

THE MINDWALKER is lovingly dedicated to my dad, the original MacLaren, and my wonderful husband Jim, who encouraged me to write in the darkest times and whose courage for daily living takes my breath away.

CHAPTER ONE

On this brittle November day coming on the end of the year 1861, Buck Ross, lean, tall and just turned seventeen, rode into the town of Validation. His hometown had crept slowly out of the flat Kansas grasslands in response to the needs of those willing to travel between Independence, Missouri, and the unknown wilderness of the far west. They were drawn by tales of Indians and rich pickings and driven by the grinding need to live free and unencumbered by the opinions of others. It had a collapsible air about it, did Validation, much like that of a twelve-man-and-a-bearded-lady traveling show, but it did own the essentials.

The livery stable stood at the west end, directly facing the clapboard church, painted white but peeling at one end. The Black Diamond Saloon—the only building with a bona fide two floors—stood right in the middle of the one street, flanked on either side, at an appropriate distance, by the offices of the land agent and the doc. The general store stood near the church, most likely because Mr. Grant, the undertaker, was the proprietor of both. The stretched-out timber yard stood opposite the Black Diamond and just up the way from the water tower.

Nothing much had changed since he was last here, in August. It was a much quieter place in the fall—no panicked noises of any description, and the debris of the huge emigration west had mostly been moved by the straight-through, strong autumn winds. Buck thought the place smelled better, but he knew he would miss overhearing the conversations of hope and the tall tales of what the emigrants had left behind.

Buck was carrying a shopping list from his Aunt Jenny. She needed threads, a bolt of denim, which had finally arrived from out east, ammunition for Uncle J. T.'s new Colt revolver, and, most important, a bag of those new kind of nails that weren't supposed to rust. Finally, he was to get the best clean timber money could buy. Aunt Jenny deserved a brand-new privy, and she wanted it done before the snow hit hard, and the war, now that it had started in earnest, took all the best her new state could offer—goods and men especially. The pecan harvest had been an especially good one this year. He could get some of that hard candy that Cousin Duncan really liked, if there was any. Buck had unchristian thoughts about his older, darker, and big-bellied cousin.

"You and J. T. will have to build my new lavitorium without Duncan's help," Jenny said. "He's far too weak in this cold. It'll most like go for his chest again."

Buck and J. T. had murmured and nodded in agreement, but each was thinking Duncan couldn't dig the shithole deep enough to last a week, let alone caulk the outside enough to keep the building dry for even a month.

He had stopped just before the timber yard, where Piddlin had found a patch of grass to nibble.

Ryan came out slowly to catch the bridle. "Your mind going for a walk again, Buck?"

"Aunt Jenny sent me to get new timber. I was recalling the talk about the new privy she wants."

"Well, it's always been my experience of your Jenny that what she wants, she gets." Buck tied Piddlin to the hitching post. "This time she wants a shelf inside so she can put a bowl on it and take hot water out into it with some soap." The two men grinned and just looked at the floor. "Must have something to do with women's things, whatever they are." Buck sounded shy.

"Probably," said Ryan, wondering if Buck really was that innocent.

"She wants some kind of rail or hook to hold a towel."

Yep, Buck really must be that innocent. He made his mind up to have a word about it with J. T.

"Would you mind delivering it to her, along with the other stuff I've got to order from the store? Sometime next week be fine. Got to dig the hole first after all."

"Sure, Buck. Need to see the famous Colt 1860 your uncle bought."

"Have to get him some ammunition today. Don't know why he didn't get any in the first place."

"Most likely the army has first dibs on it."

Buck wandered out again and remounted Piddlin. "See you in about a week or so, then?"

"Most likely, Buck. You take care now." He waved his hand once at the departing tall figure and thought about how alike the boy and horse were. Both were tall and pale. Ryan was sure they had silent conversations while Buck just sat still on his horse. Piddlin would sometimes shiver or her ears would twitch just as the boy took off his slouch hat and scratched the very top of his head, all the long, dark hair flying about as he did it. It wasn't so much his mind wandered as it went for a walk into the beyond, Jenny had told him once. He wasn't slow in his thinking, and there was no harm in the boy at all. It was because he came into this world too fast, Jenny said. He'd been born in the back of a buckboard wagon, that's how they gave the child a name. Head first into trouble, Jenny said of it, what with his ma dying just as he took his first breath and his pa having been shot just before. It was God's great blessing Buck had an aunt and an uncle to take him in. For some reason Ryan felt—and maybe it was a bit of the Irish in him—that when he spoke to Buck he was speaking to two people. He shivered a bit and commenced to choosing Jenny's wood.

Buck's next stop of the day was at that most wondrous of places: The General Store and Ian Grant, Undertaker. As far as Buck was concerned, apart from all the amazements on the shelves the best treasure was a sight of Mary, the redheaded eighteen-year-old woman who happened to be the daughter of the place and therefore due much respect and honor. He loosely tied Piddlin (in case he felt the need for a quick getaway) and launched himself onto the porch while he undid the door latch. This time he ducked under the lintel, because he'd nearly knocked himself out cold the last time he was here.

"Well done, Buck. You've learned to duck." Mr. Grant was looking up at him from behind a glass-topped counter that displayed all manner of knives at one end and a half-dozen jars of candies at the other. Rolling baccy was available by the half ounce and matches could be had by the small or large box. "You look like you've grown even more, lad."

"They tell me I'm six feet two inches."

"I believe you, Buck, I surely do. How's everyone at J. T. MacGregor's Pecan Farm today?"

"All's well, thanking you. How's all here? Aunt Jenny sends her felicitations." He could feel someone hovering in the background.

"We're just fine, aren't we, Pa?" Mary, with a voice that sounded like a cat that hadn't decided whether to purr or not, materialized out of the semi-darkness in the back of the shop. It was—as everyone knew—the mortuary area. It was probably why the shop was always kept on the chilly side and never smelled of anything but the damp.

"Mrs. MacGregor's order has arrived, but I notice you haven't brought transport with you, Buck."

Buck's mouth was dry, and he thought his knees would give out. "Ryan says he'll take it when he delivers the best wood next week, so that I can build, or at least my uncle and I can build, the new outside convenience that Aunt Jenny wants before the first bad snow, and she's hoping you've got the new nails that aren't supposed to rust. Duncan's not allowed to help because he gets a bad chest in the winter, so Uncle and I will have to get a hurry on." He knew he was blushing, and knowing it made him worse. Mr. Grant was grinning at him, but all Buck was aware of was the top of the little man's hat and the reflection of Mary's face in the glass countertop.

"Here's her list. I'll pick it up after I do some business with Mrs. Haggerty at her bank."

He launched himself out the door and was grateful for the instinct that had told him to leave his horse on a loose rein. It would have been as quick to walk to the tiny bank not known to many people. But having made, he felt, such a fool of himself, well, a man could only ride away from a situation like that. It proved he had some dignity. When he arrived not a dozen steps later Mrs. Haggerty was just finishing off some land agent business with a stranger, so Buck waited. The top of his head tingled, so he paid a bit more attention. The man was very dark and looked like he'd spent years in the sun. His left ear lobe had been sliced in half lengthwise. Maybe years ago it had held an earring. He looked at the ground, tutted to himself, and smiled at his imagination. The man opened the door and paused briefly to stare at Buck, who just stared back. It was awkward, but it was over quickly.

The stranger turned to look at Mrs. Haggerty, touching the wide brim of his worn, dark leather hat. "Thank you very much, ma'am. A good day to you." The stranger had an odd way of saying his words and sounded like he had a sore throat—like he had a rasp in it. Buck had an extra moment to notice he had gray hair tied back at his neck by a leather thong. He had no eyebrows over the narrow blue eyes, which held nothing but cold. Buck nodded, waited for the man to step into the street, took off his own hat, and entered the bank. His head stopped tingling and he realized the man's presence had made him feel sickly.

"Wonderful to see you, Buck. All's well at home I trust?" The tiny woman with piled-up dark hair closed her receipt book on the counter.

"Yep, thanks, Mrs. Haggerty. I've come to put a bit of my wage aside, if that's all right."

"You had a good harvest, I hear. Are you starting the new MacGregor convenience?"

"How did you know about that?" Buck was stunned.

"Your auntie was planning the new convenience if the harvest came up to her expectations, and your uncle's new Colt if it was possible to afford both."

He was staring at her and he knew it. Did everyone know everything?

"Don't need to let your mind go for a walk, Buck. What women plan they finish, as long as menfolk don't get in their damn way." He was aware of closing his mouth as he watched her add up his bank book. "Will I keep it behind the counter as usual?"

He nodded. "Yes, ma'am, I'd be obliged."

"Tell your auntie I'll look forward to seeing her at Christmas service if the weather keeps fairly sensible."

"I will, Mrs. Haggerty. The big day's only about five weeks away now."

He gave a short nod to the lady and retreated to the street. Wondering about the stranger in Mrs. Haggerty's, he gave the top of his head a good going over before he replaced his hat. There was something familiar about the man—something he had seen or heard before. At any rate the itch on his crown warned him to be careful if he ever saw him again. Personally, he preferred the itch on his crown to the sights his eyes would see sometimes. Generally the itch didn't make him sad. Some of the stuff he had seen or heard that would happen to other people was awful bad. Aunt Jenny told him never to say anything, though. It would scare people. Buck didn't want to scare anyone, but Aunt Jenny had said that other people would either be scared of him or want to take advantage of him. No, he decided, he would never say anything—well, unless he could help stop someone dying or getting hurt. Then it would be up to the person to decide what to do.

He became aware that his mind was walking—the main reason the townsfolk were gentle with him—so as the day was wasting he strode back to The General Store to fetch the ammunition. He ducked in again, nodded to Mary, ignored the candies, paid for the whole order, and thanked Mr. Grant as he left, taking the very last of his dignity and the ammunition and nails along with him. The cloth and threads could be delivered with the wood.

"He's sweet on you, Mary, I'm telling you."

"Oh, Pa."

"Now girl, you're just past old enough to be thinking of things."

Mary tidied up and was grateful no one else was in the store. "He's odd, Papa."

"Well, yes, I grant you that his mind goes for a leap at times." Mr. Grant polished his countertop.

Mary watched Buck ride toward the livery stable. "It's more than that, Pa. It's like he's too big for his own body or something. Sometimes he stops to look at me, and I feel he's looking right into my very soul." She had stopped dusting. "It's like he knows my future but thinks he shouldn't say anything."

"I guarantee you he has plans for your future, Mary. He'll say something when the time's right, you trust me, girl." She tossed the duster at her pa and picked up a broom to give the front porch a good seeing to. Her father resisted the urge to suggest she'd be better with a shovel for the leftover snow, recognizing she had gone out to be inquisitive about Buck's comings and goings.

Mary watched him go toward the livery, probably to make sure the horse would be watered and fed before he left for home, and then ducked inside in case he saw her staring. It was a good thing she did because four rough-looking men rode past the door, setting off what was the last of any dry dust of the year, mixed with the first snow. The dirt would have clung to her skirts if the door had been open. She watched Buck striding toward the saloon, then turned to start fixing her pa's lunch.

"Welcome, Buck. Come in, lad, come in. You're looking strong, boy. Yes, good and strong." Pete, the owner and proud proprietor of the Black Diamond Saloon, was the only man in town who was tall enough for Buck. That was probably why he didn't make comments about height. "Jenny will take me to task, but can I offer you a warming shot on this bloody cold day?"

It was the first time all day Buck hadn't seen his own breath. He was grateful for the warmth of the place. The Black Diamond was built to purpose, the long L-shaped bar containing two wood-burning stoves. There wasn't much to drink on display. Two wall lamps framed the mounted pair of Sharps rifles above the bar. Pete "The Knife" Tait kept them there as a warning, not a threat. They were always clean, and everyone knew it. The saloon always smelled of lemon oil, for some reason.

Buck pushed his nickel over the counter to indicate acceptance of Pete's offer. "Nah, Buck, call it a birthday present, being I couldn't be there and all."

Buck's day was looking up. "Now, you'd better have some chicken soup and a chunk of bread, just to keep your innards warm for the journey home. Then you can say I gave you some proper vittles."

Pete had an astounding belly laugh that could drown out some of the noises from the bedrooms upstairs. The soup turned out to be chicken and vegetables of various consistencies, but once he added extra salt it tasted mighty fine. Pete's lady friend and business partner Miss Poppy was one of those fine buxom women who could cook a feast out of any old thing. She ran her kitchen on joy and her upstairs girls on strict motherly love. She refused to call them the new term of "hookers." To her they were still fallen doves—so much more genteel. She waved to Buck briefly from the end of the landing.

The dark man from the land agent's office appeared on the long top landing, came down the stairs, spurs jangling on his black but old leather boots. He found a seat at one of the round, green baizes-covered tables facing the door. He dragged the brass spittoon a bit closer, dropped his tobacco pouch on the table, took a small pinch, and filled a chunky, deep-curved white pipe. He lit it thoughtfully, warming the bowl as he did so. His actions spoke of a man needing some thinking time. The few others in the place tried not to watch, or catch his eye. Pete brought him a bottle and a shot glass. All Buck heard was a grunt from the man. He felt a lurch in his own stomach and tasted what he'd just eaten. The man was making him feel unwell again. A cold sweat trickled down his back and decided it was time to get home.

Pete followed him out. "Stay well away from that man, laddie, him and his four cronies. They're on the wrong side of the law, such as it is; may even be pro-slavers. Stay well away." Buck nodded and walked to the stable. He picked up Piddlin, who shivered as soon as he sat down.

The four cronies Pete had warned him about looked him up and down as they walked from the bunkhouse to the saloon, and his head started to tingle like it never had before. He took off his hat, tucked his fair, bowl-cut hair behind his ears, and out of the corner of his eye caught Moon Feather, his Cheyenne spirit guide, watching him.

She only ever showed up to warn and protect him. The first time was when Duncan told him the reason Aunt Jenny said bees could sting was to keep him away from the honey in the tree. Duncan had said Aunt Jenny wanted to keep the sweet golden stuff all to herself, and all he had to do was reach his hand down. Moon Feather stepped between him and the tree and motioned him not to. She seemed to shimmer in the sunlight. Duncan must have seen her, too, because he ran to his mother screaming about a loose Indian. Young children could see plenty before they were told not to. Buck was only about three, but he felt very happy to walk out of the pecan orchard holding Moon Feather's hand. He accepted she was his spirit guide.

Now he settled into his saddle, nodded to her in acknowledgment, patted the pale dappled gray on Piddlin's neck, and told her they'd better make good time before dark. He rose up in the saddle and asked her to trot. It wasn't like him to fret, so to stop his mind talking to him he thought instead about the new boots he needed to make for himself. He'd like to cut the leather before he started the privy in the morning.

CHAPTER TWO

Once he got to the Kansas River he was only half an hour from the farm. An urgency came over him. He felt sick and began to breathe the way he did before he had one of his "future looks," as Aunt Jenny called them. Piddlin picked up on the fear building up in his rider. Buck lifted himself out of the saddle to give his horse a good chance to gallop for home. He was aware of watching the ground rush past him as he bent over the neck of his mount and willed her to go faster. All they had to do was bend around the corner before he could see the home gate and the painted sign above it. His head was really bothering at him, and Piddlin's ears looked like they were attached to two different animals. She was edgy and acting all nervous—snorting and puffing. He kicked her sides and let loose her reins. If it were possible for a horse to fly, Buck was sure she could. They raced like they were being chased by a full troop of graycoats.

Now, in the distance, he could see that Aunt Jenny had her head low in the water trough for some reason. J. T. was nowhere to be seen, Duncan was absent but most likely in the cabin enjoying his afternoon nap. There was still plenty of life left in the day, but there was a quiet in the air that wasn't natural. Jenny should have heard him pounding into the farm on the hard, cold November ground of the trail home. She should have been shouting at him for mistreating his horse. J. T. should have been temporarily stirred from his normal walking stupor (caused by too much hard work) and stopped to stare for a minute. Duncan should have jumped out of bed to enjoy the telling off he'd be getting.

Piddlin slowed herself, still agitated and puffing. She walked right past Jenny to the front door of the cabin. J. T. lay halfway outside, his right arm reaching toward his wife, broken bones of two knuckles showing as if something had been ripped from his hand. Most of his head was missing; the top bit. What had happened to Duncan? Buck shouted for him, and he kept shouting for help as he slid out of his saddle. Jenny's head was floating sideways in the trough, the long, graying hair trailing behind her, no longer framing her small, chubby face. He rolled her over, the water sloshing over his boots and making a cold day colder. Her chemise floated beside her as if trying to reattach itself. She stared at him with clouded blue eyes—anger still in place. Her throat had been slashed and her jaw broken; the lower one didn't seem to fit the top of the mouth, and there was a sign that she had bitten through her bottom lip with the few good teeth she had. He pondered why she was showing marks on her wrists.

"Yes," he whispered as he gently crossed her arms over her substantial white bosom, "those are definite fingermarks."

He hastily pulled down her skirts and wondered why they had been above her waist. Only part of him noticed the red stains on the inside of her nearly white leggings. Again, he screamed for Duncan.

"Oh, God, help me." His legs weakened, so he gave in to his feelings and sat on the cold, wet ground at Jenny's shoeless feet. He stared at Piddlin without seeing her, trying to comprehend what had gone on.

Where was Duncan? He called for him, he searched for him, he screamed for him. He looked around every one of the fifty pecan trees Jenny had come across all those years ago. They reminded her of the chestnut trees in Scotland. It took Buck a while to realize he'd been crying so much his throat hurt. He wandered into the middle of the ancient forest of tall pecan trees, trying to understand. He was alone. He had to do the right thing. Piddlin was fretting. Yes. He should do something normal first. He still hadn't taken off her saddle. He gathered up Piddlin's reins and led her to the small stables, where he heard Thunder stomping and snorting. Duncan's horse was tied into his stall. The tall, old animal must have heard the commotion and really got himself into a state, judging by the panic in his eyes and the damage done to the railings. Buck thought the best thing was to let him run free for a bit so he could let loose his worries. Thunder didn't like a pat on his neck and shied away. Buck opened what was left of his stable door, smacked his rump and shooed him to freedom. He started and stopped a bit before he decided to make for the river. Buck sighed in sympathy. "Just checking to see if you were safe first, eh, old fella? Well, I'm not too crazy about Duncan either, Thunder, but I'd still like to know what happened to him."

He wondered why the criminals who did the rest of the damage hadn't stolen Thunder. The well seemed to be intact, as was the privy, but most of the fencing was gone and the small chicken coop that Jenny was so protective of had been smashed to fragments. God alone knew where the chucks were.

He became aware of Moon Feather while he was caring for the horses. She said nothing because nothing was needed, but he felt better once he realized she'd been there all the time. He must be settling down a bit if his awareness was returning.

It came to him that his aunt and uncle should be buried in the tiny boneyard that had been set aside for family. Aunt Jenny's mother was there, along with his parents. Alasdair Ross and Johan MacGregor died the nineteenth of September 1845, the same day as his birthday. The carving said they were murdered, and something about the love of money. It still made no sense. Buck didn't have any money apart from the silver and gold bits that J. T. had given him to hide in the latrine. He'd been told not to tell Duncan because it was the only inheritance Buck was likely to get and J. T. wanted to help if he could. Jenny and J. T. were land-poor.

He finished feeding and watering Piddlin, took off his checked wool shirt, the one he'd put on clean this morning after he'd given his face and hair a wash in case he saw anyone that mattered in town. Jenny had clucked a little but smiled and let him get on with it. He stopped to let his mind go for a walk, this time into the not-too-distant past, about the man in the bank, but cut it short to find the shovel. He shouted for his cousin a bit more, then found what he was looking for and went to the yard to dig the graves. The sun was setting rapidly now, and Buck wondered why it always seemed to speed up while it was setting and sneak up on him in the morning before exploding into life. He didn't want to leave Jenny and J. T. as they were overnight. Thinking he could go for help in the morning, he probably didn't dig as deep as he should. The place was so quiet. All he could hear was the sound of his own breathing and the slap of the shovel as it dug into the hardening dirt. After he burrowed three feet down for each of them by about six long and two feet wide he was exhausted and had to go back to the cabin, where he hoped he could find some water to drink. There was always the well and he could see the rope, so maybe the bucket was still attached. His hands burned with cold.

Putting the shovel against what was left of the old wooden fence surrounding the yard, he took a deep breath before straightening his long back and marching the forty paces or so, stepping over J.

T. without looking at him too closely. He heard flies, he thought, but that may have been his imagination. He covered J. T. with one of the pecan husk rugs and took another to Jenny so she could lie on it overnight. Maybe she would like her favorite crochet blanket to be placed over her.

There was a pot of soup on the small range. He added a bit more wood to turn up the flame. There was a jar of water, so he swallowed a mite and then added some to the lukewarm meal. There wasn't much bread left; he broke it into what was going to be his dinner. Without thinking, he said the little prayer of thanksgiving that Jenny had always insisted on…

"I saved you some." Duncan's girlie voice snuck up on him from the dark back corner of the cabin, where his bed was.

"I called for you." Buck didn't turn around. He felt a level of anger that was new to him. He didn't know anger could be a stranger to him. Anger had its own life. He could stand beside it and let it walk with him. Anger was quite possibly a friend. Funny how it made him feel as if his back were straightening and his eyes growing hard.

"I was scared."

"Who did this?" He held the pot of soup in one hand and a spoon in the other as Duncan lit the small paraffin lamp that always seemed to choke the atmosphere with black smoke.

"How would I know?" Buck sat at the table to eat straight from the pot, no longer fussed about how hot it was.

"Did you see?" His voice was steady.

"I saw them coming, and Ma told me to hide in the wood shed and not to ever come out until I knew I was safe."

"So you knew you were safe after you watched me dig the graves?" Anger was beginning to smile inside him. He knew it would one day soon show its teeth—it had been growing for nearly eighteen years.

"I knew to fix you something to eat."

"You'll help to take them to the final resting place, then. In the morning." Anger was getting damned hungry.

"I'll do that."

Buck finished his beef stew, not soup as he had thought, in silence. The bread was soggy. He sucked at it.

"Your ma's dead. Your pa's sprawled in the doorway and you ain't bothered, are you?" Duncan sat down opposite, in what had been J. T.'s chair. Jenny had always sat with her back to the stove. He folded his arms to rest his head and began to make sobbing noises.

"I turned out Thunder. Had the spooks, I guess, because he ran for the back of the trees near the river." Buck hadn't raised the pitch of his voice. He was only stating a fact. He tapped his spoon a bit on the table—keeping a beat to control his heart. Moon Feather had taught him this many years ago to help him while someone blamed him for something Duncan had done.

"That's good, thanks." Duncan wiped his nose on the tablecloth. "I'll put a bit more wood on the fire for you."

Duncan and fire were not a good mix. Once he'd tied dried, long grass to a dog's tail, lit a match to it and watched the dog chase it to put it out. He had laughed until he peed himself. J. T. had poured water over the poor animal, but it died later—of shock, probably. No one ever said anything to the perpetrator, but the story would mark him for a very long time, if not the rest of his life.

"Why would I want a bigger fire? You can help by throwing a matt under where Jenny's going to have to spend the night. Then we can toss her blue blanket over her to give her some dignity. That all right, Duncan?" Buck couldn't look at him, so he put his dishes in the basin and wiped his hands on his pants. He picked up one of the matts from the floor, handed it to Duncan and then got the special one, the one Jenny had spent months making for the day she had a settee and could use it as a throw for visitors.

"You've got snotters on your chin."

Buck took a large step over his uncle while Duncan minced past a leg and a shoulder, not having the length of leg of his gangly cousin. Buck used his sleeve to clean himself, but he glared at his cousin's back.

"We'll have to figure a way to get her out of the trough without making her messier than she is. Ma was always tidy, wasn't she?"

"Whatever we do, the sun is just about to vanish into tomorrow, so let's get a hustle on, cousin."

Buck unrolled the matt on the ground beside the trough. Buck took the bottom half with Duncan at his mother's head.

"We'll move her on three. Good thing she taught us our letters and numbers." Duncan had changed his voice from that of girlie to grown man. "One, two, and three." The boys laid her onto her side, but both got a jolt when she groaned. "Dead people do that sometimes, Buck. Pa told me once." Still, Buck put his ear to her cold mouth and nose to see if he could hear any breathing.

"Better give her the blanket now, Buck."

He stood up and Duncan tossed it over her. Buck tucked her in as best he could around her head and feet.

"Do you want to say any words?"

"As you said, the sun's just gone so we'd better see to Pa. We'll have time for words when we lay them to rest tomorrow."

Buck followed him into the cabin, anger retreating into a shell of grief for just a flash. Duncan flung the matt over J. T. and announced he was going to turn in. There were bacon and eggs in the larder outside, he said, if Buck wanted to have some in the morning. Duncan knew he hated eggs. My, oh my, how Duncan could change from minute to minute, so he was glad to see the fat little bastard retreat. His anger was building into rage, and Buck felt the desire to kill him.

He went out for a while to seek Thunder and found him creeping around the stable. Piddlin whinnied at him. Buck led Thunder in and fed and watered him. Thunder stomped a bit and swished his tail, but he had relaxed. Buck hoped he would tolerate being groomed in the morning. The young man returned to the house, put more wood on the fire now that it was probably safe to do so, and began to carve the names of Jenny and J. T. and the date they were murdered.

It was a turning point in Buck's life. Duncan now owned the farm. It was time he left, anyway, especially if he needed to take a wife. He would have to find somewhere to live while he made arrangements for his future. The thought of being at his cousin's beck and call made the top of his head tingle again. Jenny would have been furious if she'd seen Buck wearing his hat in the house so he removed it very quickly, in case she was still here. He swore he heard her laugh. Once again his imagination, he thought. He carved November 29 1861 on their crossbar and made his mind up to use one of the special nails Ryan had given Jenny as a sample to pin the cross together after their burial the next day. He fell asleep in the chair and was woken by Duncan going out to the privy. Then he heard the horses getting restless, so he jumped up to get J. T.'s rifle from the bracket above the door. It was missing. Buck left the cabin in time to see Duncan walk both horses from the stable.

"You sleep light."

"Where you going with my horse?"

"Just thought I'd get an early start."

"I can see that. Where exactly are you startin' for?"

"I like the idea of south. It's warmer there, I'm told."

"Fine. Don't blame you, but leave my horse."

"Don't think so. Might need a spare, after all."

The boys were now face to face and standing between the two horses as Duncan held their reins.

"Can't leave just yet, still got things to do, ya know?"

Buck had never punched Duncan in spite of the many grudges, but this time that odd feeling of cold anger gave him permission. There was a prolonged tussle because fat rolls once it's on the ground, but once Duncan was down Buck had every chance at knocking him out. After well-aimed three punches at Duncan's nose, Duncan was spluttering and bleeding. Buck picked him up as best as he could by the collar of his jacket and marched him to the trough Jenny had died in. He ducked his head a couple of times.

"Now you're at least cleaned up, you slimy pig." Buck slammed the forehead of the horse thief into the edge of the trough, hoping to knock him out. It worked. He rinsed his hands and dried them as best he could on Duncan's clothes. He turned his back and returned to the horses. Thinking they might enjoy spending time with each other in the trees, he removed their saddles and reins and let them wander.

It was dawn. Time to get on with the job. He didn't want to be on the farm one more minute than he had to, so he didn't bother to dig the graves any deeper. He managed to get J. T. into his grave by dragging him. Maybe it was a good thing Kansas was so flat. Jenny was a bit more difficult, mostly because burying her was harder for him. He got the cross he'd made and, after covering them in with another matt, he said a few words he could remember from church and went looking for Piddlin.

His job was done here. He checked Duncan on the way out. He was breathing but still out cold. Buck felt he could safely pick up his stash from the privy.

CHAPTER THREE

There hadn't been much to rescue from the farm, but he did salvage a skin of water, a blanket, a wool-lined jacket, his faithful old buffalo hide, and J. T.'s cutthroat razor. As usual, he checked that his Colt dragoon was well packed in the bottom of his saddle bag. He'd never had to wear it, but if he was going to head for the hills he'd better be prepared. He didn't know why he took the razor—it wasn't like he had a good enough growth for it. He took a little hay and oats as a treat for Piddlin, who hadn't been at all hard to find. One whistle brought her to him.

He saddled her and left, noticing Thunder relaxing well back in the trees. His owner could recapture him once he woke up. The gelding's black color would make him stand out against any coming snow so if the poor animal was trying to hide he wouldn't last long.

"Unlikely we'll be back now, Piddlin. Let's see where we can go to keep out of the snow." The sky was full of slow-moving clouds, gray turning to black. He slowly breathed in the cold air past his gritted teeth in order to heat it, enabling him to taste the weather before the frost got to his lungs. Moon Feather taught him to use all his senses to increase the level of his sixth one. He could hear himself making a steady hiss as his shoulders lifted. Snow on the way—definitely—he could smell the damp threat. He controlled his exhale. The wind was settling, no doubt before it came back to create a white, swirling nightmare, so Buck gently encouraged Piddlin to move away from the carnage behind them, to extend the distance from their past.

They took a track on the farm side of the river, avoiding any people or overly familiar places. He glanced behind him once and saw Moon Feather raise her arms to Heaven. It seemed she was sending him one of those blessings people were given in the little church. He sent his mind for a long walk, a daydream of his future, but Piddlin seemed to keep her mind on her job. When he brought himself back from thinking about Mary he discovered that he was in a forest he had always meant to come to but never could because of work or some such reason. Buck wasn't used to feeling closed in. The smell of dead leaves crunching under Piddlin's hooves combined with the sound of birds taking flight from the trees, made him feel squirrelly. The clouds were darker and lower.

For the first time in days, his head wasn't tingling. He could remember Jenny saying that this sense was his birthright and would stay with him forever. His mother wasn't there to protect him, so she'd left him that legacy instead. She warned him he'd never be able to tell his own future. The sixth sense didn't work that way.

He shivered himself back to the present. He was cold, and the sun was setting ahead of him. Large flakes of snow were starting to fall on his hat, and the wind found them when they came into a more open stretch of forest. The young man observed more frequent flakes melt one by one on the back of Piddlin's neck. Both of them needed shelter, and damn quick. He looked for branches lying about that he could use to build a windbreak if nothing else, and made a movement that told Piddlin he was going to dismount.

But the horse seemed to sense something and did an unscheduled lope for a few paces. Buck tried again. This time the horse gave an even stronger warning she wasn't going to listen. She wasn't normally so ornery, so he pulled up his collar and let her have her head for a little. She stopped. She just plain stopped and shook her mane, probably to remove the snow that was beginning to rest on it.

Buck cursed his tight boots and slid off the saddle to find he was at the entrance to a cave. He'd heard talk about a series of white caves near the woods and up a ridge, but never paid much mind.

"Clever girl, Piddlin. Much obliged, as they say. Looks like there may be room inside for both of us." He ruffled her mane and enjoyed her turning to him as she blinked some flakes from her eyes. Her ears were alert but not twitching—and neither was the top of his head.

It was dark inside but big enough for both of them to spend the night or even longer if the snow took its time to blow out. He took her by the bridle and slowly walked in, hoping that he wouldn't come across a bear—or worse. Retrieving a bit of the hay he'd taken with him he took a match from his tin box to light it, then relaxed. The cave was empty. Someone had been here not long ago and made a small circle of stones to mark a fire. He tossed the lit hay into it and kicked about for small sticks, dropping Piddlin's reins onto the earth away from the fire.

He wondered where J. T.'s rifle had gone. Duncan didn't have it in a saddle holster, he knew that for sure. He had the ammunition for the Colt, but where had that gun gone? It wasn't on J. T. Or Jenny. Why had someone attacked the farm in the first place? Who did it? Buck's brain was full-on busy. The Bible was missing, too. He'd wanted to say real words, and he couldn't find the very book that Jenny had taught him to read from. His fire was getting big enough to warm him. He dug out the accouterments of life: a pot and a steel mug. He poured some water into the pot, the last of what was in the skin he'd taken from the farm, and put it on the fire while he explored.

Most caves like this had a Native hunting pack stashed in it somewhere, so he searched for it. He knew when he found it, as he did, that it would have a bow, arrows, and another blanket, perhaps even more food. He took nothing that didn't belong to him, although he did borrow the blanket. It was made partly out of hide and partly from fur of some kind, and whether it carried ticks or fleas didn't matter. With any luck the weather was too cold for them to survive.

He removed Piddlin's saddle, dropping it beside the fire. Using a bit of hay, he gave her a rubdown of sorts, threw his own blanket over her and fed her a nosebag of oats. He wondered how he could water her. The snow would melt a bit if he brought some inside. They might both have to use it.

Beef jerky was hiding in the bottom of his saddle bag. He sat sideways on the saddle, chewing it, while he waited for the water to heat, adding dry sticks that were conveniently lying near an old fire farther back in the cave. Maybe he should build some kind of windbreak—but no, it was too dark for that. The wind, just as he thought it would (being a true Kansas expert in these things), was rising into a frenzy, sneaking around the corners of the cave, throwing the occasional dry twig to him. Snow appeared to be flying like Jenny's clean white sheets in the spring wind—almost, as she would tell anyone, directly horizontal. Jenny knew big words like that.

He poured himself a bit of hot water, grateful for the heat on his fingers. He left his boots on, dreading how his feet might feel once he took them off and not being willing to find out if he could get them on again later. He rubbed his toes as best he could and pulled his buffalo hide around his shoulders.

A Native appeared at the mouth of the cave. He wasn't overly tall, but he was broad enough to block the last of the sunlight.

They stared at each other. He flipped back his fur-lined hood, exposing large black-brown eyes, receding hairline, and a long, thin ponytail. Piddlin started up. The Native placed his hand on the horse's neck. She settled.

"Getting cold, young man. Is there room at your fire?"

"Yes, sir. Sure is. You the owner of the hunting pack?" Buck stood to meet the man, not knowing whether he should be as nervous as he was. There was no tingling. No tingling at all and Piddlin was calm.

"No." He came to the small fire, stoked it until it took a real grip, and then sat on a matt he had magicked from the pack he was carrying. Buck wondered where he'd learned to talk American.

"You got any coffee?" The deep voice rumbled but wasn't loud.

"No, sir." Buck wondered what it was about the man that made his Sunday manners come out.

"I do." He conjured a coffee-making pot from the pack.

Buck lowered himself back down onto his saddle. They watched each other's movements.

"You want a smoke?"

"No, sir."

The Indian smiled at him and then rumbled a laugh. "You don't drink coffee, you don't smoke, how do you feel about women?"

"I'm sparkin' Mary in Validation." Buck felt defensive.

"Glad to hear it." The Native dusted the snow from his leggings. "You sure you don't want coffee to go with that tack?"

"Well, if you're offering."

The man poured two mugs of it and offered one to him. It felt so warm on his hands, much better than just plain hot water.

"You are Buck."

"Yes." He nodded, wondering how the Native knew. "You are?"

"Mark."

"Mark? I thought Natives had fancy names."

"It was given to me in the Christian school. Luke and Matthew had been taken. I got Mark, and my brother got John."

"Is that why you talk so good? Because you went to the school?"

"I talk my own language better." The Indian made himself comfortable. "My daughter came to get me. She said you need help. She will meet us here after I help you to clear the dirt of your day."

"Who's your daughter?" Buck voice was so loud in the cave it made Piddlin wake from what had clearly been a deep snooze. This time he soothed his own animal. Mark grunted an approval when he sat again.

"Moon Feather is my child. She came to tell me of the darkness during your day. She has asked me to help you clear your memory of it so you don't drag it behind you, so you don't let it bump into you when you're not needing it."

"My aunt and uncle were killed. My cousin Duncan had something to do with it. I don't care now. I am just moving on, leaving, getting away, and carving new wood somewhere else. I'll start once the snow lifts."

Mark's brown eyes looked deep into him. The smoke from the fire began to smell like sage. "It is time you began to learn your path."

"I can go wherever I want now."

"You are born to be a healer, young Buck. I will teach you your first steps. I will teach you how to heal yourself." The fire crackled and spat.

"I'm never sick."

"No, but you have been wounded and more wounds will come to you. They are the price you pay for the abilities you will collect later. Now, listen to my voice. I will return you to yesterday." Buck felt Moon Feather join them.

Mark's voice dropped lower and became slow. He was telling a story of trees and colors. Buck's mind started to see what he'd come across on the farm. It was like one of those screen shows he'd heard of. One picture at a time stuck with him. First J. T. with his head shot off. It would probably have been done with a rifle. Was it his own? Then Jenny with her head in the trough. Her eyes were open in fear. Buck couldn't stop his mind looking at all the blood on the inside of her legs. He recalled her buttocks. They had been sliced open from front to back, from her ladies' areas to the bottom of her backbone. Why would anyone do that? Why? Jenny had always been a pure woman. Duncan's face came to his mind. Did he have something to do with it? Had he organized the raid of his own farm? None of the animals were left. Not even one of the six chickens Jenny was so proud of.

Buck shivered all the way down his back.

The fire was now big enough to show the paintings of buffalo and Natives on the walls of the cave. Shadows created by the flames made the tribe appear to be moving. He enjoyed watching the action, feeling he could hear the hunting cries and whoops of command as the chiefs organized the hunting party. All three, Moon Feather, Mark, and Buck were taken to another world. The protective aroma of sweetgrass and sage enveloped them, the beating of his heart a silent, steady drum. He felt Piddlin come closer, expecting to join them wherever they were going, but which world were they in? Buck felt a peace he didn't know existed. He felt settled. Changed.

At dawn, on a day that didn't show any sign of snow, he had a deep dream that he stood to face the sun and howled into it. He had come to terms with things. He had been given many gifts by the Great Spirit. He must carry them with a firm but gentle grip, and it was up to him not to share them with others until he was asked to. He would not be able to tell his own future, only create it as his life came to him. He would most likely walk alone. Mark was still with him. Piddlin was standing behind him and shivering. Moon Feather had moved to the back of the cave.

"Have I been asleep?"

"Some tribes would say you've been on a vision quest. It's taken three suns to finish." Mark said. "Here, have a sip of warm water. We'll have some bacon before we head back to Validation."

The snow had ended. The light meal was taken in silence.

"Come." Her father, a man in white robes of what was probably arctic fox and many other furs, re-saddled Piddlin, and tossed Buck onto it as easily as a sack of fresh cornmeal. He must be a well-traveled man, this Mark. How else would he have white fur?

"It's a fine thing you care for your horse, boy."

The poor horse was shivering like she meant it, but she tolerated being remounted. Mark took the reins as Moon Feather strode ahead, leading them to what Buck would regard as safety. The Native village was closer, but going there would have caused trouble on both sides. The men of the tribe would have wanted the horse, the women the skins and pots, and Buck would have wanted to keep what he owned and go back to his own tribe in Validation.

"You have done well, boy."

Mark was speaking, not to congratulate, only to acknowledge.

"Are you real?"

"Only my daughter is in the spirit world. You and I are in the same one."

"We're alive, ya mean?" Buck felt sore all over. "Just tell me one thing please Mark?"

"If I can."

"What is that white fur you're wearing?"

Mark laughed gently. "I'm a trader. Two arctic fox for one buffalo pelt. Got them in Sault Ste. Marie, Hudson Bay Company." He was shaking his head. "Moon Feather's mother was very angry." The party moved quietly, each focused on their own thoughts. "Your people have named you well. You are a true Mindwalker. You listen and think before you act, especially when you are warned what will come of things. It is not to be an easy life for you." Mark started a soft chant.

Buck's head fell on his hands resting on the saddle horn in front of him. Mark's arm came from behind to support him in his seat. Vaguely, Buck could hear the elder crunching through the snow beside him and speaking softly to Piddlin in what he thought was most likely the Native's own language.

It looked to others like Piddlin had done the rescue all by herself because Mark stopped just outside of town and of course no one else saw Moon Feather guiding the old mare.

Joss, the stable apprentice, heard the noise of a strange horse and poked his head around the corner to look at the cause of the commotion. He ran across the paddock to catch Buck as he slipped out of his saddle, and shouted for help from Pete, who was in the feed barn.

"What the hell, Buck? What the hell?"

"Piddlin. Take care. Piddlin."

"Lad's passed out, Joss. Take the horse out of this wind and then go for the doc."

"I saw Ryan moving about. I'll get him on the way."

"Nah. I'm here, Joss. Just get the doc."

Joss slipped and slid all the way down Main Street in the snow, shouting for Doc the whole way, so other folks were mighty disturbed. People stuck their heads out of windows and doors, asking what was the to-do.

"Buck and horse half-dead," he yelled into the wind.

"Who?" Mrs. Dawson, the baker's widow, sounded angry.

Joss kept running and sliding. He was about to bang on Doc's door, but Doc had heard the ruckus. He was halfway dressed and running toward Joss.

Pete and Ryan had moved Buck onto a haystack near the wood burner. Buck was mumbling names and shouting out nonsense about murder, but the two men put that down to fever. Joss went straight to Piddlin and began a warming rubdown, applying lineament to her legs and then giving the horse food and water. He threw a warm blanket over her. Joss thought the saddle was ruined with all the frost and snow but with the right attention he knew that the horse would be fine and that once the doc and all the busybody women in town had notified Jenny, Buck would be even better. He smiled to himself. Duncan wouldn't be pleased about his ma concerning herself with Buck. No doubt there'd be trouble from that direction.

Mrs. Haggerty joined the company.

"I saw you chasing toward the barn. Thought someone was real poorly." She always had an air about her that ensured people paid attention. Some said she used to be a school marm, but others weren't so charitable about a lone widow woman traveling on her own to set up shop, even if it was government business.

"Well, Doc, what's to do with him, then?"

"I'll have to take him to my office to have a good look, but I can tell you he's got a fever."

"Well that's why you're the doctor, then. You get away with stating the obvious. Take him straight to my office, please, gentlemen. There's a good, draft-proof room in the back where I do my accounts, and I have a long settee he should be comfortable on until we can take him back to Jenny."

There was no argument. They put a saddle on one of the horses, put Joss in the saddle, then Buck across his lap, stomach down. Someone threw a buffalo hide over him.

"Look at the state of his boots. Golly God, they look like they've walked the whole way, wherever he's been." Pete put his hand out to touch them, causing the first sound Buck made—a yelp.

"Let's go. He'll be fine when he gets to my place." In a jiffy Buck was in a warm room for the first time in over four days. Mrs. Haggerty stirred the fire.

"Thank you, gentlemen, you can go about your business. Doc and I will let you know how things are doing. Try to get a message to Jenny, of course." She held the door open for them.

"We'll have to start by cuttin' off his boots. They look so tight they might be cutting off his circulation. I hate to think what his feet will be like. That was one definite scream, that's for sure."

"Would his feet be bad enough to give him a fever?" Mrs. Haggerty asked.

"Wouldn't be the first time I've seen it, not the first time."

Both of Buck's feet were white with frostbite. The little toe on his right foot had been trapped underneath the fourth one and was starting to turn black.

"I'll give him a few hours to see which way it goes." Doc looked at Mrs. Haggerty's shocked face. "I may have to take it off."

CHAPTER FOUR

Duncan put his hand out and found the edge of the water trough. He opened his eyes, shook his head purely out of reflex—and was not rewarded for his effort. He puked as he watched the home in front of him move in and out of focus. For the next little while he sat still on the cold, wet ground, his vomit the only warm thing around him. He watched the steam rise from the small pile and tried to remember how he'd got himself into this disgusting state. Where was Ma? Oh, yeah. She was dead and, Duncan presumed, buried. He smiled at the thought of Buck having to do that all by himself. Well, not everything is bad. He finally had all of them out of his life.

Things were coming back to him as he stood up, holding onto the trough and anything else that was handy. The bucket at the bottom of the well was empty, bobbing up and down against the sides, and the sound of it, steady and hollow, seemed to shoot bullets at him, making his head throb. He staggered to the cabin the way he would if he'd had too much of Ma's medicinal. He began to feel real good, apart from a tetchy headache. A raven or two were circling the bone yard. If the bodies weren't buried deep enough, well, that didn't worry him none.

Hell, it was a good day to burn the whole place down. No wind yet. That would come later, after he'd be long gone. It'd be a great way to celebrate.

Pa's new Colt and the old rifle were worth taking with him when he left the farm. He wanted to be gone by noon. He found the small bottle of whiskey Ma had kept in her cupboard for medicinal purposes, stoked the fire, threw the bacon in the pan, and toweled down before he changed into his dark-blue outfit. It wasn't the color he wanted, but Ma said any lighter and he'd be suspected of being a Confederate and in her part of Kansas, the Union part, the abolitionist part, he would not be having supper in her house. He'd nearly told her he could accept that, but he still needed the clothes for his escape, however it happened, so he kept private.

He liked his hat, though. The milliner in the big town said it was the style worn by some in a place down south, a big enough place to be called a country, but it was called Texas, and it had cattle and desert, Natives for the killing, and adventure. The idea of Texas and the style of the hat fired Duncan's imagination, but not his will. The big hat suited him and the rest of his size. He especially liked the extra height the peak of it gave him. He put on his plaid shirt while he forked bacon onto a china plate. Ma said proudly that this suit was to be kept for the best days. Getting rid of his whole family in one day made it the very best day of his life, especially since he couldn't get the blame for it. Even if Buck went squealing all the way to Validation, no one would believe that Duncan had watched the whole thing and hadn't been hurt, what with Buck being so famous for his mindwalking and all.

The grease ran down his chin. He got the towel to make sure it didn't stain and then took a swig from the bottle, which made him choke slightly. He felt like a man for the very first time in his life. He had organized a couple of killings, supervised a rape and a shooting, and watched his cousin weasel out of digging a couple of good deep graves only to have the soft-heartedness to carve the names and date. Duncan laughed out loud at the thought and then did it again to see if he could sound anything like the man with the half earlobe. He had admired the man so in Leavenworth at harvest time, when he and Ma went to deliver the pecan crop to the buyers on the eastbound train. He wondered why the man's name was Silk and made up his mind to ask when he saw him again—real soon.

Buck thought he was going south. What a fool. That wasn't where the cash was. The South was going to die, Duncan had said to his pa. The real cash was in building things, not in growing things, cotton included. The money was going to be in gold and trading goods. The biggest cash would be in the railroads. Everyone could get a license to build one real soon. There were rumors that they'd only cost a buck dollar. He took another swig and suck at the bacon, his teeth not being strong enough to chew it. He would take some of the harvest money that Ma had kept in the dresser and get himself a new set of those teeth they told about in the eastern newspapers.

He threw his leavings into the yard, took the Bible out from under his mattress and went to the privy for the last time. He was nearly finished with the Book of Revelations and most of it had been good wiping paper. He'd just leave the book when he was done. He did his britches and left the smelly hole, wiping his hand on a near-frozen piece of grass that had survived the first snows. It would be the only thing still standing when he left because that's what he thought of the whole place—wasn't worth a shit on a dark night.

He stoked the fire again, got his brand-new jacket, finished the bottle, and threw it into the fire, where after a time it exploded. He went out to whistle for Thunder, who came quickly for a change. He saddled up and watched as the place took fire. What a good thing he'd managed it before noon. In Validation people might have been able to see the smoke and flames if it were night, and the sun was leaving early these days.

He whooped, whirled his new hat in the air, and took off for Leavenworth, the large town to the east where his real life was to start. Thunder had blown his chest, the cinch slipped, and Duncan wound up in the dirt. He should have known. He wasn't used to putting any saddle on any horse—Buck or J. T. always did it for him. The damn animal kept running, the saddle fallen to the ground because he hadn't tightened the cinch before he jumped on. The horse was laughing at him and wasn't in any mood to come back when whistled. It must have been after high noon when Duncan lashed the horse for running away, then re-saddled him (giving him a good hard knee to the ribs to make damn sure he exhaled this time).

"This time, you old bastard, you'll do what you're told." Duncan flipped the reins on Thunder's neck. He needed to be well on the road before nightfall and the cold set in. Maybe it would snow, maybe it wouldn't, but right now that didn't matter because the past was past, his shiny, new future was anchored in what he did with his present, and his present had been bought.

There were a few things he hadn't done, and the doing of them would make him a man to be reckoned with. He would go to town, have a shave—maybe create the beginning of a stache—then get a bath, a woman, and go to a saloon without Pa. He'd have more than one drink. Hell, he had enough money to buy a round of drinks. That's what real men do, and Duncan wanted to live up to the ideal.

He realized that being dumped in the dust by his horse had done him a favor: he would look more trail weary than if he showed up looking like his clothes were new on and had been made by his ma. He gave Thunder a fright by giving him a perfunctory pat on the neck. The steady old horse danced a bit but settled quickly when his rider flicked him with a rein. He was nearly there, he thought, because he could hear iron banging and smell the making of liquor. The wind was picking up and coming toward him. The aroma made his mouth water.

That cheered him up some because when Ma had taken part of the husked crop to the rail yard at the Leavenworth, Pawnee & Western Railroad for shipment to Chicago in October, he had caught a whiff of this and she had tutted all the way to town. There, she mentioned it to a few folks, who nodded and said they knew the moonshining was going on and who was doing it but that there was no law in writing against it and no one to carry out the prescribed warrant if there were. Well, no one willing who hadn't taken advantage of the source. Whiskey from the east was at a premium now the war had started, so people had to put up with privations. In the case of hooch, people were forced to make do with homemade. Some of it was mighty fine as medicine, they said to Ma. Once she heard this she bought the small bottle that he had finished this morning. He was comforted that the still remained in business, and his nose told him the premises may have been extended a mite.

He could see Leavenworth in the distance at about the same time Thunder came up lame. He got off and checked the horse's foreleg, discovered a stone in the shoe, and pried it out with his knife. Duncan struggled to get back on without the trough to stand on. He remembered from old times that Pa sometimes found a rock to give him the extra few inches of boost to enable him to remount. He searched in the dead sunflowers at the side of the trail and found a rock that would do.

"Bloody weeds will really be back in force next year." Duncan was starting up a sweat. "Good thing I ain't going to be a farmer."

He loaded himself inch by inch across Thunder's back, eventually settling down, but after just a few steps Thunder showed he still wasn't happy. Duncan slid down again, checked all four legs, rescued the mounting rock, and got back on, but still Thunder snorted and limped.

Duncan had had enough of the fuss. His new clothes were sticking to him under his buffalo hide, right up the crack of his backside. Out of pure frustration he looked to see if anybody was watching, then checked Pa's old rifle had a cartridge in it. He stood ten paces away and shot the horse. He got a bit sprayed in blood as Thunder collapsed, but only enough to make him explain what happened to his old, beloved horse and how he had done the right thing, putting him out of his misery. Duncan picked up his saddle, having to cut it out of its stirrups, and carried it toward what he considered to be his promised land.

He was wondering how he would get from Leavenworth to anywhere else when he heard a buckboard coming up the road behind him. At least he wasn't staggering anymore. The headache was worse, though.

"That your horse, kid?"

It was the man he respected above all others. It was the man with the ripped earlobe and the huge laugh. It was the man they called Silk.

"Yes, sir. That's old Thunder. He did his very best for me and got me here."

Silk stared at him for just a hair longer than was natural. One of his gang sat in the buckboard. The others trailed behind on their horses. Not for one moment did Duncan feel threatened. He was one of them, he felt, or at least would be soon. All he had to do was have his shave, his bath, and his woman, then buy them a drink. That would make him part of this gang, he felt sure. Silk gave the cross-eyed man sitting beside him a nudge with his elbow. "See to the horse."

"You'll be needing a ride then, sonny. Better have a seat beside me for a spell. I think we've got business to finish."

Duncan tossed his saddle in the back, noticing a few large cases covered with coarse, dirty blankets.

"You buying some of that whiskey from the moonshiners?"

He got into the buckboard, his weight making it lean considerably to one side.

"No. Not whiskey." Silk spoke softly. They were coming into town, and there were more people about.

"Things went well at your farm, but we didn't find that gold or money you were talking about."

"As I told you, I've never been rightly sure it existed. I've only ever heard whispers about it."

"Don't you concern yourself, me lad. I know for a fact there's money or a title to it somewhere about that house."

Duncan knew there wasn't. Hell, he'd even searched Jenny's underwear for it and only left off when he heard a horse that turned out to be Buck coming hard down the road. Now was not the time to tell Silk he'd burned the place down.

"I brought your pay with me," Duncan said. The buckboard lurched on an unseen stone. "I'll give it to you later in the saloon."

"There better be the grand you said."

"Yup. Every penny Ma saved over the last five years; less expenses, of course."

The conveyance stopped outside the bathhouse.

"I've got to pay for a new horse, the bath, the shave, the woman, and the drink. Shouldn't come to more than twenty dollars, though."

Silk put his head down into his chest and smiled.

"You'll owe us twenty dollars, and you will work it off. Is that clear, kid?" He looked straight into Duncan's dark, piggy eyes.

"Why you shoot your horse, kid? Just get sick of it?"

Duncan's mouth went dry as he looked into the face of a cold future.

"Yeah. I guess." The cold wind whipped into his eyes. "Make sure I don't get just as sick of you."

Duncan didn't say anything, but he thought, *that works both ways.*

CHAPTER FIVE

"We can't let him warm too fast, Shona." Doc Fraser examined the rest of Buck's extremities as he spoke, failing to recognize the silence he had created by using Mrs. Haggerty's first name. He looked up at her, his blue eyes remaining professional.

"Who gave you leave to speak that name, please, Doctor?" Mrs. Haggerty was genuinely offended.

Doc grinned at her. "We can't say any more than we need to right now. Let's just leave it that I know, and you know, you haven't always been a land agent and a respectable banker." He felt her shuffle in her tight bodice. "Let's get on and take his wet clothes off. Any dry ones about, do you know?"

"Why don't you run to the Black Diamond and see if any of the clients have left something behind, Keith."

"You remember me, then."

"Only as the doc that actually read medical books."

"Thank you, Mrs. Haggerty. We are both fully capable of discretion, then."

"I think so, Doctor Fraser." She smiled at him from under her eyelashes, still long and dark even after five years working with the girls in Leatherneck. What an unusual time and place to find and rekindle a bond, even if it had only ever been one of kinship to the old country and the circumstances of life.

He stood upright and slapped his knees, finishing the conversation with a final exclamation. "You calm that fire a bit. We don't want him heating up too quick. I'll see if there's a dry nightshirt at Pete's place and if I can get hold of Mary. She'd be a great help right now, and it's not like she hasn't seen a male body, what with helping her Pa to dress the deceased."

"You do that very thing, Doc." Mrs. Haggerty winked ever so slightly, as if she had a twitch. He replaced his wool hat and tried, unsuccessfully, to prevent the wind from slamming the door behind him as he left.

She stripped Buck down and began to wash him with coldish water knowing that he had to be brought back to life real slow. He'd be in horrible pain when his blood came back. He was talking to himself about murder and Piddlin and a moon feather, whatever that was, and every once in a while his eyes would open and he'd stare toward the door, having whole talks with his ma and pa.

The poor boy's brain was well addled with the cold. She hoped the weather would lessen a bit and Jenny could be got.

"Mary will be right along. That girl's got real sense." The doc returned with Joss right behind him.

"I came to tell Buck that Piddlin's making a right good go of it. Thought he'd like to know." He'd taken off his boy-sized round hat, all felt and wool, and was holding it in front of him like a shield.

"That's a kind thought, son. You'd better get closer to him, though. He's talking so much it would be good to know if he could hear."

Joss bent down within an arm's length of Buck's ear. "You got a horse with heart, Buck Ross. A hero horse, she is. She'll make it, just like you, and that means you'll need each other again, so you get well in a real hurry, just so she knows you're a fine one."

Mrs. Haggerty busied herself with the water pitcher, and Doc with his medicines. Joss straightened up with tears in his eyes. "I think he heard. Do you?"

"I do think he heard that very fine thought. It seemed to me a bit like a prayer." No one had noticed Mary when she came in. She had an elegant cloak on and was carrying a wicker basket.

"My, Miss Mary. You look right fine, even in this cold weather."

She curtseyed to Joss. "Thank you, sir, but now if you could go back to poor Piddlin, Mrs. Haggerty and I will do our very best to make Buck come back to her in one piece." Mary looked Doc in the eye. He'd told her he might have to remove a toe.

"He ain't going to lose a leg or nothin', is he?" Joss sounded startled and brought his hat closer to his chest.

"Nothing wrong with his legs a little care won't fix, and the ladies already know their work, so don't you be at all worried, Joss. Thank you for visiting." Joss nodded at the doc and then left without slamming the door, which in itself impressed Mrs. Haggerty.

"The wind must be dropping," she commented to the doctor.

"Sometimes I forget Joss is only fourteen. He picks up on everything, doesn't he?" Mary began unpacking what she'd brought. First, she withdrew a shroud. Mrs. Haggerty jumped in horror. "No, no. It's been my experience, especially when my little brothers were dying, that if we can use it as a lining under this nightshirt it'll be softer on his skin and easier to get to his legs without embarrassing the rest of him. I won't sew him into all of it, Mrs. Haggerty, don't worry."

"That is clever, miss, but what if he needs to pass, you know?" Mrs. Haggerty pointed to Buck's nether regions. "I put a towel between him and the bed, and I've got an old jam jar for the rest."

"I've brought some elderflower tea we can make up for him when he's ready to swallow again."

The doc produced a nightshirt that, as long as it was, would only come down to Buck's knees. "Been my experience that tall people take longer to come back than normal-sized ones. Must have something to do with the distance from the heart to the feet."

Buck fought them as they cut off his buckskins and long johns, toweled him down, and put on the winding sheet. He was shouting out about murder and blood and Duncan and horses and guns and moon feathers. None of it made sense. It didn't take nearly as much time to dress him because he lost consciousness again. They rolled him as Mary had done with most of her other clients, then tucked him into the shoulders of the shroud. Mary had brought a needle and began sewing loosely as Mrs. Haggerty made hot coffee. The smell of it made everyone hungry, and the hour was past lunch-time. Doc enjoyed his coffee and the bit of cake Mrs. Haggerty had left over in her cupboard as he took another look at Buck's baby toe.

"I think he may lose this, you know." He lifted the leg from the bed. "There's no darkness spreading up the calf, thank the Lord, because we don't want that. Can I leave you ladies to keep an eye on it? Let me know if you see the beginning of anything nasty just under the first knuckle…" Doc hushed suddenly. Buck was looking straight at him. "You awake then, kid?"

"Ma says you have to take it off today." He closed his eyes. It was Doc Fraser's turn to shudder.

"I told Pa he was odd," Mary said. "You don't suppose he's one of those seeing people?"

"That's exactly what he is, the poor lamb."

"We don't know exactly what mind or even what world he's in right now. Medicine has never figured it out."

"Ah, well you see, Buck always knows where he is and usually where others are meant to be, so it can be very difficult for him to make the two match." Mrs. Haggerty sounded like she had experience from the old country.

The room was quiet and settled for the first time since they had brought Buck in. Mrs. Haggerty began to straighten up; Mary washed Buck's feet and legs with slightly warmer water. Doctor Fraser excused himself to go to the Diamond again but this time for a stiff drink. He knew, every instinct in him knew, that Buck had been right. The toe had to come off. Now. Just because he hated the thought of sawing into bone, the smell, the noise, and the blood of it, didn't mean he didn't have to do it. The chances were that doing so now would save the kid's life, and that was his job. No one else but a proper butcher was capable of the cutting—except in the butcher's case there was no life in the carcass.

He encountered Pete coming over to see the goings-on. Pete was a good man as far as the doc knew. He was bringing a pot of chicken stew and dumplings freshly made by his buxom partner, Poppy—"the original Diamond," he proudly called her. Doc told Pete what he was planning and asked him to help, saying they may need Ian as well. The ladies could go to the saloon with Poppy, or to Mary's, for the hour or so it would take.

"God, I wonder how he got into that state. Will I tell the womenfolk when I deliver this and then meet you at the Diamond?"

"Better let them enjoy their meal first. I'll go over and tell Mrs. Haggerty after I've had a drink or two and gone for my tools and medicines."

"Ian closed early, being no one can get anywhere except on foot, and if they need anything they know where to find him. You can ask him when you see him. There's a small card game going, by the way, so try not to make the request for help too public. People can be so queer about wounds and wanting to watch."

The men parted company for a little. Doc headed into Pete's strongly built two-story establishment, leaning on the bar for the first shot and taking a chair to sip at his second. Poppy was probably in the kitchen so Clara, one of the younger of the three fallen doves, worked the bar while her services weren't needed in a bed.

Ian sat at the card table near one of the small wood-burning stoves, but obviously wanted to finish his hand. He had acknowledged Doc Fraser, and that would be half of the discussion because Ian wasn't a stupid man. He knew Mary was busy with Buck. It would be unfortunate, but his professional skills may well be needed. He had noticed her leaving with a shroud and a towel, and thought the tea was for Mrs. Haggerty.

It was true, Doc thought, people would love to watch him take off Buck's toe. They would brag about not fainting or even say he'd done it all wrong and it just proved he wasn't a real doc. Yeah, people were funny. He stroked the rim of his shot glass. He'd toyed about volunteering for the Union in this war, but a fifty-five-year-old widower whose hobby was keeping the cold away with a bottle of whiskey wouldn't have done any real good. He'd lost his nerve a while back in a New York hospital. There was too much sickness in a city. Wasn't that much better here, actually. He knocked down the last of his courage and stood up, jerking his head in Ian's direction.

When the two men were outside, standing on the snowy boardwalk, he asked Ian if he would hold Buck's torso. Ian nodded. "Pete should have told Mrs. Haggerty by now," Doc continued, "so the women should be leaving as we get there. I'll have to go home for my scalpels and saw. See if you can find a bit of wood that I can put between his small toe and the one next to it, will you? I don't want to cut two off." He gave a shout of false laughter and a manly punch to Ian's upper arm. "I've got some of that poppy juice, works wonders on pain. I just hope we can get a dribble into him before we start."

Mrs. Haggerty and Mary were wrapped up and struggling against the wind. They had decided on the company of Poppy Diamond to bring them comfort through this darkening night.

"You'll find another lamp under my counter," Mrs. Haggerty said. "God be with you, Doctor Fraser."

"You'd better get in, ladies. I'll send Pete for you when we're finished. Try not to worry too much. I have done this before." He nodded to them in a comforting manner, but he thought, if they only knew I had to cut off my own wife's leg. He started to shake and knew he'd have to take another drink from his private stock at home before he could begin what he considered to be a mutilation.

CHAPTER SIX

Silk stretched his back and legs once he got off the buckboard at the livery stable in Leavenworth. The size and busyness of this city, which was what Leavenworth was becoming, always made him feel good. New cities, new people, all desperate for something or another, made it a certainty his brand of skullduggery would be required. A black market was always good for a growing economy—especially his. He began to release the team of his four horses, unmatched in color but matching in strength. Even as a young boy in Yorkshire he'd had a good eye for horseflesh. Aye, and a healthy respect for the animals that, in his opinion, were worth more than any woman, black, white, or even slant-eyed. If a horse were treated right it would treat you right. They could be skittish, even ornery, but if a man understood his horses they bloody understood him and, without his even having to raise a hand to them.

"Take these inside and give 'em a good polish, will you, lad? I'll get the team to bedding, and we can give them a good brushing down." Silk handed the harnesses to Duncan and patted the lead bay mare who had recently begun to eat more than was usual for her. It crossed Silk's mind she may have fallen foul of a wandering minstrel, as he called them.

"Can't one of the boys inside do this?"

"He probably could, but we'll do it better."

He sauntered into the yard. To Duncan's amazement the whole team followed without a whistle, shout, or a taste of leather on their rumps.

"I was going to ask you to take care of Trixie for me, but she needs a gentle hand and you don't have a fondness for horses, do you?"

"They're just big and stupid, and they stink most of the time."

"Well, if they don't like being rough-handled, who's the stupid one, eh, boy?"

Duncan flared up. "You calling me stupid?"

"I'm afraid so, kid. Only a stupid man walks when he can pay better attention to his method of transportation and save himself the cost of a bullet, don't you think?"

Duncan stood still, looking at the horses, currycomb in his hands.

"Don't you know how to currycomb a horse, Duncan?"

"Ma used to let my cousin Buck do all the horse work. She said it wasn't good for my chest." He was using his girlie voice, and it gave Silk a terrible chill. It reminded him of a voice he'd once heard coming from a jail cell in Portsmouth. It kept calling him duckie. Come for a bit of the natural, duckie, it had crooned. Not all day and night, just suddenly, like when he was just falling asleep, or scrounging a piece of food from a dead man's plate.

"You just clean up the harnesses. I'll get the boys to help, as well as one of the stable staff. You sit in that corner near the door, where I can keep an eye that you're actually doing the work. Don't forget the bits and don't leave them lying about. Keep them nearer the heat so the team doesn't have a cold bit of steel shoved into their mouths first thing. And, Duncan... I've seen every slimy trick in the book, so if you want to eat and ride with us, don't think for one minute I won't notice you accidentally dropping them in the snow just to see if the temperature will bother them."

Duncan threw down the harness he'd been putting a cloth to and stomped toward Silk, declaring, "I am tired and damn hungry. I'm going to the saloon to get a whiskey and to get my teeth into some real hot grub. You ain't paying me. I'm paying you, remember?" He stuck his chin out, brushed his hat against his city-slicker pants, and began to leave. Silk grabbed him by the throat, getting nose-to-nose with him. He held Duncan until the brat turned purple, then let him slide to the dirt of the stable floor.

"What are we doin' with that fat sack of lard, boss?"

"We've got trouble. There's a cousin."

"Maybe he's got the gold."

"It's another lad. He did the horses at the farm."

Silk kept grooming the horses, more quickly now that he didn't have to concern himself with Duncan for a while.

"How old we talking?"

"Don't know. Have to keep this kid Duncan alive until we find out more." Silk was talking quietly and quickly. He dropped the last brush in the last bucket and poured the water out the back door. He was careful to make sure it didn't pool and cause an ice patch. All he needed was a lame horse or worse if one of his team had an accidental fall.

Duncan was moaning. Silk thought briefly, very briefly, about giving him a kick in the head to keep him out of the way a bit longer, but decided a better idea was to get the kid drunk. He would find out everything he needed to know. Yet he wondered if he really wanted to know. Something was niggling at him. When he sailed the eastern oceans he came across a nation of dark-skinned people who believed what you gave out you could get back—maybe not in this life, but it was better to be kind. The idea lived with him the way lice could eat at his hair.

Duncan had lived on the same farm he had raided nearly twenty years ago, just as he was feeling his way onto dry land. Just after he'd escaped the navy noose.

It had been on a Sunday, he remembered. The singing from the church in the three wood buildings that called themselves Validation was loud and bad enough to drown out the noise of his old gang leaving. Something, he thought, should be done about that music before the Lord our God gave up completely on the village and had it blown down by April. Only Tom was left from those days—when being a thief and liar was just an honorable way to make a go of things.

He had been a member of a three-man gang who had, they thought, been cheated by the smart Boston couple who had witnessed him killing his ship's captain. He had chased them all the way to Kansas. His gang had shot the man, stolen his watch (the one currently in his pocket) and left the woman to it, as she was already screaming in the back of an open buckboard. When he paused on the way off the farm he glanced in her direction and was weakened by the sight of a child being expelled from her swollen and bloody body. He didn't know if she died immediately, but he was sure she wouldn't last the day, so the child wouldn't, either.

The woman that was sheltering the mother in the wagon had aimed a rifle roughly in his direction. Silk didn't know if she knew how to use it. The three men, realizing they'd had enough for one day and their horses needed a good feed, vamoosed to a small town that called itself Validation. At least there was a small livery and a decent saloon, although it wasn't completely built and didn't have a name. Validation would do for a spell.

It still rankled Silk that the title for the house in Boston that the couple were supposed to own had vanished somewhere. Maybe this karma thing worked both ways. They still owed him. He still wanted to own property, and the new Homestead Act Congress was debating, didn't appeal to him. He still had a sailor's wanderlust.

The land in Boston would be easier. He could build on it. He could be close to the sea. He would be able to escape anywhere, in any direction, at any time.

He snapped out of his brown funk when he sensed Duncan struggling to his feet.

"Sorry about that, lad. Why don't we go for a drink and something to eat like you wanted?" The kid tried to nod, but his head had had a rough day and didn't cooperate well. He staggered toward the saloon, but Silk decided that the best way to handle a girlie boy was to mollycoddle.

"No, no, Duncan, let me apologize properly. Have you ever been to the hotel?"

"Couldn't afford it."

"Well, you can now. How much you got of my pay?"

"I told you. All of it less expenses."

"You don't need to buy a new horse. I'll make sure you've got a ride when the weather gets better and we have to go to pick up a delivery elsewhere."

Duncan had forgotten about the boxes in the back of the wagon. They had vanished somehow.

"Also means you won't need a new saddle for a while." He opened the hotel lobby door for Duncan who didn't break his stride. He stepped into a world he didn't know existed. His sore head was stunned by the bright lights, the carpet, the curtains, the gold, and the plush red. There were tall potted plants and gold-colored spittoons. Duncan wanted to leave.

"I can't be here without I have a bath."

Silk looked him up and down. "Do you know, you are absolutely correct. Neither of us should be here until we're scrubbed." They struggled down the street against the snow and bitter wind to find that the bathhouse was out of hot water. If they wanted to go to the saloon for a while there'd be more about dinnertime.

"Let's go, then," Silk said. "Maybe we can catch up with the gang while we're there. They could have bunked down by now, of course. It's been a right busy day."

Duncan stopped in the middle of Main Street. "Where am I going to sleep?" It was a child's wail against a furious wind. Silk wanted to leave him where he stood, but he needed to tie loose ends—and he may even need another pair of hands at the next job. He curtailed the slap he wanted to give Duncan, turning it into a grab of his shoulder.

"C'mon, I'll take you for that drink and food and then to the bunkhouse. We can skip the bath until tomorrow. The weather will have us here for a few days, I think. C'mon kid. It's bloody cold out here, and I can hear music coming from over by."

He got Duncan onto the boardwalk where they stamped most of the snow from their clothes. For the first time Duncan was aware of the chill, but he was sure a whiskey would sort him out.

"Duncan, have you still got your pa's Colt revolver?"

He gave the location away by touching his right hip. "How did you know I had it?"

"You told me, and I can see the bulge on your hip."

"Don't remember saying anything."

"When you hired us you said that your ma was going to let J. T. buy his Colt because she'd made enough profit. Remember now? It's when I knew you meant what you said about the grand."

Duncan didn't recall clearly. He put it down to the cracks his head had taken in the last day or so.

"Well, now you know the truth of it."

They marched into the raging wind and snow, Silk glad they were on their own so no one could overhear their raised voices.

"Couldn't see a smart man like yourself walk away from a brand-new gun."

"No smart person would."

"Do you know exactly how to use it? Because, well, I'll tell you how I know this once we're in the warm building—I know for a fact you can't use a rifle."

Duncan started to argue that he was the best shot on the whole farm. "All right then, maybe your eyes were blinded by tears when you shot Thunder, but you didn't do the job you meant to do. Look, Duncan, for your own sake you better let me carry the Colt until the morning. If the men in here see you with it they're likely to want to pick a fight. You got any ammunition for it?"

"Cousin Buck was supposed to pick some up, but I never saw any once he came back from town. He did get the nails Ma sent him for. He carved her name on the cross he made for them and hammered it together with one of them."

Silk now knew the name of the cousin who handled the horses for Duncan. Could it possibly be that the babe shot into the world on the back of that buckboard had survived?

"Well, I think it would be even better if you let me have the Colt before we went in. If some drunk challenged you there would be no time to explain you didn't have the bullets. You'd be dead first. Duncan, the men in here are less likely to challenge an old hand like me, and I may need you to help with a deal I'm trying to organize, so I'd like to keep you with me for a short while—if you're agreeable."

At least Silk had shown him some respect. Duncan didn't fully trust him, but he slipped the Colt into his hand. It vanished into the older man's coats, and they opened one door at a time to prevent the cold from getting into the building.

"Keep the gun a secret, boy. Don't even whisper it in your sleep."

Duncan stood in the warmth, water dripping from his coat. A woman showed up from nowhere and asked him if he needed a drink. He didn't know what to make of her, but Silk stepped in, offering a bottle and two glasses. She vanished as quickly as she'd come. He hadn't liked the smell of her. It choked him and reminded him of the texture in the air of fine sawdust. He coughed a bit. Silk had set the glasses up at the bar. There was not a seat to be found, but one of Silk's gang, the one with the woolly hat, was passed out at a table.

"All is right with the world, lad." Silk had to shout above the noise of the talking and the piano and banjo in the corner. "Want a smoke to go with that whiskey?"

Duncan had never been allowed to try because of his chest. "Got a cheroot?" One arrived from over the bar. Silk helped him light it. Surprisingly, Duncan didn't choke.

"Good man. You had more sense than to inhale the smoke. There's hope for you." Duncan knocked back the whiskey and thought his throat had taken fire. He didn't think he'd ever breathe again, but Silk patted him hard on the back, telling him cheerfully that this feeling was the same one as passing from boy to man—it was only going to happen once.

A seat became available because someone fell onto the floor, dead asleep from his drink. Silk pushed the stranger away with his foot. He made Duncan sit in the empty chair while he encouraged "woolly hat" to wake and move to the same table. It was easy. Once they were sitting down with the bottle between them, Silk told Duncan that Thunder, who was alive at the time, had his eyes and most of his gut picked out by white ravens. It had taken another bullet to put the horse out of his misery. The corpse was now a good winter meal for anything alive that would value it. This was why Silk didn't think Duncan could shoot well. He couldn't even see he'd missed the vitals on something the size of a standing horse. He would need lessons with the Colt before he let himself into serious trouble.

"Do you see my meaning?" Duncan said he did, but Silk knew that he had missed the whole point. Silk knew that this kid was capable of shooting to torture before he killed the victim. As a matter of fact, Silk thought, this kid was so sick in the head he'd do what he did to the horse, leave a torture victim to bleed to death. Maybe he would have stayed to watch if the gang hadn't come across the spectacle. They had surprised him—he thought they'd already be in the town, waiting for him. Looked to Silk like Duncan's little, black teeth matched his little, black soul.

"Now where's the cash? Because you need to go upstairs to do the essential with one of these ladies, but it you go up there with everything you've got you'll come down with nothing left, not even your drawers."

"I'm not letting you have all of it, only the thousand I owe you."

The silence between them was palpable.

"For God's sake, keep your voice down. I don't want everyone to know how many shares I have in that damn railroad."

"I'm going up, and I'll probably stay here, not the bunkhouse."

"Sounds good. Meet you at the bank after breakfast."

Duncan steadied himself as he headed for the stairs. A different woman came to meet him, and one came for Silk. He got the impression that she knew Silk very well. He hoped that one day he would have a good time with the same woman every time.

"That was well done, picking up my cue on the railway shares. Maybe you're quicker than you look."

Duncan smiled with as many black teeth as he could. He was hungry, and he craved Ma's bread and jam.

CHAPTER SEVEN

It was a blessing on this snowy day that Buck managed to take a sip or two of the opium Doc Fraser had given him. Buck had writhed and fought at first. Ian held his arms, and Pete his legs. Doc told them to rest Buck on his left side because it would trap two of the four limbs that would twitch purely out of self-defense.

Ian put all his considerably rotund stomach on Buck's top half, the doc tied both legs together with a cushion between the ankles. Pete put all his strength into holding down the thigh and calf. Both held their breath, but it was obvious that Doc had experience doing amputations.

When Buck had cried out a tad, a leather strap was found so he could bite down, but the worst was the snap of the bone and then the smell of burning bone and flesh when Doc performed the cauterizing to stop the bleeding. Mrs. Haggerty's fire poker would never be regarded in the same light, not ever being thought of as something that could save a foot, let alone a life. Once the poppy juice had taken effect, the operation took five minutes between turning Buck on his side, placing the wood between his little toe and the one beside it, and working the saw and a piece of equipment that looked like snippers common folk used to pull old nails.

It was all over real quick, and Buck managed a bit more of the poppy juice before he went to sleep. Doc Fraser was so calm afterward. He threw the toe into the street, thinking a rat or some other feral beast could have a meal, came back into the comparative warmth of the land office back room, and began to tidy his tools.

Ian couldn't look at the wound. "I'm all right with the dead, but seeing the living all cut up with holes in them always gives me the shudders." He cleared his throat. "Well done, Doc. Don't know how you can stand it." Ian's awe and respect sounded through his words and showed on his pale, round face. His small eyes seemed larger. The dying flames in the wood burner reflected in his round, silver spectacles.

"Ah, the fire is getting low. Buck will need to be kept warmer now." Doc examined his patient's legs for the last time and pronounced them improving. He then found a piece of best brown paper and a piece of red lint. He placed the paper over Buck's damaged foot and then tied, with what appeared to be a silk ribbon, the piece of lint around the young man's heel, arch, and toes to dress the wound without damaging it further. "I've found that people who care for the injured are likely to forget exactly where the injury is, so I draw attention to it by using something red."

Pete stretched from his position at the leg end of the business. "My, my. I didn't know you'd done a great deal of mending."

"I worked in a hospital out east, you know that, Pete. There's a great deal goes on in big cities." Doc smiled at him. Pete nodded and accepted that Doc wasn't in a talking mood. "Better go back to yours and get a refill of whiskey." Ian volunteered to fetch one of the ladies so that Buck wouldn't be left on his own. No one noticed the windows rattling, but all felt the blast of winter when the door opened.

"You're shaking, Doc."

"Just because I know it's a job that has to be done doesn't mean I have to like doing it, Pete." He gratefully collapsed into one of Mrs. Haggerty's chairs, padded with horsehair, covered with old brocade firesides. Pete put another small log on the fire and returned the poker to its original use. "Do you think he'll make it?"

"Don't see why not, as long as he can accept he won't be taken for the army unless he can march for weeks and fight for days. His feet will never manage that now. Once frostbite gets hold the tendency is always there, it seems."

"Didn't know he was aiming for the army."

Doc snorted in derision. "All sixteen-year-olds think they're grown men and immortal. Don't you remember? I know I did."

"True, I suppose. Much more pleasant being in our forties."

"Yup. Especially when I'm in my fifties and can kid myself about it." The doc pulled a pipe from his left trouser pocket and proceeded to light it using a taper and a light from the wood burner.

"Didn't know you used tobacco, Doc."

"Sorry, Pete. Can I offer you some?"

"No, not right now. I'll wait until I get back to the Diamond."

There was a companionable silence that lasted just long enough for Buck to stir and Mrs. Haggerty to come home.

"Ian told us how well the lad did and how calm you were, Doc." She hung her warm coat by the door and wrapped her shawl over Buck's torso. "I don't think we need all this much light now, do we? The fire's helping, and the sun is starting to peek through, just in time for this day to end." She turned down two of the lamps, ever practical, ever frugal. "With any luck the snow will give us a bit of peace tomorrow and we can go tell Jenny what's happened. She must be worried out of her mind."

"You can give him some of that tea Mary brought if he'll take it, and I've left two doses of the poppy for him," Doc said. "One at dinnertime if he's awake, and the other if he wakes during the night. If you need more I can let him have some in the morning.

I think he should manage, though." Doc was putting on his coat, patting the pockets, looking for something known only to him. He was relieved when he pulled out his matches. "Don't know what I'd do without roll-ups. Hope the war doesn't have a bad effect on the supply of tobacco." He did up his huge wooden buttons. "Be awful if I had to go to Leavenworth to get some, wouldn't it?"

"Doesn't Ryan grow some tobacco behind the coral?" Mrs. Haggerty was not as innocent as people thought.

Pete and the doc shuffled their feet.

Buck moved a little and whimpered as his toe brushed against the top sheet.

"I'll make a little doodah that'll lift the sheet away from the problem, don't you worry about it. I think there's a cradle kind of thing somewhere. I'll jig it up somehow." Mrs. Haggerty was coming into her own as the organizer of nursing care. "You boys go off to the saloon and send Mary over, will you? We'll need to get some kind of timetable sorted out between us."

The men were shocked at the strength of the cold wind. Their extended time inside had given them a sense of security that shouldn't exist at this time of year. Bracing themselves, they stamped the snow from their clothes on the boardwalk outside the Diamond and jumped inside in an attempt to keep most of the cold air out. The few patrons laughed at the sight of them.

"Any closer to Christmas, you'd be taken for Saint Nick himself." Poppy helped them out of their damp clothes. Pete returned behind his bar, the place he was most familiar and comfortable with, and poured a shot of whiskey for himself and one for Doc Fraser. He toasted the success of the operation and the fact that Validation must have the best medical man in the West.

He asked Mary, who wasn't at all happy sitting in a bar of any kind, to join Mrs. Haggerty if that was agreeable to her. Poppy knew that Mary was sweet on Buck but had kept mum. She asked Mary to come back to the kitchens with her so she could get her some soup and fresh bread to go with it. "There's enough for all of you, but promise me you'll get some rest. You can't stay up all night. After all, Mrs. Haggerty is strong enough to share the load." Poppy ladled soup into a carrying pot. "Just because you're sweet on him…"

Mary began to blush.

"…and don't try to tell me you're not because I'm an old hand, girl, and you, my darling, are showing me the wrong color to be innocent of your feelings for him. Blushing is always the big admission. Matter of fact, you'll have to stop before we go back out or the men there will know. That would be the end of your little secret that everyone knows, except you and Buck." Poppy patted her cheek lightly and then helped Mary on with her coat.

"One day I'll figure out a way to make money taking people's coats to hang up so they come back warm and dry. At this time of year I could make enough money to pay for a rail ticket to New York if I wanted to go there." Mary and Poppy shared the laugh, and her blush subsided.

They walked to the front of the room together. "You are going to see she gets there safely, Ian?"

Ian rushed to his coat, Poppy helping him on with it. Father and daughter took the very short trip to Mrs. Haggerty's. Behind them Poppy screamed, but they saw the Saloon door close as they turned to see what may have happened.

"Don't run, Mary," Ian said. "March. March quickly. March like you mean it. The hounds of hell are after us."

Mary caught sight of movement in the flickering daylight. The sun hadn't completely set. Shadows were forming behind them. They heard growling. The land agent's door was shut but they could see the light inside. It would be five more quick steps. The door opened. "Hurry people," Mrs. Haggerty called. "Run, for God's sake, run!"

Ian was sure he felt the nose of a wolf sniffing at him before Mrs. Haggerty jammed the door shut. She and Mary leaned on it.

They heard clawing as the wolves tried to dig their way through the thick wooden door. Mrs. Haggerty propped the chair Doc had been sitting in again the latch. They heard shouting. It was no reason to relax. A wolf had discovered that the frame around the window was weak. A claw and a tooth were showing, the snarling persistent and determined, the smell of its rank, warm breath sneaking into the corners of the room.

"Have you got a gun?"

"I never carry one when I go to the saloon, Mary."

The young redhead took the fire poker, heated it a little and shoved it past the lintel into the wolf's jaw. It retreated, yowling, but returned to the doorway, where they could hear its labored breathing just outside. Mary was panting now. Ian had both hands on the door, trying to hold back what was behind it. Mrs. Haggerty, small as she was, sat in the chair in the hope her weight would defend them a little longer. If Pete was out there, so were others. Help wouldn't be long coming.

The sound of a shotgun firing both barrels one after the other cracked the air. The growling continued. The clawing at the door stopped. There was a thud just outside on the land agent's porch. Someone fired again. They heard more shouting, then Doc's voice came to the door.

"Stand back, please. Is anyone hurt?"

"We're all in one piece, thank you." Mrs. Haggerty's voice sounded strong.

"The wolf lying in front of your door is only wounded, so I'm going to do the right thing. Stand back in case any splinters come your way." They could hear him organizing the shot. His feet moved, he had a quiet word with Pete, followed by the noise of a gun they hadn't heard before. Pete preferred them because to him they seemed to sound quiet and businesslike, not lethal like a musket or rifle. Maybe it was just the clear air so close to the door. It could be the sound of Pete's Sharps rifle—no one had ever heard it being used.

They could hear someone move the wolf's body. Ian opened the door and slipped out.

Buck spoke from where he lay. "Well done, girl. You didn't even spill the soup." He closed his eyes again.

CHAPTER EIGHT

The morning came to get Duncan long before he was ready. The woman who'd done what she was told last night was still sitting in the chair across the room, just as she had done all night. If she had stirred he would have woken as soon as jump, so the money would be safe down his britches. The day didn't seem to be as bright as he needed it to be. He gave her the two dollars plus a quarter as a bonus, and told her to get lost.

"You might come across as a hayseed," she said, "but you're as evil as they come, you disgusting little rat-toothed piece of scum." He played at giving her a slap, but she ducked out the door, and he nearly lost his balance.

There was a knock on the door, and without waiting for a by your leave, Silk walked in, obviously feeling better after getting his pirooting the night before.

"Man has his needs, boy. Don't you just know it now?"

Duncan just looked at him like a fawn would if caught at the sharp end of a gun. "Lord, boy, you did make use of her, didn't you?"

He shrugged. "She did what needed to be done."

"Sometimes you give me the shivers, boy—the shivers."

"Can we get eggs and bacon here?"

"I can smell the coffee brewing and the bacon frying, can't you?" Silk slapped his flat stomach. "Let's go downstairs."

"And then I'll go for my bath and shave like I was wanting to yesterday."

"That sounds like a good plan, because the boys and I will have to set up the next deal. The man I'm meeting won't want a stranger around while we're fixing it."

The two of them walked down the wide, carpeted staircase to the dining room. The gang wasn't there. "Are the men coming later?" Duncan asked.

"They stay in the bunk house, so they'll most likely get better and fresher food over there. All this fancy living isn't for them. They don't like it—well, maybe Tom does a bit these days." Silk pulled out one of the padded dining chairs at a table built for the use of four and motioned to Duncan he should do the same. "No, I think Tom is getting a bit too old for all this running up and down the country. I think he needs to find a place to stash his saddle."

The cook came out of the kitchen carrying a massive plate of eggs, bacon, and biscuits in one hand and a jug of coffee in the other. She looked big enough to have sampled all her cooking before the clients. She almost rolled to the table and back. Duncan was amazed at the puffing and groaning she did. Her ankles looked as puffy as her chins. Silk gave him a poke to snap him out of staring before she caught him being unmannerly. "Watch it." He leaned forward to whisper. "If she catches you staring, it's been known that she'll spit on your eggs." Duncan shuddered to think what she'd be able to cough up.

She came back with a plate of the same for Duncan. "You didn't treat my girl right last night."

Silk had been pouring coffee into his cup, but he stopped in mid flow to stare at this stupid child.

"How do you mean, Lizzie?" The sailor kept his voice low, his eyes fixed on his eggs and bacon.

"Didn't let her touch him, didn't let her sleep in the bed, paid her half what's expected for a lady's time and then made to slap her on the way out of the room this morning." She dumped the greasy food down on the table, handing him a fork. "Enjoy your breakfast, sweetie. You're not welcome back." She turned to Silk and told him not to collect another bad apple. "You've got enough to be going on with."

Lizzie stared at Duncan through her little puffy eyes. They didn't like each other one bit. He wanted to roast her on a spit; she would like to have rendered him for fat. Silk felt the tension increase.

"Thank you, Lizzie, I'll be happy to take that advice as soon as I return him to Validation. His momma is waiting for him, you see."

She jammed her fists into her hips and roared as much laughter as her stout form would allow. "Oh, I see," she said. "He's one of those boys." She patted Duncan's shoulder. "Never mind, sweetie. It takes all kinds. I'll tell my girl there's nothing she could have done. Nothing at all. Let bygones be bygones, then. Here, I'll get you both some fresh. Everything will be cold by now."

In a flash she removed the food and provided fresh grub.

"What was that all about, Silk?"

Once again his hand stopped while pouring coffee. Surely he knew that some men didn't take to women. Surely he knew the facts of real life. "I really don't know. You'll have to tell me why you didn't bed the girl while you had the chance, but not till later. It's private, isn't it?" Silk was actually feeling out of his depth, not a position he was used to.

"If"—Duncan leaned forward as the older man had done previously—"I'd let her do her business, she would have found the money down my britches. If I'd let her sleep in the bed she could have stolen it. I made her and paid her to sleep in the chair and watch me give myself a hand. That's all. If she'd moved out of the chair, I'd have woken and caught her. The fake slap was only a tease." He leaned back to eat his eggs. "I thought you knew me better by now, Mr. Silk. I would never hit a woman." The way he looked into Silk's eyes made him pay attention. "I pay other people to do it, don't I? So who's the worse person, Mr. Silk?"

A man and a woman entered the room. She stood in her stiff collar and corseted plain dress, hands folded in front, deliberately eyeing everything before she nodded at the man and allowed him to pull out a chair for her. They nodded politely to each other. "Lots of snow and wind today, I think," he said to Silk and Duncan. "Wife and I were planning a trip to Lawrence for to visit with her sister and family over the Christmas period." The man looked like he was selling medicines. He rubbed his hands together. "Eggs good, then?"

"Yup, and so're the biscuits. Might be going that way ourselves, but if the snow's as bad as you say may have to stay over a bit." Silk stood up, forcing Duncan to join him. "Maybe see you later then." He tugged his imaginary forelock to the woman, took Duncan's arm, assisted him into a coat that didn't belong to him and forcibly escorted him to the front door. Duncan started to object, but Silk just opened the front door and ejected him through it.

"What's wrong with you?" Duncan demanded.

"Seen that little man before somewhere and didn't need him to start thinking about it. Let's go to the bunkhouse. See how the boys are."

The boys were much better than Silk and Duncan had been. They were warmer, drinking a nonstop supply of whiskey and coffee and tucking into a real steak, cooked medium rare. All the Chinese cook ever did was to stick a long fork in one end of the meat, put it on a sizzling hot grill, and then turn it over after a few minutes. He did exactly the same with pork rib. The smell was spectacular. It made men feel they had gone back to the times when eating meat was a natural thing to do, not something that had to be fussed and fought over the way women did it. No, this was food for the joy of it, the taste of it, the smoke, the smell, and even the burned edge of it. This was where men could be themselves and enjoy a whiskey without a bad conscience to go with it. Rye Carp, the man with the woolly cap, belched a long, comfortable passing of air. No one said "tut" or "sorry," and no one cared, not even the smallest mouse hiding in the nearest straw bale, busy with his mate and so paying no attention and caring even less.

"I think the wee man that hangs on to the coattails of Benjamin Walter MacLaren is in the hotel," Silk said. "We'll have to get out of town now."

"We can't, Silk. It would draw more attention to us if we skaddled than if we took our time." Pat McBride, the man in the gang who tended to ride tall in his saddle, spoke sense when he wasn't mooning about a lost woman. "Means you'll have to go over to the hotel on your own, boy. You can give back the coat you took by accident and tell Lizzie we're going to stay with the horses tonight. The wind is making them fractious."

"You want I pay the reckoning?"

"Aye, lad. Good idea. You can take it away from the expenses."

"Who's this Benjamin guy?"

"He's the son of a bitch who's been hunting me since I jumped ship in New York. Now move it, kid. Chances are his horse and buggy are in the livery. I don't want to run into him at the wrong time, do I?"

Duncan didn't like being used as an errand boy, but he wasn't in a position to do much else for the time being, so he walked into the hotel lobby to find there were people shouting and fussing about the missing coat. He was in the process of taking it off when a screaming woman attacked him for being a thief. It was the woman with the stiff collar he'd seen at breakfast. He explained that he'd taken it by accident. Lizzie stepped between them, telling the couple he wasn't all that right in the head and nothing had been meant by it.

"Poor lad doesn't even know what to do with a full-grown woman," she whispered loudly to the man who looked like he sold medicines.

"What did the cook say about this weasel?"

He was mightily embarrassed, but the husband hushed her and shooed her back into the dining room. Duncan finally understood what Lizzie had meant this morning. His color was up.

"I'll pay you for the rooms, the food, and both women." She could tell he was affronted, but then so was she, so she wasn't going to let him get away with it. "Rooms ten dollars, breakfasts, two, eight dollars, I'll take off what Mr. Silk paid for his girl and the two dollars you paid for yours, so that's twenty-one all told." She shoved her fat palm right under his nose. He didn't know if the price was right or not, but he knew that making a fuss would mean drawing more attention to the gang in the bunkhouse, so he turned, took the paper from his britches, and gave it to her exactly.

"How'd it get wet, you little bastard?" It was like she knew, but Duncan just said it was probably sweat from her dirty, woolly sheets. He took his own coat from the rack and left, slamming the door behind him. It didn't give him the satisfaction of bouncing back at her or smashing into pieces. It took him a minute to warm himself in the cold air and to come to terms about what he thought were his true feelings for women. Nah, he thought. He liked pictures of tits and things. He heard the snow crunching under the boots his cousin had made for him and let Buck's fate cross his mind for a minute.

The door to the hotel opened behind him.

"Where is the telegraph office, please?" He heard the voice of the man Silk didn't like.

"Just turn to your right," Lizzie responded, "and you'll find it a few steps away. Have to let your family know you're stuck here for a bit, I suppose." Lizzie was being a busybody. "Maybe I know them?"

"Hear of the MacLaren family just outside the city, near the church?" the man said. "My brother Benjamin is heading this way for the holiday season."

"You say hi when you see 'em will you? Nice bunch of folks."

The hotel door closed.

Duncan shoved his hands in his pockets and headed for the bunkhouse.

Joseph MacLaren, Benjamin's brother, checked on his wife and then slipped out to the telegraph office, which was working in spite of the snow.

CHAPTER NINE

On hearing Buck's words, Mary snapped around. The pot of soup in her hand was still intact, just as Buck had said.

"That wasn't his voice, was it?"

"Hush girl, you must be tired." Mrs. Haggerty took the pot from her hands and placed it gently on her own wood burner. Mary wasn't sure if her shaking hands were because of the wolves or the fact that Buck had woken just long enough to comment. She tightened her shawl and rubbed her back and her shoulders.

"Don't tell me you're coming down with something, Mary. Please don't."

"I'm perfectly fine, Mrs. Haggerty, just a bit shocked is all. It's not every day I'm chased by wolves. Where did Pa go?"

"He's just out with the other men. We'll keep an eye on our laddie here."

"What's this contraption over his foot?"

"Just something I rigged up to keep the pressure of the sheet from bothering his feet. It's just a couple of books at each end and a ruler resting on them. Seems to be working." Mrs. Haggerty checked to make sure the top of the sheet was off his feet.

"Have you had anything to eat?"

"Just had a bite in the Diamond. Miss Poppy is a good soul, isn't she?"

Shona had other opinions. The ten years she had on this lovely young woman had made her, of necessity, more worldly and wise.

"I'll stay here with Buck if you want to go to the saloon and get something more than soup. She may have some peas and beans left."

Ian knocked on the door and walked in, as he did so, bringing snow and water with him.

"Close my door, please," Shona shouted. Buck jolted, sitting up to see what was happening, then collapsed slowly back onto the bed. Shona made a dart for the protective contraption she had engineered and managed to rescue him from more pain. The doc had warned her he may not realize his toe had been removed. Doc said he didn't really want him to until he'd had a chance to sleep and heal through most of the troubles he'd endured, whatever they were.

"Thought you'd like to hear that it seems the wolves are gone. We'll know better in the morning, of course." Ian couldn't stop staring at Buck's face. "He's a poor color isn't he?"

"You'd understand better than most the definition of poor color, Ian Grant." He hurried to look at his shoes.

"Nobody hurt, was there?" Mary tried to dispel the tension.

"The horses were skittery, but no, the doc's services weren't needed apart from the use of his gun. The good thing is that we've got three wolf skins now, and if there are any hungry pigs or dogs, the meat will do them a power of good."

"Speaking of food, Mrs. Haggerty needs something to eat." Mary turned to Shona. "Would you like my pa to take you to the saloon? Just to be on the safe side, I mean."

"That would be very sensible, Mary, but are you sure you'll be fine on your own?"

"I'll keep the door shut behind you, don't you worry."

Ian and Shona looked at each other.

"Well, it's a good thing Buck is as quiet as he is, otherwise your reputation could be tarnished simply because you are a young woman alone in a house with a young man."

Mary sat down in the old but comfortably padded chair. "Well, between the wolves and the no good Buck and I might have got up to while Mrs. Haggerty was having a spot of dinner, I'm sure the ladies of the church won't know what to talk about first."

Ian grinned into his chest, Mrs. Haggerty actually giggled, and Buck seemed to snore once. They opened the door, the snow came in, Mary shut the door hard and turned to stir the pot of soup. It had turned cold.

"Actually, it's a fair point, Ian. There was no service today. Snow aside, I wonder where Reverend Parker was."

"Think there's trouble up at the Pulaski place? I'll know only too soon if my services are required."

"Did you know that you speak very differently when you're being an undertaker?"

"No. How do you mean?"

They were nearly at the Diamond. "You just turn all formal and proper, your voice gets quieter, and you even slow down like the hearse is behind you." Ian opened the door for her to a loud chorus of, "shut the door you lousy couple of bushwhackers." That was a huge insult, of course, so the two of them slid in without drawing further attention to themselves.

Pete came over to find them a warm chair by one of the two small wood burners. "The doc and I will join you in just a minute. We need to talk, don't we?"

The door opened again, this time to another chorus of complaint from the twenty or so men, women, and children that had taken refuge from the cold and the prowling animals. Reverend Parker, all broadly built and flat-footed, stood inside the door, shaking the last bit of snow from his specially made—Eskimo style, he said—parka jacket.

"Saw the wolf skins. Praise the Lord, no one was hurt. Scraggly looking beasts, though."

"Shot of whiskey for you, Reverend?"

"Thank you, Pete, would be grateful, mighty grateful indeed. Got anything to eat? Anything at all will do. Hot food, even better."

Poppy knew what he wanted as soon as she heard his booming voice. He only ever boomed like that when he wanted to attract the attention of a willing contributor to his well-being. Folks knew he wasn't a bona fide minister of the cloth, but they didn't care because he actually did practice what he preached. He was there in trouble and joy, sickness and sorrow, health and well-being. He couldn't marry people proper—couples had to go to Leavenworth or Topeka for that—but he did supervise jumping over the broom, and if the union lasted for the year, he would gladly organize a nuptial and take the couple in a horse and buggy to the proper man of the cloth or justice of the peace, as they preferred.

He didn't need to be asked, he just sat with Shona and Doc. "Something wrong with your little establishment, Mrs. Haggerty?" Doc told him he most likely would need his help in the morning if the snow had lessened a little. Buck was ill and currently staying at the land office. He was deeply unconscious so Mary was with him to make sure he was still breathing.

"And that, Reverend Parker, is why there is a woman of good repute in a saloon. She's hungry, and we all have to discuss what action to take over the next day or so."

"Many apologies, ma'am. I have no desire to offend your decency."

"No, of course you don't, Reverend. Certainly not a man of the cloth who is sworn to be charitable and forgiving of all sins, just like our Savior, the Lord Jesus." She smiled sweetly, her green-gray eyes as cold as slate.

"Saved you some pork and beans in gravy, Reverend. Just as you like it. There's some black pepper out the back if you're needing any." Poppy always flirted with Reverend Parker. Pete thought it was amusing. Shona thought she was demeaning herself. She never took her eyes off the reverend when Poppy put the same treat down in front of her.

"You've been working so hard today, ma'am. I sincerely hope this gives you good cheer." That comment turned Mrs. Haggerty's head toward Poppy, whose eyes were soft and brown. Instantly, she felt guilty. "Thanking you so much, Miss Diamond. I am very grateful indeed."

Pete joined the table. He gave Poppy a quick kiss on the cheek and nodded toward a table that had a family with two children. "Have we got any room for them, anywhere?"

She nodded. "I'll fix something up, don't worry."

Pete sat down beside Doc, who was picking the little bits of carrot out of the pork and beans because he always said they gave him indigestion.

"Any kind of orange vegetable has been given to us to feed to the pigs so we could gain strength through their meat. Amen."

Mrs. Haggerty blessed herself and then tucked into her meal, carrots and all.

"I wonder why the wolves came here."

"They're starting to go hungry. Not nearly as many buffalo as there were," Pete said as he stirred a stew that arrived with his third whiskey.

"That's a scary thought," Shona said.

"I wouldn't leave my child outside right now, or a cat or dog, for that matter," Ian said. "Horses can at least kick a bit."

Shona suddenly had tears in her eyes.

"Oh, sorry, ma'am. Forgot about your old ginger tom." Ian was having a night of placing his foot where it didn't belong.

Shona's cat had passed away in his sleep a couple of weeks ago, and she hadn't really got over it, as stupid as it sounded to many, but not all. Miss Mary had understood for some reason, although Shona had never marked her as being particularly fond of animals. The young widow was learning quite a bit about quite a few people today. It gave her heart.

"How many wolves do you think there were?"

"It looked like a pack of about ten, but still, I wouldn't trust them to keep going east, the way they were headed." Doc Fraser sounded like he might know what he was talking about. "They might just hole up around that end of town to see what pickings they can get in the morning."

"Do you think they'd eat their own kind?" Mrs. Haggerty was shocked.

"Why not? We do, if we're hungry enough."

She pushed her bowl away. "How do you know that, Doc Fraser? That is unheard of, surely."

"Rumor is that Napoleon's troops did it during the winter campaign in Russia." Doc used his finger to get the last of the gravy before he realized what he was doing. Everyone at the table was looking at him as if he was an eater of human flesh.

"You weren't there, were you?"

"Pete, I'd be a great deal older than my forty-five years if that had been the case. No, I just read the medical journals when I was living in New York. That's all. Fortunately, I've never had to think about it again until now, so can we get down to why we're really here? If the weather's better tomorrow, I suggest that Pete and Ian check on the outlying farms. We need to make sure our nearest neighbors weren't invaded by the wolves. You can, if you go west and then south, check on Jenny and the rest of the family. Tell

Jenny that Buck will be here for a while and what has happened to him. Does that suit?"

"I'll do that. What about you and the reverend here? I have a patient just down southeast toward Leavenworth—and the reverend better get hold of Ryan and even Joss in case of another pack of wolves."

Mrs. Haggerty stood. "I had better get back to Mary, then. We'll have to sort out some kind of schedule of duties to keep Buck comfortable and ourselves rested."

"There are other ladies in the town that may be willing to help."

"I'm sure you're right, Doctor, but I'm not willing to let them into my private living space." She pulled her skirts straight and organized her long, woolen, worsted apron, trying not to compare it with Poppy's linen one. She allowed Pete to help her into her long winter coat, adjusted her knitted scarf and hat, and pronounced herself ready to be escorted home by any gentleman willing to brace himself against the weather one more time.

This time the reverend got the job. "I don't like you, Reverend Parker," she told him as they walked. "I'm sorry, but for some reason I can't take to you."

"Don't concern yourself, Mrs. Haggerty, I don't like you, either. It's probably because I'm no reverend and you haven't always been virtuous. It's a mutually exclusive secret, isn't it?"

"It seems to me that people who come to small towns in the West never ask about a person's background in case their own is exposed." Shona had stopped just before her door. She could see the last of her paraffin lamps burning. "Would you do me a good turn, Reverend?"

"If possible."

"We may need more fuel for the lamp and wood for the fire before morning. Would you be so kind as to get someone to organize it for us? I wasn't expecting visitors, after all."

"I'll just go to see Ian right now. His store will have all that. You go in and stay as warm as you can." She turned to her door as he walked away, but she heard him turn. "Our semi-secret, then."

"Maybe one day the truth will come out about all," she replied. "But maybe not. It will be as it will be and will have to be faced at the time—not a minute before. Good night, Reverend Parker. God bless."

CHAPTER TEN

"C'mon then, kid." Everly Plastow, who seemed to grin all the time, was about to give Duncan a swift kick on his fat rump when Silk told him to let alone.

"Let him sleep, for God's sake. He'll just get in the way of our business."

Everly grunted and sloped away unsatisfied.

"He's not the greenhorn he's making out that he is."

Duncan was awake and heard everything.

"He's very fast in his thinking, and picks up on things real quick. Trouble is, I don't know what he intends to do with all this knowing about stuff he's cottoning on to."

Silk and Plastow joined the others near the door, out of earshot. Duncan rolled in his bunk but kept his eyes closed for just a quiet breath or two. The gang had tried to keep quiet, but they were all staring at him; he could feel it and hear the holding of their own collective breath. He opened his little, piggy, brown eyes. He sat up on one elbow, and smiled just enough to hide his teeth.

"Morning, all." A fleck of spit flew in their direction.

Somehow, the gang felt he was in control of what was going to happen today. Silk stepped forward to smash the rising mood, locating himself between them.

"We've got a delivery to do today. You will stay here, canny lad. Tom will take care of things at this end so you can organize our next trip. When we get back this early afternoon we are going to Lawrence to pick up something we have planned for your little hometown of Validation."

Duncan jumped up so fast he nearly lost his long johns. "I can't go there yet."

"Yes, you can, and yes, you will. I thought you wanted to go back as a hero, with lots of money and good clothes."

"But what about everything else?"

"What are you talking about? Did something else occur?"

Duncan sat down on the bed again, relieved. He smiled, ran his hand through his greasy long hair, and told Silk he'd go for his bath and haircut, but he'd be ready by noon if that was what Silk required.

"That's exactly what's required, boy. Tell you what, though. I want the money you owe me. Right now."

Three of the men had their hands on a pistol or a rifle. They weren't aimed, but the threat was obvious. Duncan turned his back, pulled out the wad that he'd had tied to his inner thigh and counted out the thousand.

"Is that real money, boss?" Pat McBride sounded suspicious.

"There's a lot of money in pecan nuts when there's a war on. This is the real thing, Pat", said Silk. "Don't you worry. Just because you've never seen so much paper doesn't mean it's phony."

"Seems to me there's a lot of money in everything when there's a war on." Rye Carp, the "woolly hat", spoke quite seriously. "Hope you've got a little left, kid. Horse and things to buy yet."

"He'll ride with me on the buckboard until we get to Validation. That won't be for at least a couple of weeks, especially if the weather hangs onto us the way it is."

Silk left, using the back door that led toward the storage area. Duncan noticed it for the first time and decided to have a look after his bath, if Tom, who was glaring at him, let him out of his sight to do it.

"You going to get spruced up, Tom?" Duncan asked. "I'm buying. Never been before and will need some educating, if that's all right."

Man and boy dressed as well as they could against the cold, getting to the bathhouse just in time to get the first hot water. The tub was like Ma's at home, except it was big enough to lie in and duck your head. Ma had to wash his head separate like. Ma had poured a jug of water over his head, soaped it, rinsed it, then put a pudding bowl on him to trim it real nice. She parted it right down the middle and said lye soap meant he'd never get lice. He did, though—every September.

He had no idea hot water could feel so good or soap smell so sweet. He also had no idea that his time in the bathhouse was limited to twenty minutes, and he should have been out of the tub five minutes ago. A little Oriental man came in to Duncan's bathing room, throwing towels and words at him. Duncan was standing in the bath with a towel around his waist when Tom, all done and dusted, came in. He calmed things down with many bows of his head to the Oriental man.

"Your time is up. What is it about your nature that has to hang around everywhere? You've made one hell of a mess, and you'll have to pay extra. Hurry up, get toweled off, get dressed, and get out of here. I'll try to give condolences to the owner and the next guy who's now going to have to wait while this whole room is scrubbed, let alone the tub. Hot damn, kid. Look at it. Never seen such a ring of dirt, not even from a cowhand who's spent two weeks on a desert saddle." Tom sounded like J. T., another man who didn't understand how special he was. He shrugged as Tom slammed the door behind him, but he did get out of the tub and room as quickly as he could.

"Your twenty-minute scrub turned into a full hour." A woman who may or may not have been Oriental spoke to him in a language he could understand. "You made such a mess it will take me and my coolie another half hour to clean up. You owe five dollars." Duncan began to object, but Tom showed up at his elbow. "It's about time you learned that little boys who play big have to pay for it somehow. This is cheap at the price. Cough up and shut up."

Duncan added the four extra dollars to his payment. She took it, put it in her cleavage quickly without any sexuality being expressed, waved her hand at him in dismissal, and walked up the stairs to his mess. Tom bowed his head to her retreating back. They heard her say, "Aw, shit," when she opened the door to the room.

"If I was your Pa, I'd leather you. Actually, if I was your Pa, I would be mortified that I hadn't taught you better in the first place. What are you, some kind of momma's boy?"

Duncan had been stomping off toward the barber. He turned on him. "You should know. You helped murder them both. Where do you think Silk got the money?"

He continued to the barber shop, accepted a chair, waited for the apron to be swished around him just as he'd seen it done for his father a few years ago, and asked the barber for a hot shave and a smart new cut to match the high-peaked hat he'd bought in this town just a couple of months ago.

Tom came in behind him. Their eyes met in the mirror. Tom sat in one of the waiting chairs made out of old hickory. The matts on the rough wooden floor were pecan husk. The barber wasn't happy about the change of atmosphere in his normally cheerful establishment and kept up a conversation, mostly one-sided, about the weather and the railroad that was going to make life so much easier for trade and moving around. "May even see passengers going all the way west one day," he said. "Yes, all things were possible in the new, modern world. Even the guns they were using in the war were better, and of course the Union had to stay the Union. Slaves were never a good thing. Unchristian, don't you know. There's talk of a whole regiment of black soldiers being formed at the fort."

He quickly finished Duncan's shave and started on Tom's, but all Tom wanted was a beard trim because no beard in the winter was a mighty cold thing as far as he was concerned. Duncan sat in the chair and stared at what the barber was doing with the razor. Tom was a much older man, so he didn't have the same amount of hair on his head, especially on top. Five minutes later the boy paid, complimented the barber on his fine work and the razor the blacksmith kept in good order for him. They left to go to the saloon.

The barber took a deep breath. He folded the razor, grateful there were no other customers in the shop because he felt his face flushing. When that happened he began to shake a bit. His wife said it was because he ate too many pork sausages but not enough beans.

On the way to the saloon Duncan saw the man that appeared to spook Silk the evening before coming from the telegraph office. Tom didn't seem to recognize him, but the man definitely recognized Duncan.

"Sorry about my wife last night, son. She can be a bit high-strung at times, but now you've got your own coat back there's no harm done." Duncan nodded, smiled, and just kept walking.

"Who was that?" Tom was rarely curious.

"Some relation of a Mac-something. Silk didn't take to him last night. As a matter of fact, I think Silk came close to running away."

"Silk? Silk would never be running from anything. Well, unless it's the husband of a woman he's been misbehaving with." Tom chuckled. "I've seen that happen. Yes, I've certainly seen that happen, but that was years ago and well up north. It's where he got his fancy watch, so I've been told."

The snow was lessening and beginning to melt. The sky was building high, but the clouds were a lighter shade of gray. Both Duncan and Tom were considerably hungry.

As they opened the door of the saloon their noses were caressed—that was the only word for it—by the smell of beef stew, onions, and gravy. The host seemed to be a decent man, burly in his white apron, displaying a huge waxed moustache worthy of envy. The assistant appeared much younger and was clean-shaven, so probably not a son or relation. His apron was not so voluminous, his eyes blue and cold, unlike the host, who was jolly. They spoke a language Duncan had never heard. Tom told him it was most likely German. Germans, he continued, had funny ideas about what made food good, but they were right so many times, it was worth trying the stew and dumplings.

Tom added he wasn't so crazy about the sausage, but it wasn't on the menu today, so it didn't really matter. The point was that the Germans liked everything to be clean, for some reason. It didn't make the food bad, and Duncan had to admit it was the best he'd ever eaten. They ordered a full bottle of whiskey because Silk and the rest of the gang would probably need it when they got back. If not, they could just take it with them. The host insisted they have beer with the meal, but supplied the glassware essential to a shot of the real stuff. There would be no extra charge, he said.

"That's because he's built the price of the beer into the cost of the stew, Duncan," Tom whispered.

"What was Silk delivering today?"

Tom didn't see a problem in telling Duncan now that the business was over. "A consignment of Sharps rifles combined with a few army Colts. Why?"

"I've got a Colt. Silk's keeping it out of sight for me. They're not cheap."

"Neither is the ammo. Hope you've still got a bit of money left."

"How did Silk get a whole consignment of weapons?"

"You'd be better asking Silk, but let's just say he's very good at what he does, and he will do anything, anything at all, for money, provided the price is right. If he lets you ride with us, you'll be safe from the law, and you'll live as wild or as tame a life as you want. He's the best leader I've ever known, but don't do a dirty on or to him. He will kill you. Cold. On the spot, no excuses. I've seen him do it, and didn't blame him one bit." Tom had knocked back two whiskeys plus a huge jug-like container of beer while delivering this sermon. He slammed the shot glass on the table and poured another. "Three's my limit. That's the trick to life, boy. Knowing your limit. Knowing not to start or when to stop before you burn out. Yup, know your limit."

He knocked it back, finished his stew, and was nearly asleep in his chair when Silk and the others rolled in, happy as chickens loose in a cornfield.

"Stew as good as it smells, then?"

"Oh, yeah. Bought a full bottle—well, at least Duncan the banker did. Thought you might have a fancy for it." It was a good thing Tom stopped at three because he was starting to slur and was perfectly capable of sleeping in his chair, which he then did.

"Eat up then, please, and take as much whiskey as you need." Silk slid into the armchair. Rye, Pat, and Everly threw their legs over smaller wooden chairs as if they were mounting a horse. "We're going to Lawrence today," Silk announced. "The weather seems to be turning for the better and it's not that far. If we go soon we should be able to see its lights in the distance. Yup. We've got another delivery, and this time it's just for fun. You'll really like it, Duncan. It's a present for Validation—as long as the army doesn't miss it."

CHAPTER ELEVEN

Mary lifted the latch as quietly as she could. It had been a most disturbing night for everyone, but it had to have been the worst day and night for Buck Ross. He'd lost a toe to frostbite and amputation, then the noise with the ins and outs of the people coming to lean on and over him, and then, to finish the day even worse than it started, he'd witnessed a pack of famished wolves descend on Validation. Even a man unconscious and drugged responded to some of the goings-on. What he needed the most, Mary reckoned, was a good, restful sleep and something warm in his stomach.

Mrs. Haggerty, as if by some trick of mind reading, came in without stepping on the part of her floor that creaked. Everyone did it when they came to see her on business and laughed about it, because it was as if she'd planned it that way. If she wasn't at her counter she surely came from the back room sharpish. She never kept anyone waiting.

"How is he doing?"

"He's sleeping deep at the moment."

The two women stood over him, arms folded, faces concerned.

"What will we do, then?" Shona sat in the soft chair, pulling up the woolly blanket she had crocheted last year right to her chin, and smiled. "If you get me that little cushion from the stool that I usually sit on when I'm behind the counter, I'll be right as roses in June, and you can go back to your own place once your pa comes for you."

Mary was retrieving the cushion when there was a light tap on the door.

"It's Pa."

"You just go, girl. If he gets really wakeful, I'll give him what Doc said. You'll be no good to anyone unless you can take over for me tomorrow. Now shoo."

Mary looked over her shoulder while she put on her coat and scarf. Pa guided her elbow into the snow. The hour was getting toward sunrise.

When they got to their store just a few minutes' walk down the way toward the church, they were confronted by a small group of complaining people all wrapped up against the cold and all with their curiosity stirred up. Some wanted paraffin, some needed rice and beans, some wanted ammunition, an axe, and another, bigger knife. One woman had noticed Mary taking a basket of things to Mrs. Haggerty's and that she hadn't brought it back with her.

Ian shook his head because he knew that when he told people what had actually happened the facts would be built upon by the time the news about Buck got to the saddler's across the road. He cleared his throat to act as newsboy. He started by telling people that he and Pete were going to check the outlying farms to make sure no harm had come to anyone. This meant that the MacGregor farm would be included in their trip, which may last a day or two, perhaps longer depending on the weather and whether the river was running high. They would tell Jenny, J. T., and Duncan that, probably because he'd been caught by the weather, Buck had managed to find his way here rather than get home. He cleared his throat again, aware that no one was making any comment and that his short stature was a disadvantage.

"Buck is being cared for by Mrs. Haggerty. It was felt that she had the appropriate space. My daughter will assist as required, simply to give Mrs. Haggerty a chance to rest. The doc says he has frostbite. Buck has sacrificed a baby toe to this weather and as the Reverend Parker would say, please pray for his full recovery. He, by the way, and the doc himself, will stay in town with Ryan and Joss, in case any other troubles of the four-footed type come to sniff around." When he finished his little homily, standing there circled by ten people all looking down on his brown trilby hat, he felt a flash of sympathy for any dying animal surrounded by white ravens.

Customers came and went, and people being people they tried to find out exactly how the doc had cut the toe and what was being done for poor Buck. There was something avaricious about the questions, something nasty about the greed for detail. Mary and Ian answered all politely and decorously, both feeling, as they told each other later, sick to their stomachs about having to relive and repeat the tragedy of it. Only one customer asked if he would be able to fight in the war, stopping all other conversation for a second or two. Mary had looked blank. She said it had never occurred to her to ask, especially since it would take him a while to learn to balance again—if he lived. People finished their business in a hurry and scooted from the store. Mary burst into tears as Ian shut the door on their retreating backs.

"You're tired, Mary." He drew her to his shoulder, giving her a quick squeeze. "You've been up all night. Why don't you have a lie-down for a bit? I'll straighten things here. Look, the sun's coming up, and the snow's slowing down." He pointed out the small window, just as he would have explained things to her when she was four years old. He felt useless to her. She escaped his hold and retreated to the back, sniffling, leaving him in an eddy of his own fear for her.

Ian met Pete at the stable where Joss had saddled their horses. "You want some of my ma's beef jerky?" He had some wrapped in a bit of brown paper. Pete nodded his thanks knowing full well that Joss's family was making a huge contribution toward their journey. "How 'bout you, Mr. Grant. Want some bacon? If'n you don't use it, maybe Jenny and Duncan would like it."

"Well now, you tell your ma thanks from me and Jenny. Looks like there's enough there to share." Ian bent down to receive the gift, placing it in one of his less full saddlebags. His rifle nearly got in the way, but not quite.

"Look at Piddlin. She's real missing Buck, isn't she?" Joss clicked his tongue in her direction. She twitched her tail but otherwise stood stock still in her stable, head sagging, just waiting, it seemed, for everything to be over. Pete wasn't in his saddle so went to give her an encouraging pat on the neck. "He'll be fine, girl. He'll be fine. You get your strength back. He'll need you real soon, I think." Piddlin lifted her head in a start, snorted, and then settled back.

"I think she knew what you said, Mr. Pete. Thank you for helping her just a bit." Joss was all smile, no beard yet, and had a few of the young man's developing skin problems. Pete ruffled his long blond hair. "You remind me so much of myself when I was thirteen."

"I turned fourteen last month." Joss sounded indignant.

"Now you see, that just proves my point. I would have said exactly the same thing."

He mounted his horse, Buchanan, named after the last president before Mr. Lincoln.

"Ready, Ian?" Ian nodded sharply, just once, and they left Validation behind them, riding side by side. Ian wore his brown trilby hat to match his coat and boots, Pete his black floppy one that Poppy had insisted she line with sheep's wool just for the winter. They had thrown buffalo hides over their shoulders, which made Ian look even tinier on his big brown mare, Annie, called that because Mary thought it would be a good name.

Joss experienced a new emotion as he watched them ride away. He wanted to go to see things. He wanted to explore. He was, he thought, experiencing what his mother would call jealousy. He would ask her tonight when he went to his home behind the lumberyard. Maybe he would sign up for the war. He returned to his duties in time to see a stranger ride into town.

The heavy man kept coming down the street, not in a rush but also not taking his time. He rode right down the middle of the street, looking at every shop front. When he rode past people he doffed his unusual, dove-gray hat. It couldn't be a Confederate, Joss thought. The color wasn't the right gray, and there were no badges or swords, only a feather, probably one belonging to an eagle, stuck all jolly-like into the three-striped, red, white, and blue hatband. The stranger kept coming, eventually stopping his horse in front of Joss. He dismounted and pulled off his long, black leather riding gloves.

"You got room, boy? For my Black Satin, I mean."

Joss was speechless but managed to nod.

"Let's see, then." Joss picked the reins from around the stallion's back and led him to a stall near the wood burner. The best one as far as most people told him, but the truth be told, Piddlin had the best stall because it was nearest to food, water, heat, and a bale of straw to make a bed.

"It's not the best you've got, but Satin won't mind giving the best to a lady. Must be one of the regulars that manages to pitch his horse in that stall near the food and water."

"That is Buck Ross's horse, Piddlin. He's in town getting better, we hope." Joss's voice let him down again. Around the time he said

"Buck," his voice cracked, and by the time he said "getting better," he sounded like a man again.

The stranger had a warm, round laugh. "Smart Mr. Ross. Is he staying at the saloon, then?"

The stranger hadn't noticed, thank the Lord. "He's real sick with frostbite, and Mrs. Haggerty, the land agent, is caring for him because the doc had to take off one of his toes." His voice lasted his whole statement, but he knew he was blushing and hoped the stranger thought that was just because he was standing near the heat.

The stranger went quiet and looked at Joss so hard it seemed to Joss like he was trying to look through him. Joss was feeling defensive, so he stared back just as hard.

"My name is Benjamin Walter MacLaren. What is yours?" MacLaren extended his hand, a hand so large that when Joss said his name was Joss Stretcher he felt like he'd never get his own hand back again because it just plain vanished. It hadn't hurt at all, though. The stranger impressed Joss as a man who knew about horses. That usually meant he'd be honest.

Benjamin asked Joss to fetch and carry, but he did the actual work of feeding, watering, and grooming by himself. "Can I leave you to get the blacksmith to check all his shoes for me? I'm going to the saloon for something to eat and even more important, something to drink. I'm parched dry."

Joss agreed it would be no trouble at all, and Benjamin Walter MacLaren threw him a half dollar. "If you're thinking of signing up to fight, don't try, son. At least until your balls drop. It's a dead giveaway you'd be lying about your age." Then MacLaren drew his gloves on, replaced his hat, and touched two fingers to its brim before he chinked his silver-colored spurs down the road. He opened the door to the Diamond to see Poppy serving a huge slice of pie to one of the people who'd had to stay overnight. MacLaren left Joss feeling as if he'd been acknowledged by the president himself.

Benjamin MacLaren was used to people admiring his clothes: his wolf-skin-lined wool coat, high-calf, black leather boots, and specially made western-style hat that was catching the fashion in Texas. But he was absolutely not used to seeing very small children in a saloon. MacLaren was not in the knowledge of how to do with creatures that were two-legged and very small, let alone experienced with those that looked right at his tanned, square face with its tidy black beard and screamed like he was a devil that had escaped from hell itself. He just sat down in the nearest chair and turned his back.

The mother ran past him up the stair, the child still screaming in her arms. Poppy came over. "Any chance of a whiskey," he asked, "or even a glass of rum?" She returned with the rum. "You want it heated?" The whole room could still hear the child screaming. "No, thank you kindly."

"Child's probably just tired having to spend so much time awake in the snow and the excitement of the wolves last night."

"I wondered what the howling was. Couldn't have been very many if they were looking for more of their kind." Poppy stared at him. "You mean you were out with them when they were prowling?"

"I was coming from Salina down here, yes. Why?"

"Weren't you worried they'd pounce on you or something?"

Ben could feel a legend starting, and he'd had enough rumors following him for far too long. They'd started to get in his way. They were preventing him from doing his job. He was fast getting to a point where he had to fight every escaped felon, just so they might be able to say they'd shot him or killed him. No, being a bounty hunter wasn't easy if you had a reputation. Ben didn't need anything but handcuffs and a gun, if he had to use anything at all. Usually all he needed was to look the man in the eye, tell him he had to go quietly, and they knew the jig was up. They just did what he asked. Normally there was no fuss.

"If I could hear them howling I knew they were far, far away, and I rode in the other direction. I'm not looking for trouble. What happened here?"

Poppy told him about the three skins the townspeople had taken. "Where did you get that one?" She was still looking for a legend. "Actually, I bought it near Chicago, Illinois, and a European tailor whipped up the whole coat for me. He had some leftover leather and made these gloves. Not bad, but they tend to get cold after a time. Is there anything hot to eat in your kitchen?" Benjamin was tired of the small talk and the kid was screaming still, now hiccupping once in a while. "Would you mind if I put a bit of wood on the stove and sat nearer? I'm still cold from last night."

Poppy told him there was coffee with cream or porridge with cream or he could even have both if he wanted it. The alternative was the usual bacon and eggs with biscuits.

He could hear movement coming downstairs so he asked Poppy for the usual, adding that since the cornbread was fresh made this morning he would welcome a slice or two. He got to the other chair in time to avoid seeing the mother and child again. He really wasn't happy about a babe in a saloon, but he was a newcomer, so didn't feel he had the right to say anything.

Poppy returned with a huge tray of food. "My, my, girl. Do I look like I eat all this?"

She blushed a bit while she began to pile the food on the table. "Yes. You do look like you need a good feed." Benjamin felt like a child being put in his place.

"Actually, you're right. I do eat lots, especially if I've been out of the warmth for a while. Now, tell me two more things, if you've got the time." Poppy stood with her tray leaning against her knees. "Do you have any spare beds?"

"I'll have to check that people aren't in the rooms, but I think there's one at the back. It's near, but not too near the cludgy. You can't smell it at this time of year anyway. If you need company in the room I can arrange that with one of the girls. They're all clean."

Benjamin Walter MacLaren paused a minute while he looked her up and down. "My other question is, has a man, an old sailor with one earlobe torn, calls himself Silk, been here of late?

"Pete, my man and the owner of this establishment, didn't like him and was glad to see him leave, but we heard he was going to be back."

"Ahh. Did he give any clue to when that might be?"

"Pete got the idea it may be soon, definite before spring."

"Thank you, ma'am."

"Your eggs are going to get cold, sir."

"My name is Ben. What's yours, please?"

"Poppy Diamond, Ben. I'll see to your room."

She marched into the kitchen in a way she hadn't in a very long time. "That stranger's name is Ben," she announced, "and I don't think he's afraid of nothing—no wolves nor any man—but a crying child, well, that's a whole other thing." Clara was scraping plates and pans.

"He's not the prettiest man I've ever laid eyes on." She was trying to hide while she peeked around the corner of the door. Her colorful dress of green tulle and silk was very gaudy and didn't vanish into the surrounding dark wood.

"You look like one of those merry men in the forest," Poppy said, "you know, Robin Hood and such. Get back, girl." Clara tutted and giggled but she obeyed.

"Does he want a room?"

"Yes, Clara, but he hasn't asked for any company. Why don't you go ask him if he wants another rum?"

Clara ruffled her skirts back into place, took off the little apron, and swished behind the bar like she'd never noticed he was there. She stopped, then walked over. "Howdy do."

"Ma'am."

"Anything to drink apart from coffee? Want me to top it with whiskey or rum?"

"Rum would be good, thanks."

He hadn't even looked at her. She came back slowly, making sure she rustled and swayed.

"Heated won't take but a minute, sir."

"I'm sorry, girl, but all I want right now is a clean bed and to be woken up just as it starts to get dark. Could you do that for me?"

"Yes, sir. Of course." Clara dropped a dip of a curtsy and went back to the kitchen.

"Maybe another time, then, Clara."

"Maybe, if I can be bothered. He's a strange one, isn't he?"

"He knows himself, is all. Doesn't need direction or suggestion. He's like Pete in that way. Take him as you find him or don't you even bother yourself trying, Clara. Besides, you're young and beautiful yet. Too young for the likes of him."

Ben looked toward the kitchen door, lifted his coffee mug in a gesture of thanks, and then pushed away from the table—everything, absolutely everything, completely finished.

CHAPTER TWELVE

Duncan lit a good fire once they realized they were going to have to spend the night. The weather had turned frosty, the path too frozen to let the horses draw the buckboard with any safety. Uphill was slippery, downhill risked the equipment sliding into them. Anyone riding on it would most likely be thrown off. When they saw a small wooded area at the top of the next hill they decided to take advantage of the shelter it might offer.

"Didn't think there were so many hills in the Great State of Kansas," Silk said.

"You know, boss, the way this kid is showing flame you'd think he was signaling someone," Rye said. "You got friends in the Rebs, the Indians, or just counting on help from some bushwhackers?"

"Why would I want any help?"

"You found us by accident when you and your ma were in town to offload your harvest. You're an evil little bastard as far as I'm concerned. Any person that can set up their kin to be slaughtered the way you did must have something missing in their head." Rye spat a solid mass into the wind.

Duncan stood up, his hand holding a branch of burning wood.

"Well, that's enough of that, boys." Silk removed the branch from Duncan's hand. "I'd tell you to tend to the horses but you wouldn't know where to start. Can I trust you to remove the saddles? Will you put them into the buckboard for us without cutting any of them or otherwise creating damage?"

"I wouldn't do that." Duncan was offended.

"Yeah you would, kid," Everly said. "I did at your age. Got a whipping for it. Nearly killed me." He never stopped grinning except when he said that. He didn't look right without his grin. He looked just plain dangerous, more than a little crazy. It occurred to Duncan that Everly might be the looniest of the loony.

"Tamp down the fire a bit, will you, Tom? Rye's right, we came here to see the lights of Lawrence, not to warn them we're coming to help ourselves to something special in the morning." Silk was cheerful.

Pat McBride had been on lookout to the west. He came back in a real hurry. "We've got company." He looked straight at Duncan. "It was probably the fire that little idiot made, feeding it like it was hungrier than we are."

"Armed?"

"No more than normal for wagon people, I think. Oddest damn thing, though. Painted and wooden topped, not cloth. Same curve though, and looks like there's a cook stove inside it, because there's a small chimney and smoke coming from it."

They heard wheels crunching on the ice toward the gang's campsite.

"Stay polite, everyone, until we find out what's occurring. Put that pot of coffee on the fire now it's settled a tad. We can show a welcome. It's too cold and the air too clear not to carry the sound of gunshot all the way back to Leavenworth let alone to Lawrence, so let's avoid it if we can."

"That's why he's the leader, kid. Good common sense, but he'll kill if he needs. Don't think too much, just do what he tells you. You'll be alive in the morning." Tom had come closer to Duncan as Silk moved toward the fancy wagon.

"Howdy, strangers. Cold night. We just settled here for a bit to give the horses a rest and ourselves a coffee, if you'd like to join us."

A man sat alone on the double seat, but Duncan heard noises coming from inside. The team of horses looked to be in prime condition, their harnesses fancy-like. There wasn't much light, but the flames from the campfire reflected to Silk and the boys that the tack was made from silver and polished leather. The big man continued to loosely hold the reins as he took his time to observe each member of the gang, one by one. A woman appeared from behind the wagon, no gun, just a cast-iron pot. "Can I put this on your fire to keep warm, good sirs? I think you are hungry, maybe. This is a good Hungarian beef stew. You will share, please. We will not partake of coffee, thank you. We will have tea, which we will also share with you. Then, once our horses have rested and eaten we will be on our way," she said. "We will do no harm to each other, yes?"

Silk was in awe of her, everyone could tell. "All right with you, boss?" he asked the man on the wagon. "Share the stew?"

"Been a while since I had a proper cup of tea. Miss and I would be thanking you for it." He swept his arm toward the fire and told Tom to make it wider, not taller.

"Space is always needed for a feast. Trust me, this will be a feast, not lunch, not dinner, a proper feast."

"My husband's name is Froika, and I am Rebecca." She put the large pot on the fire, pausing to look at Duncan. Then she returned to the wagon to help her man down from the rig. He busied himself with their horses.

Her clothes were very different from those worn by the local ladies. Yes, her skirts were long, but there was a color in them, and a natural movement. Her bodice appeared to be puffy in the shoulder area, and both their coats were definitely made from fur—perhaps bearskin mixed with a wolf trim around the neck. He was wearing a spectacular wolf-skin hat that seemed to sit on top of his head like it would never come off. It completely covered his ears and part of each cheek. Duncan thought he might be quite frightening to look at in daylight. He had no discernible beard.

Not tall, but broad, and obviously a man who could take care of himself, he walked purposefully and silently to the fire, as a man of the woods should. She brought a small stool for him and he spread his legs, showing the sight of loose-bagged leggings and ankle-high boots. He removed his fur gloves and put his hands toward the fire for the heat. He spoke to Rebecca in a foreign language. She returned to the back of the wagon, and Duncan heard noises of china and glass being moved about before she came back to the fire with her husband's plates and cutlery. Once she had served him he made a circle in the air around the fire.

"Froika says you may sit and join him now."

The gang hadn't noticed they'd been standing, nor that the horses were starting to wander. "Pat, get the horses back, quick," Silk said. "Duncan, do what I asked you to do and be quick or you'll get nothing at all to eat. Rye, rescue the harnesses, and Tom, please make sure there are chuck stones behind the buckboard's wheels. I'll see if we have any food at all that we can share. I'll at least get the tin mugs from each of you for the coffee."

There was the usual scuttle of organization. The fact that they were being watched by a woman they were sure would be beautiful if she took off the long fur hat that was part scarf, made them move so quickly and efficiently that for a minute Silk wondered about getting a woman to join the gang on a permanent basis. She'd have to be a tough bitch and have a bit of look about her. She'd also be great to do a con, if he could find the right woman with the right frame of mind and experience. Yes, Silk mused. Maybe not too bad an idea.

In less than twenty minutes the work was finished, the gang sitting at the fire on blankets or saddles, with cups of steaming tea in their hands. Rebecca had made them materialize as if by magic. Silk looked at his pocket watch. He sighed contentedly, relaxing back with his elbow on his saddle, his legs stretched out on the blanket underneath him.

"Used to sail the seas, ma'am. Had this once in Saint Petersburg. Lovely city."

"We too have sailed a sea, but now we travel land, and it has been good to us."

"Are you with one of those traveling shows, then?" Everly tried to get closer to Rebecca as he asked, but Silk stopped him with his leg, looking him in the eye, shaking his head in warning. "These folk are of the Gypsy persuasion, Everly, and you'll be advised to show respect for people whose history goes back thousands more years than yours."

"Most people are wary of us, sir." Rebecca was dishing out a stew of beef, onions, and beans, and adding to the mix something she called noodles. The men were suspicious of these things until they saw Silk slice through them with his spoon. Pat was the first to try one and pronounce them edible. Then everyone else tucked in until there were none left. Rebecca said if she could find more eggs in the market in Lawrence tomorrow, she could easily make more. Duncan asked if he was tasting whiskey in the stew. She laughed lightly and assured him no, it was only a glass of wine. "You have a taste for the finer things in life, young sir."

Tom rolled his eyes to the heavens. "Came to us a waif and stray, miss, a waif and stray. Seems to be doing a bit better now we've got him a shave and a haircut." Duncan was glad it was too dark for them to see him blush. He sensed Rebecca watching him.

She passed his plate back to him, the steel plate he'd given to her to fill. Their fingers touched. Time stopped for him. He ate his meal, not tasting anything, only aware that he was chewing, swallowing, chewing, swallowing. He sipped the hot water she called tea. His heart was fluttering, his head floating, but he wasn't anywhere near that campfire. He felt he was between worlds somehow. When he drew pictures in the dirt or on his school slate—that was where he was. He didn't belong anywhere. It came home to him that he could be pure evil, but why he would want to be was beyond his thinking. He liked the idea of being sinful, but why did it take the touch of a Gypsy woman to point it out to him, and why now? Was he supposed to do something about her?

He finished his meal. He found himself staring at her, and her coolly watching him. Froika only lifted his head. No one, none of the gang, was included in this group. They may have been sitting there sharing laughter and coffee and making plans to fetch more eggs, but he heard nothing.

"You have a dark soul, boy. You have already killed and will kill again and again unless you are stopped." Rebecca leaned forward to touch the middle of his chest with the palm of her hand. "You were given gifts to use and thought yourself too good for them. Draw one more picture before you die. You will become famous for something beautiful, not something ugly. People will wonder how such a man was capable of both. Then, in a hundred years or so, the beauty will vanish and the ugly remain. Beauty always fades. The ugly thing gets uglier. You have time to repent and find redemption. Go home and confess."

Silk was standing over him, shouting at him to get up and get going. It was very cold. Apparently he'd fallen asleep in front of the fire. Had he dreamed all of it? Maybe he'd had a drink, but at any rate, he felt discombobulated, unattached to his surroundings. Rebecca was up and sitting, ready to drive off in the painted wagon.

She looked at him and placed her hand over her chest where he thought she had placed it on his.

"Don't exchange messages with a Gypsy girl, boy," Silk said. "They know things they shouldn't and can tell you things you don't want to hear." It felt to Duncan like she'd had an effect on Silk. He was uncomfortable in his own skin.

Duncan stood. He seemed to have grown a bit. He'd certainly lost some weight, because the suit that Ma had bought him didn't fit none too well anymore. Silk took a step back. "You had a talk with her. I know, because your eyes have changed."

"So did you, Mr. Silk" Duncan said. "Unless I'm mistaken." Silk shuddered as he looked into the kid's now jet-black, dead-looking eyes. They reminded him of a shark or a dolphin—always hungry and not caring what they ate, even if it was one of their own.

He marched away. "Watch him," Silk told the others. "He's dangerous now. The Gypsy talked to him. He knows his future." Silk mounted the buckboard and motioned to Duncan to join him up front.

"Don't turn your back on him, lads. Ever."

The painted Gypsy wagon started down the trail to Lawrence, the empty buckboard trailing behind.

"Not too slippery today, then," Duncan said.

"No, we should be there in a couple of hours." Silk dug his watch out of his top pocket, deep inside and underneath his coats.

"Where'd you get that watch?"

"Gift from an old client. Want to look at it later?"

"No, that's all right," Duncan said. "Just had a mind that I'd seen it before somewhere."

"Only if you'd been in the right woman's bedroom, kid."

"I'd rather you didn't call me kid."

Silk put his watch back and tapped it home. *I was right. The Gypsy got to you. Well, maybe she's given you a good start, so fine, I can't promise, but I will try not to call you kid. Hey up!"*

The Mindwalker

He flicked the reins so the team wouldn't get cold or bored. Holy Jehoshaphat, that horse looked pregnant. As if Silk didn't have enough to worry him.

"When we get to Lawrence we're going to stable up for a bit while I see to our delivery."

Duncan looked at the flat scenery around and about him. Everything was frozen and white-frosted, even the spider webs he could see between the unharvested cornstalks and sunflower stems. "Are you going to tell me what we're getting this time?" He was hoping it would be something big and useful, like the Gatling gun he'd heard tell of.

"He wants to know what we're picking up, boys," Silk called. "Will I tell him, do you think?"

"You'd better disappoint him now, not later. I'd hate to see him embarrassed and shocked while he was standing in the middle of Lawrence," Pat enjoyed himself.

"Get me the clothes in the chest behind you." Silk told Duncan.

They turned out to be a suit a parson would wear. "Now, do you think you could take the reins just long enough for me to change into the shirt and the dog collar?"

Duncan was fired up and eager now. "I can do that, all right."

"Just hold them, just so the team knows there's someone paying attention." Silk was anxious about this but reassured when he saw Tom come to the front of the lead horse. He handed over the reins. The team skittered a bit, and Tom and Silk exchanged looks. Tom moved closer to the team, things settled, and Silk changed. "I'll put the dog collar on while I drive. Thanks, Duncan, I'll take the reins back now."

"What are you planning, robbing a collection box?"

"No, young man, there's a church organ, a smallish one, admittedly, about to be delivered to the army at Fort Leavenworth. I thought I would pick it up for them, being that I'm passing through from Kansas City, Missouri. Then, my friend, we can deliver it as a present from you to the people and church of Validation. It will make you look good, as you wanted, explain where you've been, and give me time to look for the paper I came for. Must be somewhere in that town if it's not at Pecan Farm, don't you think?"

Well, if he could find it in all that rubble, good luck to him. As for the organ, well it was a good joke. For the first time in days, possibly the first time in his life, Duncan laughed like a grown man with a purpose.

CHAPTER THIRTEEN

Pete and Ian rode most of the way to the outlying farms in silence. They spent their first night away in the home of the McMenemys, who welcomed them as if the family of eight children and three adults (one being the wife's mother of seventy-two years) hadn't seen anyone in years. In fact all eleven of them, even the one-year-old, showed up to church as often as they could. It was a good thing, really, because if they were all present, they formed a choir and drowned the reverend out. The poor man couldn't hear how bad and monotonous he actually sounded.

Pete and Ian were more than comfortable that night. The McMenemys provided a fabulous feast.

"There's your rations on the big wooden table, and the countertop as well." Nancy McMenemy stood with one hand on her hip, using the other to hold a ladle as a magic wand. "Find what you can and don't apologize for eating it, even if you have to stand up to do it."

Pete chose a good bit of the mutton, to which he had always been particularly partial. Ian tucked into a fire-roasted section of pig's ribs.

Great Ma McMenemy handed him an old piece of cloth. "Wipe your mouth afore you have to wipe the floor." She was right. Grease was running down his chin. He had been standing up as well, so she was right, he would have created a slippery mess on the rough wooden floor.

In the middle of the meal, someone began to tune a fiddle and a squeezebox. Ma was sitting with the babe in her arms. Father was helping the older ones feed the pigs with the leavings and bed down the animals outside, so the girls cleared the table, scraped the dishes and sat in the four double-sized chairs. All chatted while the musicians were getting ready and before the four older family members returned.

"We heard the wolves going past the house." Ma was feeding baby Coltilde. We've only got two old rifles, but they work, and we've got fire for them."

Pete told her about the three beasts they took down. "Looks like you could do with one of the skins over this winter. Maybe keep a draft or two away." He was thinking about the wind coming up her skirt from the floor as he could see the flimsy fabric it was made of moving around her ankles. A wolf skin would make a great rug.

"That would be mighty handy," she said, "if the price was right."

"Well now, Nancy, I understand that you're a proud woman and that you have every right to be, but you fed us and you're going to give us a bed for the night and we've come totally unexpected. So if it's all the same, I'll get one of the boys to drop it on by in the next few days if the weather stays good."

She knew what he was saying. "That would be mighty kind, Mr. Tait." Nancy lived in a two-room sod house. It was comfortable for temperature but needed more space now the family was older, so they had made plans for the spring. A wolf-skin rug would do a power of good and look mighty nice. One day she would like to cover the walls with paper that didn't come from the back and front cover of *Harper's Weekly*, even if it did serve the purpose of teaching the young 'uns their letters.

"You wouldn't have heard anything from the other farms at all?" Pete changed the subject. He'd seen enough prairie wives show the glazed look in their eyes that meant they were wishing and hoping, so he broke the wandering from the what-ifs and if-onlys by forcing her to remember there was a now that had to be lived through and dealt with.

"We've been held in here for three days, Mr. Tait. Mind you, it's unusual that we saw smoke coming from the direction of the MacGregors. Mr. and Mrs. MacGregor don't usually burn the left-over husks until the beginning of December. She likes to use them for fuel before Christmas because otherwise the pile is too large, she says. She saves any wood-burning logs until the New Year. That way it's like getting rid of last year's waste before the beginning of the new season."

Pete glanced at Ian. Sounds like there's been something untoward happening." Ian nodded his agreement. "You'll be sorry to hear that Buck is unwell and in the town, being cared for by Mrs. Haggerty and Ian's daughter, Mary." He explained how Buck had been found and had a toe amputated. The men had just come in from the shed, catching the word "frostbite" as they did so.

"We don't know where he had come from or even how long he'd been away." Pete cleared his throat. "We do know that his horse rescued him."

The children sat at his feet as if about to hear a bedtime story, the adults perched anywhere they could find as Pete and Ian shared Buck's story. At the end of their tale, Will McMenemy, tall, strong, and usually reluctant to say his thoughts, said, "That's only partly a bad thing."

"Why is that only partly a bad thing?" Grandma was awake in the corner, near the cooking fire.

"It means he won't be able for this stupid war." Father sat down and pulled off his boots. One of the women had knitted a remarkably good pair of thick socks. He replaced the boots with a wool-lined pair of moccasins. "Did you know that Buck could make boots, shoes, and moccasins?"

"That is a true talent. No, I didn't." Ian was flummoxed. "He's a right strange one. Says nothing, stands still in his own world, and works away quietly in the background. I wonder what else he gets up to."

"He sees things."

Pete smiled at the little girl whose name he couldn't remember.

"Haven't you ever seen him talk to people that aren't there?" The serious, big blue eyes were standing within a foot of his face.

"I have to admit I have," Pete said, "but I thought he was having a conversation with himself."

She nodded fiercely. "That's right, the other part of himself. The one that walks beside him." She appeared satisfied with his answer and went to sit near a big sister who had picked up some fleece and was beginning to card it. The light wasn't all that good, so Father got another lamp from the next room, and the party began. They played music into the night, but because the family had to rise early, they respected the routine. The oldest children gave up their sleeping spots, one up the bed and the other down along, joining with the younger ones, who acted like bed warmers and lay in-between. The two men kept their long johns on. They were both grateful there were no untoward holes in their drawers so no cold wind could sneak its way into their private regions.

In the morning Nancy offered coffee and porridge in an attempt to keep the company from leaving. Pete and Ian accepted, understanding her feelings, and not upset by delaying their departure from a warm fireside chat. She gave the men goods to take to Jenny if they wouldn't mind and oh, she saw how they admired Father's socks, so here was a pair for each of them. Grandma couldn't work as well on the homestead as she used to and her eyes weren't much good for long sight, but there was no one in the house that didn't have warm feet. Nancy even lifted her skirts up, just above her boot calf. It was only a little scandalous, but it proved to Pete that she wasn't as cold as it appeared to him.

The colleagues rode away, again looking mismatched but both with such full bellies they wondered if they would have to dig a hole in the river's edge before they reached the farm.

"That was a strange thing."

"What was?"

"The girl that said Buck talked to the part of himself that walked beside him."

"Her name is Persephone."

"I did wonder."

"Born in spring. Think it's the goddess of spring, Persephone. Could be wrong."

"Even if you are, it's a strange name to give a child."

"Just means she was born in the spring."

"She's not the only one that thinks funny, Pete Tait."

They encouraged a bit of speed from their mounts.

The sun was coming up, steam lifting from the grasses, cracking of tree branches against the warming of the weather, a man's breath warmer than anything around him, except his horse. This is a perfect day, said Pete to himself, but they crossed the cold river with care. It was running fast, but not dangerous yet. Ice formed around the edges, but Buchanan was steady and led the way for Annie and Ian.

Back on dry land they were relieved to see the sign above the gate for Pecan Farm. They could see the massive trees all looking asleep and waiting to start their job again in spring. No doubt J. T. would have painted pitch pine on their trunks to protect them from parasites. The boys would have been able to help this year.

Well, Buck would have. Duncan had always had a weak chest and may not have been up to much.

"Oh my. Oh my." Pete stopped Buchanan to help him understand the devastation he was staring at. "Look, Ian. Look."

"Oh, sweet Jesus. It's burned to the ground. C'mon!"

They kicked their horses into a canter, realizing that it was too late to be able to save any of the building but hoping against hope there would be life somewhere. It turned out there was. A pair of wolves was in the small graveyard. Pete didn't think, he reacted. His rifle came out of his saddle holster

"You bastards, you mangy bastards," he screamed. He shot one stone dead while he was still in the saddle. The other was bold enough to lurk in the trees. "You just wait there," he muttered. "You'll join your mate in hell." He slapped his rifle back down into its saddle holster. On trotting back to see Ian waiting for him at what used to be the front door of the house, he noticed that the privy was still standing. It looked untouched. Snow around the base of it, nearly up to the door handle, had maybe saved it.

"I wonder what the wolves were doing in the family plot?"

"Eating something."

They rode to see. A carved cross lay on the hard, cold ground. There was still snow on it. Ian slid off Annie. "Says, 'Jenny and J. T. November 29 1861'. Buck would have carved this."

"We'll have to get them deeper into the ground somehow."

"Good thing I'm here then, isn't it?"

Pete had forgotten Ian's profession. He couldn't look at the rotting corpse of Jenny. It felt disrespectful to a truly great and courageous woman.

Ian took his saddle blanket and put it over what was left of Jenny MacGregor. J. T. seemed to be buried deeper.

"Where the hell is Duncan?"

"He must have done some kind of runner, Ian."

"Well, his body isn't here."

"Can't see Thunder, either."

"I'll check around, see if he's wandering around the trees any."

"I will probably need help with the digging, Pete, but I'll work a while with Jenny here. Make sure she gets a bit of dignity, poor woman. Lord almighty, can't even put a decent shroud on her."

Pete rode off a ways because Buchanan, like most horses, didn't like the smell of decay and was showing skitters. Annie was more used to it, so Ian just left her to find some grass to nibble, being that the plot had been partly a garden and had some niceness attached to its upkeep. In a while, Pete came back.

"I've started a small fire and put on some coffee. Want to warm up a bit before we dig?"

"It must have been just one person that did this work. The first grave is well deep but the second is just deep enough. Either the light got bad or the digger had no energy or even a smattering of both, but the work was pretty well done. I only had to go down another foot or so, and I hate to say this, but there really wasn't a lot of Jenny left. She'll be safe now, though." Ian leaned on the small, wooden fence that was left. "I'd be grateful if you would help me tuck her in, so to speak."

"You're not going to believe this, but I found the family Bible in the privy. We can say words over her if you've a mind."

"We can take that back for Buck. I 'member him saying he learned his letters from it. Jenny taught both the boys."

Pete picked up the shovel, working like the devil was coming for him if he didn't hurry, while Ian recited the twenty-third Psalm from memory. He waited for Pete to finish and then said, "Amen."

Pete put the cross back where it belonged. "Buck must have done this on his own, but how did the MacGregors die in the first place? Did he see it happen and take the wrong way coming for help? Did he get caught in the snow and lose his way? I know I'm repeating, but where has Duncan gone? Thunder is nowhere. I can't find the buckboard, unless it was burned in the fire."

Ian encouraged the fire. It had nearly gone out while they were finishing the horrible but essential task. Pete walked calmly to his saddle, slowly removed his new Sharps rifle, lifted it to his shoulder, and put the other wolf out of its starving misery. Ian hadn't seen it sneaking up on them, but the noise of a shot in this brittle air seemed to echo from the trees. It felt like giving Jenny a ten-gun salute.

"A little warning, man. Damn good thing I wasn't pouring the coffee." Both of them laughed a bit to relieve the tension. "I'll skin one if you do the other. The ravens can have what's left. By the look of the poor beasts, they'll get precious little."

They lapsed into their comfortable silence while they let the coffee warm them. Without speaking, Ian skinned the wolf in the graveyard, and Pete did the one that had been lurking in the trees. It would have been better if they'd managed to hang the skins a bit, but needs must so they removed the skins and left the carcasses for the scavengers. Leaving them behind would be a complete waste and show no respect for the lives of the animals. It would be good to get back to Validation and their own homes by nightfall.

"The only person who'll be able to tell us what happened is Buck. I hope he comes round soon. Got the Bible, Pete?"

"Yup."

They headed back, knowing that they were traveling with two fresh-smelling pelts in the dark, with more snow threatening, by the look of the sky.

"Nice rifle, Pete. Reloaded, I hope?"

Pete grinned, spurred Buchanan through the river, and aimed true for home.

CHAPTER FOURTEEN

Pete was as sore and tired as he'd ever been by the time he handed Buchanan's reins to Joss.

"Feed him up well, will you? He's been working real hard and steady." He did the rubdown himself, but he knew that Joss loved this horse and would be spoiling him with treats of carrots, as long as he wasn't caught doing it. Joss liked to think he kept it a secret from Pete. Buchanan's teeth weren't as good as they used to be so, the secret wasn't truly hidden; traces of carrot gave away Joss's frequent generosity.

"Who does that beast belong to, Joss?" Pete threw a loose forefinger in the direction of a magnificent black but nervous-eyed stallion a side stall.

"That is Black Satin. The owner is Mr. Benjamin Walter MacLaren." Joss seemed pleased to be trusted enough to take care of such a spectacular specimen. "Came into town yesterday. Straight down the street from the east. Stupendous tall, gray hat." He showed how tall he thought the crown of it was by stretching his hand about twelve inches above his head.

"Still has an eagle feather in it, I hope?"

"You know him?"

"Old-time drinking and whoring buddy."

"What?"

"Sorry, Joss, you've got it all ahead of you yet. My days of fast living are far behind me."

He patted Buchanan's large, black rump. "Say hello to your Daddy, big fella."

"Black Satin is your horse's sire?" Joss was astounded.

"Every chance of it, Joss. Every chance." Pete smiled as he left, aware that he had once again shocked little Joss with a lie. One day one of them would learn not to tease the other, but he enjoyed himself for the time being. The jest cheered him up a little and made him feel a bit younger, so he left the livery bouncing along a bit.

Ian caught up with him, Annie steadily following on behind, reins slung over her saddle.

"Can't tell Buck about the wolves and what they did to his family." Ian kept his voice low. "Told Ryan that we'd had to bury Jenny and J. T. and that we wouldn't know what happened until Buck could tell us. Said Duncan wasn't anywhere to be seen. And he said if there'd been any trouble the little snake would have slithered into a dark hole somewhere until it was safe to come out. Asked him to take the pelts to the tanner because we'd come across the beasts and put them out of their misery in case they had the frothing crazies. Didn't say anything about having to rebury the family in case Buck heard that Jenny had been defiled. Told him we were giving the pelts to the McMenemy people for putting us up that night."

"Fine by me. You noticed there were a few cold spots in that patched-together house as well as I did."

"Yup. I think a new floor covering would do some good there." Ian stopped just short of the saloon. The lights were on, and someone was tinkering with the piano. Not too many customers then, he thought. The sound of the music wasn't being drowned out by shouting or laughter.

"Need a drink?"

"Later on. I'll check in with Mary first." He slapped his hands together in the hope of stirring the blood and restoring the warmth to his system. Stamping his feet up and down, he formed the opinion that he was too old for this gallivanting. The only people who should be out in this cold were the already dead.

The men shook mittened hands as best they could and Pete entered the saloon, taking his hat off and whacking it a couple of times on the door jamb to get rid of its frozen stiffness. Poppy ran to him and threw her legs around his waist as she grabbed his head for a kiss. The room of about a dozen cheered her on.

"Get off, girl, you're making a show."

"A fine show it is, Pete "The Knife." A very fine show indeed." Benjamin Walter MacLaren stood up. Poppy clung to Pete's hefty waist as the two old friends clasped their large forearms in reunion. Side by side, Pete and MacLaren were the same size and build. Both were broad-shouldered and could look each other clearly in the eye. They shared an old and mutual respect.

"I've come to this town looking for a blaggard and found an old scoundrel instead. How fares thee?"

"That's enough of the old country blather, Benjamin MacLaren. Plenty of enough. Sit, sit. Tell me all that's brought you here."

Benjamin liked to be called Ben, not the full title. Everyone in the saloon that night, including Doc Fraser, had heard the truth of his life and how he had met Pete many years ago in a Chicago hostel, as he termed it. Everyone realized it was a place where the ladies would ply their trade, but no one mentioned the obvious. A blaggard called Silk, who had escaped justice from the Royal Navy after being sentenced to hang, had also been a guest and had gotten into a tussle with Ben over, of all things, a pocket watch. Now,

Ben knew that it belonged to one of the ladies and told Silk to give it back. He refused, saying it was his right to keep it because the woman hadn't given him full cooperation. Ben had pointed out that women who've been slapped seldom cooperated well and fully. The sailor rounded on Ben with a knife. Pete, who just happened to be in the way of it, caught the sailor's arm and bashed it against the staircase, forcing him to release a truly magnificent dirk. It had a case etched in silver that matched the handle of the knife. There was the most highly polished, golden cairngorm crystal in the hilt. Ben had given it to the lady in question so she could defend herself in the future. The sailor made a run for it during the disorder he'd created.

Ben had gone to the establishment to find this very man on behalf of the widow of the man Silk had murdered. Silk had been on board his ship and disagreed with the captain of the vessel, saying that he hadn't been at sea long enough to pass wind, let alone find any to sail with. There had been a tussle. Silk had shot the captain with a gun that would normally have been used under a card table— in other words from five feet away, in the most cowardly of fashion.

"Until this Civil War of yours started I had lost track of him, but as wars often do, they bring the best and the very worst of society to the surface. I knew if I lurked about the military establishments, the armories, the trails between North and South, I would catch up with him. Midshipman Silken would always show up for profit. I am, of course, counting on the fact that he doesn't know I'm looking, that I have, in fact, given up." Ben sipped his warm rum. "I haven't. I want that watch back. I know who it belongs to, and I swore to return it."

There was an almighty cheer from everyone and, as he expected, mumbling about a mighty fine tall tale. He sighed and raised his glass to Pete.

"Here's to the legend, Ben. Where would we be without them? Life would be helluva dull." He moved Poppy from his lap, asking her for something, anything to eat because he hadn't had a bite since the morning. He leaned forward. "The woman you made the promise to arrived in this very town just at the end of August." Ben scanned the top-floor balcony.

"No, not up there. She is now a woman of good reputation so I'm keeping her confidence, as is Doc Fraser—here sitting beside you, by the way. She's the land agent, Mrs. Haggerty."

"Can you warn her not to recognize me?"

"I will. As a matter of fact, I'll excuse myself to the privy for a bit and do that very thing. It's good she hasn't come across you yet."

"I spent the day in my rooms resting. Your girl Clara woke me up as I'd asked her to just after it was dark. I've been sitting here eating and drinking. As you will remember, I'm good at it."

Pete went to the kitchen end of the building, telling Poppy he'd be back in just a minute.

As soon as the back door closed on him, a young woman's voice called from the front. "Is the doc here, please?"

Doc stood up. "Right with you, Mary."

"He's awake."

"That's good, be right there. Is Mrs. Haggerty with him?"

"Yes, but she's needing a break from it all so she'll come here while you see to him."

Doc slipped his coat on, passed a look to Ben, and went to see his young patient.

"I'll go check on Satin, I think," Ben said. "Can we meet here in about an hour?" They all walked out together.

"Mr. Benjamin Walter MacLaren, I have the honor of introducing Miss Mary Grant, daughter of Ian, our general provisioner and very part-time undertaker, thanks be to God." They stood on the sidewalk in front of the Diamond. The wind had settled enough that lifting the voice was no longer necessary. Mary extended her hand as she'd been taught by her mother just two years ago, before she died. Mr. MacLaren took it and bowed, just as Mary had been taught to expect. She was impressed. It was the first time she'd been introduced like a proper lady and treated like one. She remained, as far as Doc Fraser could tell anyway, as calm and unflappable as usual, so he presumed she was quite used to this.

Ben knew better, being much more a man of the world than the doc, in spite of all the book learning. It warmed him to see that a young woman had managed to remain just that, in this hard, western way of life, hard especially for a lady. So many had taken the route that Shona Haggerty had taken after her young widowhood and now, unless the truth of things was respectfully managed, the luck she must have created for herself could turn on her. He wondered if Mary could accept or even needed to hear the slightly older woman's past. They could only be ten or fifteen years apart. Maybe they got on well enough that Shona could tell her if and when she chose to.

He touched the top of his brim and excused himself to go to the stables. Mary and Doc went to visit his patient. Doc wasn't looking forward to telling Buck he would have to learn to walk again, let alone ride. It wasn't impossible, of course, but re-learning would take time and the doc remained concerned about infection. He asked himself if Buck was aware of the loss of his toe, or would he be one of those who never stopped feeling it.

Mary opened the door without knocking but shouted that the doc had come. Mrs. Haggerty had been doing some crochet. She was wearing tiny, wire-rimmed glasses that sat on her nose. No wonder she always appeared to look right through people.

"I had no idea you needed help for close work, Shona." She glared at him.

"That's a lovely name, Mrs. Haggerty." Buck covered Doctor Fraser's faux pas with grace not usually found in a seventeen-year-old. The room felt serene and smelled of sage, the same sage a visitor to an Indian teepee or campfire would smell. The sound of wood crackling in the fireplace added to the aura of peace, as did the low lighting of the small paraffin lamp. Doc also felt something added, something extra. Doc knew now what Ryan meant when he said he felt like he was talking to two people when he spoke to Buck, and what Mary meant when she said there was something odd about him that she couldn't put her finger on. She would always go silent when she said that, like she was supposed to be observant of some kind of higher power. Quite frankly it gave the doc the shivers because he was—and he hadn't mentioned it to anyone—absolutely sure that another pair of hands, invisible ones, had covered his that dreadful night when he had to mangle this young man's body.

"You're awake, Buck." The doctor sounded brusque and professional.

"I've been awake for most everything, Doctor Fraser. Thank you for being so quick when you removed my little toe." Buck tried to sit up a little. Mary and Mrs. Haggerty sprung into female flap and reaction, one helping him to sit and the other plumping the cushions.

"There's some pea soup if you're ready for it."

"I'm really hungry, so a bowl of soup would be a good start, I guess."

"You've been through a bumpy time of it, Buck. Don't eat too much until maybe breakfast tomorrow," Doctor Fraser said. "How's the rest of your body feeling? Pins and needles?"

"Not bad, thanks, Doc. Right leg isn't very pleased yet. Hands are fine."

There was a slight rap at the door. Shona answered it.

"Just stepping out to have a quick word with Pete," she said. "He needs to tell me something." She tossed her shawl over her shoulder and closed the door behind her.

Mary brought a bowl to the bedside, intending to feed Buck, but he took it from her, putting it on his lap. "I'll get a towel for a bib, laddie. I'm not wanting what's left of my mother's good linen to be stained, and green is not my most favorite of colors."

"I'll wait for you to finish before I have a look at the wound." The door let in a waft of cold air as Mrs. Haggerty rejoined them, smiling at Mary as if to tell her there was nothing amiss.

"I know I wasn't supposed to hear," Buck said, "but Moon Feather is with us and says to ask how Mr. Grant and Pete Tait got on at the farm." It was a very good thing that Mary hadn't been handling the bowl. She would have dropped it.

"What is a moon feather?"

Buck looked at them one at a time and sighed. "Everyone here calls me "The Mindwalker," but you think I'm not aware of the affection that it shows me. One or two of you have even felt an undisclosed touch, smelt a semi-familiar smell or sensed it. I, along with others of you, am not walking alone. None of us in this room are unaware. Mrs. Haggerty especially, who speaks to her deceased, beloved Jamie every day. It is wonderful to hear, because she's been telling him everything that's been happening to me and others. I know about the three, but now five—Moon Feather tells me—wolf pelts. Seems Pete is a crack shot with his rifle. Got two while they weren't looking."

Buck handed his bowl back to Mary. "Now, thank you for that. Moon Feather is my Cheyenne spirit guide. She was about twenty when the fever took her. Piddlin would not have got here if she hadn't taken charge. It makes no never mind to me if you do think it's the fever talking, Doctor. The fact is that I went back to the farm on the twenty-ninth of November this year. I found my aunt and uncle dead. She, it looked like, had been drowned in the trough, He had been shot in the doorway of our home. I buried them as best I could, went back to the house to see if there was any food and to carve a cross for the graves." He took a long breath and appeared to age twenty years before he took his eyes from the now dying fire.

"Then Duncan showed up."

"Where had he been in all this?" Doc growled.

Shona looked horrified. "In hiding, for certain sure."

Mary was aware Buck was holding her hand very tight. "There are things I don't want to share with ladies. We had a fistfight. I knocked him out and just left. I didn't know where I was going, but I didn't want to be on the farm. It belongs to Duncan now, anyway."

He looked into Mary's hazel eyes. "I'll have to find a different way to make a living."

He shifted his look to Doc. "You'd better see to my foot, if you wouldn't mind."

Moon Feather closed her eyes and bowed her head in time with Buck. They communicated in silence while the doc did his job. She was grateful he hadn't mentioned her father.

CHAPTER FIFTEEN

"I'm tired of riding with you, Everly Plastow." Rye Carp snarled. "Any man that has to have a woman at every stop no matter whether she likes it or not has an itch in his pants that'll one day show up in his finger, and I'm not going to take that risk." He shoved himself away from the saloon table, drew his pistol, and killed Everly where he sat with a shot straight through the heart.

"Clean kill," he said, taking evident pride in reholstering his Smith & Wesson Model 1.

Pat MacBride was just a little less drunk. "You shot my compadre, you half-scalped Indian son of a bitch." He began to draw, but Silk was able to stop him in time because he was stone-dry sober.

"It's late," Silk said. "That's enough fuss for one day."

Pat and Rye were eyeball to eyeball, only a hair away from their noses touching. Pat shrugged after a while. He stepped over Everly and past Rye to get some air outside on the boardwalk.

Duncan was unconscious from the amount of whiskey he'd had. He was sound asleep in the wooden armchair, as far as Silk could see. A man, either an undertaker or the law, Silk didn't rightly know, came from outside, stepped into the middle of things and asked who was going to pay for all this: the coffin, the burying, and the rectifying of this mess in his bar.

"I'll take care of the overheads, mister, don't let it worry you, no, don't let it worry you." Silk bent down to retrieve Everly's gun and belt. "You the owner here?"

"I'm the head of the town council, so I do most things here, Mr. Silk." He was a quiet talker. "Leave the gun until the undertaker gets here—just in case he has to sell it to pay for the internment of your friend—in case you forget, I mean." The sallow, wide-girthed little man had the sand to look Silk straight in the face. Silk bent again, this time to place Everly's hat over his open eyes.

"How do you know my name?"

"Why wouldn't I? There's wanted posters, but thanks to this verdammit war you're not worth the five hundred dollars to make a fuss over."

"So your name is?"

"None of your business. Just clean up your mess and get out in the morning." Silk smiled. The speed of the little man's departure implied that the smile had worked on the weasel. Two cronies that came in while he was leaving, lifted Plastow's body like it was nothing more than rags. The taller man threw him over his shoulder, Everly's grinning head flopping up and down as they carried him to the undertaker. That grin must have been a tick life had given to him, but it gave Silk the shudders all the same.

He had to rethink now. Damn and blast Carp. It would mean he might have to use Duncan to steal the gift and the treasure he'd promised himself. Ideally, the heist should happen sometime in the next eight hours, and in the dark. It made him feel good to think again. He rubbed his gloved hands together as he walked into the town, followed by Pat, Rye and, taking up the rear, Tom. Duncan was better to be left sleeping it off.

"Just the four of us, then," he said to the others. "First thing is to see to Plastow's horse. Don't want that kid getting anywhere near the beast, so Tom, go to the livery and tell them to give it to the councilman in payment for all his trouble. Give him these two silver dollars as well. Get him to clean the animal and its tack. One dollar is for him and the other also for the councilman."

Silk was beginning to plan, to live again. He had been feeling sluggish and old lately so maybe Pat's killing of Everly Plastow, rapist, murderer, and all-around butcher of women was a good thing. Maybe not having to keep a weather eye on him all the time was even better.

"What do you want me to do, boss?" Pat had also caught the feeling of being back in action.

"We are going to the land office. Looked to be a big one so we'll have to be quick."

Tom walked toward the livery as the others walked nearer to the hotel and smaller saloon at the other end of town. Lawrence was a bigger place than when last they were here. There was more than one church and a few more streets and houses near the river. The population was bigger and a lawman, jail, and courthouse had arrived to stay, judging by the solid-looking buildings. The war had created a different set of priorities, of course, and people were mostly trying to live and let live within their own confines and their personal sense of right from wrong.

"It's a good thing we're here now. This time next year things will have changed out of all recognizing and all, due to the war, no doubt." Pat said.

"Aye, the war will get the blame for many a thing, lad. Many a thing." Silk sounded old.

They stopped just outside the land office. Pat rolled a cigarette.

"Rye, go check around the back to see if there's a door. We'll wait here. If anyone sees us they'll just think what they like and move on."

"You can read, can't you, Pat?"

"Just a bit."

"Can Rye?"

"Oh, yeah. Real good. Had proper book learning before the Indians stole him from his ma and scalped him before they sent him home." He lit his smoke, trying to hide his shaky hand by turning his back to the wind.

"Lucky he lived, then."

"Is why he wears that hat all the time. Says he can get a mite cold even in summer with only a half of his hair."

Rye came back as if he had a purpose. "Spotted a wanted poster. Some people want you alive only. Dead is no good to them."

"Councilman able to read as well as you then, Rye." Silk sounded proud of his notoriety. "Would you turn me in for the cash then, boys?" The laughter was too loud and attracted the attention of the few people still on the street.

"Not if you can guarantee more than five hundred dollars each by the end of the day tomorrow," Pat said.

"You're a man thinks like me, Pat McBride, just like me," Silk said. "I can get you that in cash this time tomorrow night, but I need you to keep that little turd Duncan out of my sight and keep watch on the front door of this place. There is a back entrance, Rye?"

The two men looked at him for a minute, both trying to make a decision about trustworthiness. Then, on that clear night at the end of November, Silk followed Rye around the back of the building.

"What we going to lift, then?"

"There's no real law here. If there was you'd have been arrested by now, so it shouldn't be hard to break into the cash drawer. You get that as hush as you can. I'm going to look for a book that has lists of titles in it. We'll go as soon as we've got everything."

"What you going to do with a book?" Rye kept his voice low.

"Sell the land that's listed in it."

"What if it already belongs to someone?"

"Aye, but the buyer won't know that, will they?"

"That's gotta be illegal." Rye ruffled his own little beard and smiled as he tried to stifle his laugh. "This is going to be great, Mr. Silken." He hopped from one foot to the other. Silk tutted.

"Very likely. Now, open the door as slow and quiet as you can."

"It's not locked," Rye whispered.

They stood with the door ajar and tried to look into the dark room. Rye edged the door a bit more.

"Coast is clear," said Silk.

"Aye, aye, captain."

"Look, the cash drawer is right in front of you,"

Silk scanned the shelves behind the counter—no deed book.

"Look, here's what you're looking for." Rye handed the thick, leather-bound book to Silk. "Can't get this drawer open."

"No need to lock the door if the cash is already locked away. Let me try." He slid a Bowie knife from inside his boot to fiddle the lock. They heard it give. They also heard footsteps outside. Standing in silence they were appalled to hear Duncan's voice. He was asking Pat where they were. Loudly.

"I'll shut him up," Silk said.

"Permanently, I hope."

"Can't just yet."

They were still whispering.

"Nice knife."

Silk looked at him, acknowledging the comment with a wink. Quietly he returned outside.

"Can't a man urinate in peace, lads?"

Duncan visibly relaxed.

"C'mon, then. We have to go to the bunkhouse. Time for bed, because we'll have a busy day tomorrow. If the weather stays good we might even go to Topeka if I've a mind. You been there kid—oh, sorry, Duncan?"

"Think so. Long time ago. Where's Rye and Everly and Tom? Oh, there's Tom. Coming from the stables." Duncan staggered toward him. Silk slid his knife back into its holder.

"Go on then, boy, Tom's just been seeing to the horses, Rye and Everly will be about somewhere, I'm thinking."

"Getting cold."

"Yes, because there's a clear sky." Silk licked his finger and held it in the air. "Wind's coming from the northwest, I shouldn't wonder. Maybe we will get snow tomorrow sometime."

They found their way to the bunkhouse, which oddly wasn't that full. Looked like men weren't wandering as much as they used to, now they had regiments to march with.

It didn't take much time for Duncan to drop off again especially after Pat offered him a good, long swig from his half bottle.

"Where will I put this stuff?" asked Rye.

"In plain sight. Go to the buckboard. Stash it under the blankets where that lump of lard sits. That'll weight it down."

"What you going to do now?"

"We'll all meet at the church as soon as you're finished. I've managed to do something legal to cover up what we've really been up to, and each of you are going to keep a straight face. You going to join me, Pat? You'll need me to tell you what the plan is."

The church wasn't very warm, but it was obviously cared for, what with the Sunday dried flowers still in their basket vases. Thanksgiving was either just about to happen or had happened yesterday. Silk hadn't noticed really. He was still a Yorkshireman at heart and paid no attention to these new holidays or festivals. Christmas and Easter were plenty. Yes, he had a fond memory of a Christmas service at Yorkminster—what a sound that organ made. Christmas was going to arrive within the next four weeks, and he was determined to finish the trade he had organized long before then.

There was a man sitting in the forward pew.

"Stay here, Pat. Keep an eye for us."

Pat wasn't a churchgoer. Rye was if he got a chance, probably because his parents were missionaries—at least Pat heard rumors they were. Tom was getting on in years and so he could be more easily persuaded toward the religious than he had been ten or so years ago.

"You the musician?" Silk sat quietly beside the man.

"Yes. You got my equipment?"

"Delivered to your address already. You should know that."

"I do, but only the man who delivered it would know the address. What is it?"

"Railway Stand, Leavenworth. Miss J. Read."

"Good to meet you, Mr. Silken. I'll have the equipment delivered to you?"

"No, my boys are here. Where is it?"

"Left it for you in the livery. Large box. Marked 'Property of the U.S. Government.' You can't miss it. Wooden though. Try not to drop it." He stood, gave the altar a curt bow of his head, dropped his Reb hat on his head, and marched from the building, his officer's saber in his uniform's sash.

"That looked like a Reb colonel," Pat whispered.

"Just another one like us but in different clothes, is all."

"What'd he want?"

"Better talk closer to the bunkhouse. With any luck it'll look like we've said our prayers for poor Everly and can go to bed with a clear conscience." They walked a few steps in silence, apart from the frost crunching underfoot. Silk noticed the councilman standing at the corner of the doctor's office, beside the undertaker. The town worthies were lit from behind, their shadows as still as they were. Silk and Pat looked appropriately somber on the street but cheered up immediately after they closed the bunkhouse door behind them. Silk took a small slug from his flask.

"You know how we delivered all those brand-spanking-new guns and ammunition to the fort, and how we managed to pilfer them from right under the noses of the very same guards? Good fun, eh?" Silk was warming to the prank he was setting up. "This is even better, because we didn't have to do any work, and this is something that, when we give it to the right person at the right place, not even a government would have the brass to demand it back. The U.S. government has mislaid a small church organ, listed for delivery to Fort Riley, Kansas." Silk whispered this information. The boys didn't know what to do with it. "I have made a huge profit for us. I will give you your five hundred dollars each after we leave town in the morning."

Duncan moved in his bunk. Rye turned the lamp down. All of them sat to stare at the drunken lump. He snorted and turned. Rye turned the lamp off. Duncan began to snore.

"What kind of an organ? Does it fire bullets in secret or something? Does it blow up when you press a special note or make a particular sound?" Rye didn't raise his voice. Pat and Tom were just as undecided.

"Tell us about the land venture," Rye said. "You have to tell all of us how you're going to sell land that is already owned by someone to someone else. If you can do that and make me understand it's good business for us, then I'll help with this organ idea. If not, well, I haven't forgotten there's a wanted poster out there."

"I think we should travel back to Massachusetts or Maine," Silk said. "Those folks only think they know all about what's west of the Mississippi. We can tell them how right they are and suggest they buy some good land to invest in, before it's in the wrong hands."

There was a silence. "That is smart, boss. Real smart. Especially as we all look like we've been here." Pat was impressed. Now he knew why it was important to Silk that someone could read.

"What do we do with the kid?"

"He's our secret weapon. Duncan will have to come off the hooch before his hand gets a permanent shake. He can draw, boys. He can copy and draw and write well. Counterfeit, lads. We own a natural counterfeiter."

"I got to visit the privy." Rye proclaimed his intention, exited the warmth, walked on a bit more, and watched the Gypsy wagon edge past slowly. Rebecca had recognized him, sharing her smile, fleeting as it was. Froika was driving, geeing up his team.

"I wonder why they always travel at night."

"I've heard stories about creatures that can only travel in the dark."

"Yes, Rye, they're called bats. Just like you, eh? Batty in the head. You'd never turn me in, would you, me old mocker?" Silk threw his arm around Rye's shoulders and joined him for the last pee before bed.

CHAPTER SIXTEEN

"Mrs. Haggerty, I'm nearly as fixed as I'm going to get, and I thank you kindly for putting me up, but it's time I found my own way, don't you think?"

Mrs. Haggerty said she agreed with Buck, but only to a point. "You're going to need a bit more help with the learning how to balance, and Doctor Fraser says that until you can ride again you shouldn't leave town."

Buck could now hobble to the privy on his own and get dressed without help. Miss Mary had tailored some denim to suit him. He didn't ask if it was the bolt Jenny had ordered or if it had been used by one of their clients because he didn't really know or care. He wasn't in a hurry to put on his right sock simply because he had to face the fact he no longer had a fully intact body. It would always be a reminder of what had brought him to lose it. Was this what Mark meant by more wounds? Was a missing toe there to remind him that his path was to be a healer?

The poor lad was so bored he had taken to reading her old knitting patterns, the *Harper's Weekly*, and then *Webster*'s dictionary.

The doc had found out and brought over his *Encyclopedia of Practical Medicine, Principles, and Practice of Modern Surgery,* and finally *Human Physiology.* Buck was fascinated by the surgery book and spent time with the dictionary looking up words that had something to do with amputations.

"Pete has arranged a special room in the bunkhouse for you if you want. You can get your meals at the saloon. Poppy is more than willing to help you out with that. She'll also fix you up a laundry girl until you can do for yourself. Joss could do with help in the livery and since you're such a dab hand at making and fixing shoes you can always earn your keep that way, at least until the spring." Shona fairly bounced with goodness.

"Fine, that's really fine, ma'am. I got to go back to the farm, though. See if Duncan's left anything that belongs to me."

"Ahh. Well, yes. I've got to get hold of Pete or Ian for that. They can go with you. Make sure you can ride fine and dandy. Have you met Benjamin Walter MacLaren yet?"

Buck had heard of him, how big he was, how unusual in speech and looks. He sounded like someone Buck could talk to about things.

"Is he living in the saloon then?"

"So they tell me. I haven't laid eyes on him yet, either. Will you be so good as to escort me there later, sir?"

Buck tried to bow but nearly overbalanced. "Who would have thought that a body needed all its toes, even one little one, just to stand up in one spot?"

"Well, you've been sickly for a couple of weeks now so you'll take a bit of time yet. Good thing your appetite's coming back."

"Now that I'm standing we might as well go to meet this legend of a man, MacLaren. Pass me my stick, please." He threw his jacket over his shoulders and extended his right elbow to Shona. She took it, aware that she'd be his other prop as they made their way through the snow and the mud. "Funny weather, this. Wish it would make up its mind." Shona was mumbling.

"You talking to me or your Jamie?" Buck's kind eyes were looking down at her.

"If anyone else had said that I'd have been hurt. You really understand, don't you?"

"My mother was murdered the day I was born, but she's never really left me. Is it true that I told the doc to take my toe off that very night?"

"You said your ma had told you to tell him."

"Well, then. Proves my point. Your Jamie has never left you either."

"He said he'd always be faithful. Even had it engraved on the watch he gave to me."

They continued along the road, trying to dodge the worst of the dirty snow and sewage.

"How do I get up steps?"

"Hang on the hitching rail, and I'll get help."

They were in front of the Black Diamond. It was only just turning noon. There was a great bellow of laughter from inside and a massive man shoved his way through the small door. He stopped to stare at the diminutive young woman in front of him.

"I remember you from years ago. Mrs. Haggerty, is it?" Shona was relieved at his discretion.

"I know your face from somewhere, sir. Can you help me get this laddie inside before you go on your obviously urgent business?"

"Not business that can't wait, ma'am. Is this the young man, Buck Ross is it, that lost his toe to frostbite?"

"That's myself, sir."

"I'm Ben. Most people have many other names for me, not all of them particular polite, but just this once I'll lift you up to the walk. Next time you'll be strong enough to do it yourself, as long as you can eat to get your strength back." He lifted Buck in one swoop, using his right arm around the young man's waist. "You definitely need to eat your taters, son. Lots of steak, onions, and taters for the next week and you'll be fit to eat proper for Christmas dinner. Got to stretch your stomach, Buck. Stretch your stomach." He assisted him to the nearest warm table. Shona followed and was glad to see Poppy. Pete arrived from behind the bar.

"No whiskey for you just yet, Buck. Got to line your ribs with good food before we burn your innards, don't you think?"

Poppy came over in a rush, as did Clara. "You don't look well at all, Buck. Pete, we'll give this young man a bed until after Christmas. Clara, go to clean the one over the kitchen right now, girl. It's the warmest. Mrs. Haggerty you'll be needing your own room and to get some rest yourself. You've been a saint about all this, but enough is enough. I've got a bunch of young women here who'll spoil him rotten without expecting any payment in return. Isn't that right, Clara?"

Clara nearly objected, but Poppy snapped her fingers in the girl's face, the implication being that Clara was replaceable at the snap of the madam's fingers.

"Are you sure, Poppy?"

"Mrs. Haggerty," Poppy sat down to speak. "I have only got one job here. You, for the last couple of weeks have had to run the land agency and the bank and take care of Buck here, a grown lad of nearly eighteen. You've had people in and out and, of course, I own you've had Mary's help a great deal of the time, but still, you have to agree that my job is taking care of people and only people. I ask that you let me help you. Fair enough?"

Put that way, Shona felt flattered.

"This is the difference between east and west, Buck. Out here we have to pull together to survive things. In the east they have to invent troubles and bring troubles on themselves to feel like they're living."

"Glad you came in, Buck. We've got something to tell you." MacLaren swept some imaginary crumbs from the table just as Poppy came back with a massive plate of biscuits and gravy.

"Don't want you to be chewing on anything that might upset a stomach that's too tender just yet. Get you some fresh milk as well. Better for you than coffee." She patted Pete's big hand. "Yes, yes, I'll bring coffee for you two as well."

"Have you found Duncan?"

"No. That's just it. He's missing, and so is Thunder."

Ian joined them. "Well done getting yourself along, Buck. Takes guts. Well done." The coffee arrived, an extra mug along with it. Poppy also sat. "Want a coffee or a whiskey, Ian?"

"Coffee's fine."

"Mrs. Haggerty?"

"Coffee, thanks."

"Are we all organized, Poppy?" Pete asked.

"Yes. We are. Now, what were you saying, dear?" She glared at Pete for a second. There wasn't a person at the table that didn't wince at the underhanded swat.

"When you told us what happened to your Aunt Jenny and Uncle J. T., you told us that you found J. T. lying in the door of the house," Pete said.

Buck tarried his spoon. He nodded, finished the mouthful, and had a sip of milk. He hard gazed into Pete's gray-blue eyes.

"So how did the farm and all the buildings apart from the privy get burned down?"

Buck was silent for such a long time people began to get restless in their seats. He continued to eat. Once finished, he looked at Poppy, thanked her exceedingly, and then asked if there was anything left behind in the privy.

"Yes. Just your family Bible. We brought it with us." Pete recovered it from the bar where Poppy had protected it by wrapping it in one of her high-holy-days-and-Thanksgiving-only tablecloths. "Nothing else?" Buck asked.

"No, were you expecting anything?"

There was another long silence while each of the adults felt they were being assessed for honesty as he looked at them, one at a time. None flinched.

"When my parents were killed, J. T. took a rawhide bag of gold and silver bits. He said I wasn't to say anything because it was for my eighteenth birthday and was from my pa. Aunt Jenny knew, too, and that's why it was always my job to build the privy. I had to hide it every time, in the very top rafter and behind the door. I knew Duncan would never look for it there even if he had been told of it, because he always felt it was a job for the poor relation and he hated the smell more than anyone I know. He must have burned the farm. He never wanted to be part of it. Must be his way of turning his back on the whole thing. Are the trees still standing?"

"It's a good thing the weather was so wet. None of them even got singed."

Buck placed his locked fingers over his full belly. He went silent again, then spoke. "He'll be on a trail somewhere, trying to convince someone he's an outlaw. He used to draw pictures of outlaws in the Bible and any other pieces of paper. Did anyone notice the drawings Auntie used to pin up on her walls?" He spoke as if it was an afterthought, then reached for the book.

Opening it at Genesis, he showed them drawings in what was most likely fire charcoal of horses, guns, trains, cattle, buffalo, and wagons. Occasionally there would be what Duncan would have thought a girl looked like with no clothes on. Truth be told, Buck wasn't any the wiser, either.

"Actually, he's not too bad for not being taught," Pete said. "What do you think, Mrs. Haggerty?"

She was staring at the book—just the book. "This belonged to my father," she said. "See? The family tree is in the front. Niall was my papa, his wife is my mother Elizabeth, and there I am, Shona. There's my brother, Alisdair, and his wife, Johan—your parents, Buck. If Jenny is Duncan's ma, and J. T. the brother-in-law of Johan, then he must have been your uncle twice over!" She traced her finger over the whole page as she whispered. "Buck, I think we're cousins."

Poppy disagreed. "No, if Alisdair is your brother then you are Buck's auntie!"

Shona laughed: "I have a nephew to be proud of then, Buck. Glee Va."

"What does that mean, Auntie Shona?" Buck had become all shy again—like he was before he lost his toe.

"It means 'well done' in Scots Gaelic, my bonny lad. Glee Va."

The newly discovered, last remaining members of the family began to enjoy their novelty.

"You didn't know your brother was here?" Pete changed the subject.

"He'd been making noises about leaving, but I didn't take him seriously at all."

"Well," Ian said, "I'm not going to pry about how or why you didn't keep in touch, but you've got to admit it's mighty odd you landed so close."

"I've got nothing to hide about that," Shona said. MacLaren glanced at her. "My father wanted me to marry a certain doctor I couldn't even like. I left home with my true love, a watchmaker, married him in Glasgow and left for New York. I have very few regrets about it except that my Jamie left me a widow." She closed the Good Book.

"Look, there's another piece of paper sticking out of the lining." It was the first time Buck had noticed an extra page—or perhaps a hidey hole.

"Let me get a clean knife or something so I can lift it," Shona said.

When Poppy came back they opened the old flysheet to find a piece of paper that was obviously a title deed.

"So, this is what Silk wanted to get his hands on all those years ago," Ben said.

"Was it this Silk man that killed my parents?"

"I don't know that for sure, Buck. If that's the case, we can find out."

"Well, this much I can tell you. The address is prime land in Boston, Massachusetts. As I understand it, Knob Hill is very swanky," said Shona. "Perhaps he was as good a businessman as Papa was grooming him to be. Be worth a pretty penny to anyone with this title, as long as they can prove they came by it honestly. These days I think the courts may not take payment of a gambling debt as valid, but I don't know."

"Is that what made him hunt for it?" Buck asked. "Does he think my pa owes him?"

"Silk is one of these men that thinks he owns everything that belongs to anyone else. Many people are like that these days, Buck. Even true of slave owners, I'm afraid." Ben was a real man of the world.

"You all right, son?" Pete was concerned.

Buck looked like he was about to fall asleep in his chair.

"Good meal's making you tired. Why don't you lie down for a bit, and I'll stir you in the early afternoon." Poppy said. "It's a fact people get weaker before they get stronger so you just rest yourself even if a little at a time."

Ben helped him hop up the stairs, told him he'd help him down again when the time came, and not to worry himself. Shona came up to see if he needed anything from her at the very moment, but no, he was comfortable and was nearly asleep as soon as he stretched out. She pulled the blankets over him and closed the thick window curtains. She had forgotten what the rich feel of brocade was like. It was one of the few things she missed from her old life.

"Coming downstairs now," she whispered to Ben. "Or are you going to give me a bad name, Mr. MacLaren?"

"I would never insult you, ma'am. You should know that after all these years."

"Hush. Someone may be listening."

The only person that heard anything at all was Buck, but he was planning things, too. He was going to kill Duncan.

Moon Feather felt helpless as she watched him sleep. Had he forgotten her?

CHAPTER SEVENTEEN

"Come with me, Duncan. Got to get Everly's effects before we leave."

Duncan groaned as he sat up. "My head hurts."

He was hung over, and he stank of stale whiskey and puke. For the first time, Silk noticed some stubble on the kid's chin. He decided to go by himself, told Duncan to stay where he was for a half hour, get himself cleaned up, and meet everyone at the livery. It looked like the snow threatened by last night's wind direction might just happen. Silk needed to be out of town and on his way before the sun came up.

"I'm gonna give you your gun back. Got some ammunition for it for you." It was a lie, but Silk was of the opinion that if you offered a horse a carrot you'd get what you wanted long before you gave it a beating. He slammed the door, such as it was, on the way out in the hope he'd create enough noise to really wake the little bastard, if not hurt him.

He had to get the kid to Validation to collect on his inheritance. He only needed his little gang until then, so once Duncan had signed over the title he could search the tree roots to the treetops of the farm if he wanted to. Silk was sure he would find the title to the land in Boston and then sell to anyone interested, make a bit of money, go to the Gulf of Texas, and maybe run his own shipping company. One ship at a time, of course. He knew he couldn't be too greedy. Once in Texas, he could also sell the land from the agency book he just stole. He could have a regular income from that. Easy living. He hoped the South won the war, though. Life would be more lucrative if slaves remained a legal commodity.

The captain he killed all those years ago had been too young to understand the ways of the world. He was a holier-than-thou little sniffer who didn't think slavery should have any part in the modern world and refused to run slaves across the water. Silk didn't see much difference between a black face in a Yorkshire coal mine and a black face in Africa. The chances were that the African probably ate better.

He strode to the undertaker, asked for Everly's accouterments, retrieved his gun, holster, and ammunition. Everly's baccy tin had no baccy in it but did contain the title to his horse—just a bit of paper that said he'd bought it fair and square. Silk handed the undertaker the dollar he needed to just bury Everly legally. No, didn't need a stone or a marker. Everly was like all of us. Here, gone, and most likely not missed. The undertaker hummed a yes, and Silk left to meet up with the gang at the livery.

He did not expect to see Duncan, and he was right. The horses were ready and the buckboard waited for its load. He found it under two blankets at the back of the building. Fortunately, it was sitting on rolling logs, so the four of them rolled, transferred the back one to the front, rolled again and so forth until after about ten minutes they were confronted by the big lift to the buckboard.

"It's not that heavy, whatever it is." Pat stated the obvious.

"There's another part to it in the back. We can get it as soon as we've got this balanced on the board."

"Why are we trading for an organ? Is it worth something special?"

"We're going to put dynamite in it, boys. We're going to blow up the place that has been chasing after me for the last nearly twenty years. I need to put it down. I need to kill the whole fucking place. I need Duncan to literally light the fuse. I have to teach him how to shoot over the next few days, so don't get in the way. He's got to be good enough to hit the hidden dynamite while he's pretending to hit me. I need the little shit to think he's going to be a hero, a big man. Then I can get most of the attached land and the four of us will have enough wealth to buy a chunk of Texas. A chunk near the Gulf." He looked at each of them in turn. "If any of you want to back out now is the time. No hard feelings. Pat, you coming to Texas with me?"

"I thought we were going east."

"Only as long as it takes to vanish again. Now, are you with me?"

"Better than joining a regiment, better than being caught up in some other bugger's war that'll probably never end. I'm with you." They shook hands on it.

"Rye?"

"Never belonged anywhere my whole life. Might as well try Texas."

"Tom?"

"I'll stay with you as long as you need me to help get this organ to Validation, but I think I've got a cousin or two in Missouri somewheres. Thanks and all, but I'm getting too old for the excitement."

"I'll miss you after all these years, Tom, but still, I can live with your choice and I'll see if there's extra in the kitty."

The men found lifting straps folded neatly in another corner and got on with the job with much heaving and swearing. They wanted a drink afterward, but time was even more essential because they had to get out of town before the cash and the book were found to be missing.

"Better get the last bit," Silk said. "Doesn't weigh hardly anything because it's only the pump thing. A kind of bellows, I've been told."

Duncan staggered in, wanting to know if he'd heard right. Was Everly really dead?

"Yup. Shot him last night. We've been told to get out of town by dawn, so it's a good thing you're here because we're running late already."

"You shot the guy that raped and killed my ma."

Silk was tossing the reins over the team, Pat and Tom were sorting out their own mounts, but all of them stopped. "How did you know that?"

Duncan looked at them, his piggy eyes dark. "I watched. You all did what you were paid to do, didn't you?"

"I suppose."

"Hate your home town, Duncan. Hate it." For some reason, Silk spat into the ground.

"Me, too." He took his seat at the passenger side of the buckboard. "Might take a fancy to blowing it up one day now that I've set the farm to light."

Silk was trying to make sense of this young man of eighteen, but couldn't. Had he overheard their conversation? They rode out of town, fixing to go west back to Validation. There was a commotion around the land agent's office, but Silk resisted the urge to encourage the horses. One man, panic on his face, ran alongside them for a minute.

"Did you see those Gypsies?"

"Sure did. Left last night as we were coming from church to pray for the soul of our dear friend Everly Plastow."

"Were they headed east, do you know?"

"Sure were. Will have a head start on you by now."

Silk was now confident enough. He held up to have a talk with the man.

"Did something go missing?"

"Some idiot left the back door open last night...Nearly five hundred dollars cash money and—strange for a couple of itinerants—a book of titles. Still scratching my head about that one. It's not like I don't keep copies in case anyone wants to check how things stand and where they stand. Stupid being fussy that way, I guess. But you say they went east."

"Sure did, mister."

"What's in the back there?"

Silk laughed out loud, the big raucous laugh that his men recognized as being nervous.

"Have a look if you want. It's an organ to be delivered to Leavenworth in time for Christmas, and I think it's a present for the little church in a tacky town named Validation. The reverend there can't sing very well, and the congregation has got him a present. It's still in its box, but you can see all the stamps and things if you like. I've got the bill of sale to prove my bona fides."

"No, no, I'm just fussy that way. Got to know what's going on in my little town. Is this the Validation with the pecan farm on its outskirts?"

"Yes, that's the one; just a little between here and Wichita I suppose would be the best way to tell you for sure. One of those towns that grows for a while, has a use, and then gets blown away in a whirliewind."

"Better not be too far away or you'll have to find somewhere to spend the night. Looks like we're going to finally get some serious snow."

"Got a little bivouac on the way. We'll be fine for a while. Thanking you for your hospitality. Sorry about the brawl. That man had always been a bit crazy. Hope he's more content where he is now than where he's been while alive." Silk flicked the reins, and they rode quietly while they left town.

"Boss, one day you'll go to the big fire 'cause of all the tattles you say." Pat was grinning.

"Hell, laddie, I've been feeling my toes getting warmer since I left my mam's hearth."

All the men pulled their collars up against the rising wind. Duncan could feel his eyebrows starting to freeze, so pulled his hat down and lowered his head.

"When did you set fire to your farm?" Silk made Duncan jump a bit.

"I thought I told you. Just after Buck came to see. He'd been in town to get supplies, remember? He came back, all were dead. I waited for him to bury them, came out from the woodshed, and got into a fistfight with him. He's not blood to me, not really, so he can't inherit. Anyway, now Ma and Pa are gone it's mine, and I don't want to be stuck with it. I'm going on the trail. I intend to be a real man, not one of those farmers that smell of shit and pig's swill. Naw, I want to wander, just like you."

Silk was pleased to hear that talking the little turd into handing over the deed would be much easier than he thought, but he still had the rest of his plan to put into place.

"I'd give you back your gun, but I figure you'd be better able to learn how to shoot real good if you used Everly's so I got it for you, from the undertaker. He threw in the holster and quite a bit of ammunition. Here. Get a feel for it."

"It's not a new revolver." Duncan sounded disappointed.

"No, it's an old-fashioned percussion revolver—a Smith & Wesson, a bit like Rye's. You'll learn about compensating for wind and light better than learning on the new Colt, which pretty well does that work for you. Make you a much better shot in the long run, and that is what you'll need to be if you come with us to Texas after we've dropped this box at your place. You'll look like a real hero if you can shoot straight, deliver a gift of a church organ, and then ride away because you don't need any of them ever again."

"Why?"

"Why what?"

"My pa would say that all I needed was someone to take me under his wing. Are you him?"

"By the time I was your age I had been at sea for nearly five years. One thing any sailor can do is to make sure the new lad can climb the ropes because a whole ship can founder if a member of the crew can't do his job, and that means the older sailor can be killed. It is self-serving. It's self-serving for me to keep an eye on you. It'll keep me alive if I teach you how to keep yourself alive. Understand?"

"Hadn't thought of it like that." Duncan never thought what the cost of all this training might be; it was his by right, as far as he was concerned. Silk had his money.

They were taking the buckboard up a little hill, the same one they had trouble trying not to slide down two days earlier. It was worse now in some ways. The sun was coming up but the ice had melted. The road was muddy and Silk could see the Gypsy wagon tracks. He deliberately drove straight on top of them in an attempt to hide their tracks. Yes, sending the townsfolk in the wrong direction after the wrong people was a brilliant idea. They'd be looking for Gypsies and the tracks in the snow had already been cut for his gang. Silk smiled to himself. It was like hiding in plain sight in the middle of a harbor.

The horses were having a little extra trouble because of the weight of the organ, so Silk and Duncan helped by walking beside them.

"What happened to Everly's horse?"

"Got sold to someone needing dog food, I think. Why? Still got money to buy one?"

"Wouldn't mind."

"Better horses in Texas. Call 'em mustangs, I think. Mostly a definition of wild, as far as I can make out."

"Old lead mare getting fat, boss. Having trouble on the heave up." Tom was most likely the best horseman apart from Silk himself.

Silk walked beside her for a bit and ran his hands over her. He felt a kick from inside.

"Oh Lord in heaven, she's in foal! God Almighty, I thought all of us called ourselves horsemen."

They made it to the top and he ran his hands all over her, speaking softly, whispering to her in a language the boys couldn't fully understand.

"Poor lass, poor lass. I'll get you safe now, poor lass. You're a brave one, my Tara." Silk started a coughing fit and hawked up a great gob of blood. At least while he was outside he could just get rid of it on the ground. None of the gang could watch. None of them wanted him to die this way, either, no matter how they felt about him. They'd all had friends who died of the flux and didn't wish it on anyone. Once he got his breath he nodded, got back on the buckboard, flicked the reins, and started off again. No one said anything. Not even Duncan.

CHAPTER EIGHTEEN

It seemed to Duncan that silence was the way in which the world should work. He loved being in his own head, where all his dreams and ambitions lay. People just got in the way of what he wanted. He'd seen to two of them, but as he sat on that hard wooden seat—hanging onto it with both hands as it heaved over the track that was supposed to be fit for travelers—he mulled over what he was going to do with his cousin. Was he worth a bullet? It wasn't as if he was owed anything. The land the farm was on would never belong to him. As to the fistfight, well, maybe he shouldn't have told Silk. There were no witnesses apart from Buck, and of course it was well known that his mind could wander at any time. It would be better to have him killed, though. Maybe Silk would agree to it. Silk was right. He wasn't a good shot. He had made a mess of shooting Thunder. He shivered and slapped his hands together for heat.

"Nearly there." Silk had a rasp in his voice. "Getting real cold. Stop for the night in Topeka."

"When did we decide we were going to Topeka, boss?" Rye was only asking out of interest.

"Nasty turn back there, and snow's definitely coming this way and in a real hurry, so plan an early night. Don't tell me you hate the idea of a night in the big city because I won't believe you." Silk straightened his back. "You been in the filthy hole they think is the state capital, Duncan?"

"Not ever." He was thrilled at the idea.

"Pat, I need you to take charge of Duncan for the night," Silk said. "Show him how to stay out of trouble, if you can. Need him to be sober in the morning in case we can move on. It'll be the first of December in two days. I'd like to get this organ to Validation well in time for the Christmas services. What would you think of that, Duncan? We'll have to find a place outside town to teach you to shoot."

"I'm happy to do that, boss," Rye volunteered.

Silk snorted a laugh. "I'm sure you are, but I need the whole gang in one piece. Can you for sure bring him back without any fingers or toes missing?"

Duncan looked panicked.

"Absolutely boss," Rye said. "No trouble to an old hand like me. I taught Everly to shoot before you met him. He was crazy, I know, and used to just shoot into the air sometimes, but when he aimed he didn't miss too often. Problem was he could only ever shoot to kill. Telling him to aim for a knee or elbow was hopeless. He always claimed he hadn't heard. Never had the idea I'd be missing him."

"Shouldn't have shot the man then, should you?" Pat said.

"You killed Everly?" Duncan asked.

"As I told him, I was sick of riding with a rapist. A man has needs, and if he has to rape, all well and good, but a man doesn't have to be nasty about it. Everly was extreme. You should be glad he's gone. More cash in the kitty."

Silence, an uncomfortable one this time, shrouded the bedraggled gang. The snow was heavier, the wind whipping itself into fierce gusts. The horses all got skittish. Silk was convinced they smelled a town just that little bit nearer. They were probably longing for food and drink just as the gang was.

A sign announced Topeka, Kansas, and a population that seemed uncertain because the numbers were placed on a board but not carved or written on it. It looked like "eight hundred and growing." Duncan couldn't conceive of this many people in one place, so he disbelieved it.

"Where I came from, in a country called England, the population was in the millions," Silk said. "God knows how many are there now."

"Now that is just plain silly," Duncan said. "What are millions of people going to do with their day? They can't all be farmers or bankers or doctors or even land agents."

Silk guided the horses deeper into the big city, trying to find one of the two livery stables he preferred because it was closer to the bunkhouse, most especially to the hotel, and truth be told to the doctor. "Believe it or not, there's miners for coal, too."

"That would be a horrible way to spend a day."

Duncan grew in Silk's estimation. "You are exactly right, boy. I was supposed to do that very thing, so I ran away to the navy instead. We're here." He pulled up, and Duncan was aware of the crackling and snapping of the ice that had formed on the harness. "Check to see if he's got room, will you, Pat? Take Duncan with you so he can learn."

"C'mon, then. Let's start teaching you to earn your keep. Have you brought any good manners with you?"

Duncan slid off the board, realizing his face was frozen and his feet not much better. "What I wouldn't give for a hot coffee." He felt that was a manly thing to say—better than crying about how cold he was.

"Good, you do have some manners. Remember them because the guy in here isn't a friend to anyone. Would probably stick you with something before you looked at him sideways."

Tom and Rye brought up the rear with their horses but waited outside the main door to make sure they were welcome before they blundered in like most folks. Most folks weren't welcome because they had taken too much for granted. Most folks didn't come back again anyway because they were scared of Bully Carlson.

"Mr. Carlson, it's Pat McBride looking to bed down five nags." He motioned Duncan to stand behind him. "Any room for the night, sir?"

A man with the largest hands Duncan had ever seen came from what appeared to be an office. Shadows danced in the light, flickering about the place. There were empty stalls. Three horses were already in the livery and looking mighty comfortable and warm. Duncan thought it would be fine to get close to one of them just to warm himself but remembered the warning about manners, so stood still, just moving his eyes.

Mr. Carlson wasn't particularly tall, but he gave an aura of warning just by standing in a way that meant he wasn't going to move anywhere on anyone's terms but his own. It was understandable that most folks would be worried of him. If he was asked he was also of the belief that it was a good idea to keep your enemies within your line of sight but then any conversation about anything other than work would have been met with a growl and a silence.

"Good to see you folks again. Got room for five. Bring 'em in." He waved his massive hands to the empty stalls, all of which were well away from the doors and out of the cold because there were two wood-burning stoves in the building. Duncan was about to ask about them, but Pat caught him with his mouth open and nudged him to shut it.

"Who's this?"

"This is Duncan MacGregor. Silk has sort of adopted him. Good kid, really, aren't you, boy?"

Pat was glaring at him behind Bully's back. "Got manners, anyway, don't you, Duncan?"

"Yes, sir." Duncan, as Silk maintained, was quick on the uptake and could bend when the situation required common sense.

"Good with horses then?"

"Well, no. Hasn't been around them much, living on a pecan farm."

"You'll have to learn riding with Silk and his lads. Where is he anyway?" Bully peered out the doorway. "I don't let any horses in here unless the registered owners know what they're doing in the first place. No sir, no city fella who can't take care of their own animal is going to pay me to do the job for him unless he can do it himself when I'm not looking. True, Pat?"

"Told Duncan the very same. If you can't take care of your own horse your horse has no reason to take care of you. Chances are a bad-treated animal will lie down and die on you rather than get you to water in a desert. Horses got pride and brains, ain't that right, Bully?"

"Horses is better than people. As a matter of fact, all animals are if they're left to themselves. Got some kind of code, I think." Bully was slipping the saddles off, hanging the reins and head harnesses, and starting to brush down and feed the horses.

"Sorry I'm late boys—had a spot of business to attend to." Silk tried to wipe down his coat.

"Good thing your mare's inside, Silk. Looks like she's about to pop." Bully Carlson ran his huge hand over her.

"Know how to clean the harness and bits, Duncan?"

"Sir."

"Well, get to it, then. Horse is as cold as you are. You'll both heat up caring for him, and then when he's fed and watered I'll give you some vittles you can't get in the hotel."

Duncan was amazed and offended in turn, but for once he turned to his work with a will.

"Carrots always work better than sticks." Silk and the others had come in quietly during the lecture on care of horses. "Duncan enjoys his grub, Bully."

Silk and Bully just looked at each other, not willing to give ground. The workmanlike atmosphere changed to an atmosphere of mistrust and danger. Silk excused himself to go to the hotel.

"Sorry, Pat. Never liked that man, even if he insists his horses get the very best. Something not right in his head. Greedy man, I think."

"Each to their own. Never done me a bad turn, is all I can say."

"The harnesses all right, Mr. Carlson?" Duncan asked. Bully checked and then hung them up on purpose-made hooks.

"A place for everything and everything in its place, just like my ma used to say. Where's your ma?"

"Dead just a few weeks back."

"Sorry to hear that, Duncan."

"Well, we found him wandering in Leavenworth and Silk took to him."

"Silk will want something from you, Duncan. Make sure you don't give it to him less'n you know why he wants it and what he wants to do with it." Bully was finishing the last horse—Silk's horse—Vengeance.

"Come for food now, all. Just fifty cents for all you can eat or until it's all finished, There was a rug of some kind of animal skin. It had golden tight fur with dark spots on part of it. "It's antelope, Duncan," Bully said." You'd probably know it if you saw it running on the prairie, but now it's dead you'd have to think." He passed out plates and bowls. "Everybody got their own spoons, I hope?"

Bully dug out a chunk of meat from the pot inside his oven. "Beef, today. A thick cut each I think." He placed the main part of the meal onto each plate ceremoniously. "Got mash, and gravy if anybody cares for some." No one was really fit for the greens, but all were so hungry they weren't objecting—especially because they didn't feel they should insult their host, even if they were paying for it.

"You feeling warmer after working with the horses, Duncan?" Rye couldn't stand watching him eat because of the way his little teeth reminded him so much of rats. He managed to catch him between spoonfuls.

"That was good," Duncan said. "I liked it."

"Well done, Bully. Known Duncan a while now. It's the first time he's said something was good."

"Glad of that, lad," Bully said. "May make a horseman of you someday."

"Silk says I've got to learn to shoot, too."

Bully's spoon stopped. "Why?"

"Says a man has to learn to defend himself." Duncan's voice was meant to be forceful, but the look in Bully's eyes told him to be careful, so he slowed down.

"Don't need to shoot anyone to make your mark."

"No, sir. I think he meant to defend myself against snakes and Indians and other stuff."

"Killing is killing."

"Think we'd better finish up and get going to the bunkhouse, Mr. Carlson." Pat could have punched Duncan if he'd been close enough.

"Now, there's no need for running away with your tail between your legs," Bully said. "This is only a boy trying to grow to a man. If he'd been a few years older, I would take real offense and slap him sensible, but right now I'm going to leave it alone, Pat, and get you and Rye here to teach him why to use a gun, not how to. I'm sure Silk will be able to do that."

"Rye said he'd teach me."

"Where you think you can go?"

"Any suggestions, Bully?"

"Right behind this building if you want," Bully said. "Can keep an eye on you. Have to wait for the snow to settle again. This is the strangest November I think I've seen. Hardly any white stuff and none of it lying for long. Surrounded in mud last week. Could hardly keep horses clean, let alone stop them from sliding." He shook his head.

"Coffee?"

Duncan felt he was on the outside looking in, and he wasn't all that sure if he wanted to be in the gang anymore. He liked being in his own head. He'd forgotten it until that moment no one spoke because of Silk's coughing attack. He found a piece of wood and a piece of charcoal. He drew a picture of Silk's horse, Vengeance.

"Now that just proves what I was saying," Bully said. "Don't need to shoot anyone to make your mark. You're a good artist, my lad. Can you draw people?"

"Don't know, never tried."

"Too dark now, I suppose, but say I find a decent-sized piece of paper. You can come back in the morning, help muck the stables. I'll feed you ham and eggs, and by noon I'll bet you'll have the beginnings of a drawing of me."

"Can only do that if Silk doesn't need me."

He was actually looking for a way out because he really didn't want to muck out the horses.

"Silk will either be with a woman or a doctor tomorrow if I know him, and I do, I really do. Isn't that right, Pat?"

Bully playfully slapped Duncan's knee. "See you in the morning, then, and don't be thinking I'll be wild if you can't do it. It'll just be enough that you tried. Rye and I will give you a shooting lesson if the weather's up for it in the afternoon. Now, how does that sound?"

"Good, sir. Thank you, sir."

The men stood up, paid their money, and ducked out the door before the snow got in.

"What a pile. Hope there's room at the bunkhouse."

"Hope we can find it in this."

"Good manners, Duncan. Nearly lost it for a bit, but good manners got us through."

Duncan had his face buried in his collar and didn't hear a word. He was in his own thoughts again. Maybe he had more in common with his cousin than he thought, but maybe Buck had had the right idea all along. Maybe he was a Mindwalker as well but it just came out different. Tomorrow was planned for him. Ma used to plan days for him. He'd just have to go along with it this time, and with any luck, he'd be out of Topeka in a week and back in Validation by the middle of the month.

CHAPTER NINETEEN

Duncan slept well that night, most likely because of exhaustion and good food. The best meal he'd had since he'd left home, if truth be told. In the morning, the first day of December 1861, he felt very different. He seemed to have come to an understanding of himself. He no longer had a ma to do for him. He had to do for himself, and he'd only just cottoned on to the idea. So now, what did he have to do for himself today?

He decided to throw some warmish water on his face. It was too cold to shave and he didn't know exactly how to go about it so he asked Rye if he thought he should try to grow a beard. Rye said it seemed to him to be a good idea at this time of year, as long as he didn't mind strange looks from the ladies while it was growing in. First beards were always the hardest to grow, he said. Duncan looked at himself in a piece of glass that was left in the bunkhouse. It was the first time he'd recognized himself to be fat. A fat, little piggy face. "My teeth are all black and pointy."

"Too much sugar candy, I shouldn't wonder," Rye said. "Don't worry, they'll either fall out or get so sore you'll want a doc to pull 'em. Understand you can get dead people's teeth made up to deputize for your real ones. Normal thing these days. Started in Europe, of course." Pat was scraping away at his chin as he spoke. It felt to Duncan like he was trying to keep a beat in time to some dance or other.

"I'll find a doc, then. Did you say Silk was visiting one in town?"

"The visit will cost you, Duncan. Still got a little of that money in your drawers?"

"There's enough."

He put his coat and unheated boots on, did a little of the cold boot shuffle as it was called—one foot hopping and then the other—and left for the stable.

"Glad to see you even if you are about an hour late," Bully said, "but I can mind, being your age. Always tried to sleep till past the noon hour, so you're doing well to be here just after nine."

Duncan had done just enough work on the farm to know that the stalls needed to been cleaned and swept and the droppings piled outside so they could be kept for fertilizer in the spring. If the winter was a long, cold one, there was no real smell, but come the new season, the steam could be seen rising from one end of town to the other. People with real money built their homes well away from the livery stables. That was where Duncan planned to live. He wanted a three-story house with the top floor completely open so he could draw things and build things. He couldn't be bothered carving wood like Buck, but then Buck wasn't at all interested in color, shape, or form. Duncan found that the way light changed things was almost like being in a different world.

One of the owners of the horses from the previous night dropped by to ask if it would be all right to keep his mare there until the snow was better. Bully said yes. "Hope I'm not paying for that extra pair of hands," the owner said.

There was the usual Bully Carlson silence. The owner fled after he bowed and apologized.

"Funny that, isn't it?" Bully said. "All I did was look at him. No gun, not even an idea of a gun, but he ran like I had one." He was grooming one of the team horses, the one Silk counted on to keep a steady pace for the smaller one beside her.

"Need to speak to Silk about this mare, Duncan. Do you think you could fetch him for me? I don't think she'll be fit to take you to Texas in January. Not with a foal behind. Poor creature be lucky to escape the birth with her life, she's so old. Got to admit she's had good care, but she's done her bit for Silk. Needs to go to pasture with her babe if she makes it." There were tears in the man's eyes. His huge right hand rested gently on her muzzle, his left on her neck. Bully rubbed his forehead rubbed up and down on her star that Silk had always referred to as her beauty mark. Duncan took a sharp breath.

"Don't move, Mr. Carlson. Don't move." He wasn't loud about it, but he had never spoken so forcefully to anyone in his life. He grabbed a piece of charcoal and a bit of *Harper's Weekly* that was just lying around for the privy. He did a very rushed sketch of what he saw. *Bully and Horse in Profile* was what he would call it. It had taken him less than five minutes to get the rough idea. Once Bully gave him the good piece of paper later he would do a proper job. He drew in what direction the light was coming from so he wouldn't forget and noted what was in the background so Bully would be able to remember how tall she was and what stall she was in, and then he finished.

"I have never let anyone speak to me like that, ever."

Duncan showed him his effort.

"But I'm awful glad you did," Bully added.

"I'll get Silk now if you want."

Bully was staring at the drawing. "You made my hands look big, which is the most important thing."

"When Ma was showing me how to do people she said to get the bit of them that meant the most to them or that explained the best part of them. I never drew a strange person, just Ma and I copied from *Harpers* so I really want to draw you Mr. Bully. It's not that your hands are the biggest I've ever seen, it's that they're so sure of themselves. That, it seems to me, is why the horses trust you so." Duncan was awestruck.

"You must miss her. I wish I'd known her. Sounds like a very wise woman." Bully sighed, placed the drawing back on the counter, weighted it down with an old horseshoe, and asked Duncan to go for Silk while he finished up.

"Would you mind doing a bigger drawing of that sometime?"

"If you get a big piece of paper."

"I'll have it for you when you get back, but don't be too long if you can help it because I think she's started. Whoops—there's the water. Could be a rougher ride than even I expected. Best run if you can, boy."

He did. Duncan ran, but the problem was he didn't know where anything was. He came across a woman in the street, but her head was deep in a bonnet and she had some kind of winter parasol in front of her and was pushing against the wind. He stopped and turned around and around, looking at what signs he could see. There was a light on in the dried goods store. He opened the door, politely asked where the hotel and doctor's office were and, of course, they were in opposite directions.

Duncan ran to the hotel. There Silk was, his arm around a girl in a pink satin dress, sipping a large whiskey. He took his hat off, bowed his head at the lady, and excused himself to Silk. Silk was very nastily drunk.

"What you wanting, you little shit?" Someone hissed from behind the bar.

"Language, kind sir. Language." The accent was apparently Southern.

"Tara is birthing a foal, and Bully sent me to get you because he doesn't think she's going to manage. Not without dying, anyway."

Silk slammed his glass on the counter, tossed the girl away, snatched his coat from the hook at the door, and ran down the street without noticing he had no boots on, just his inside shoes. They called them house slippers, apparently. They were made out of cloth. It's odd what you notice in a rush. Duncan hoped Silk didn't catch cold.

Tara was wild-eyed with fear, anyone could see that. "I got the paper for you," Bully shouted to Duncan. "Do what you said you'd do and leave us to do this job here."

Rye had seen all the commotion but understood exactly what was going on. He got a rope and tackle organized in case the foal had to be dragged out. Tara was really starting to panic. Rye left, saying too many people would do no good. He stopped Pat and Tom from coming in as he was leaving. They made gestures to Duncan to get out, but he pointed to Bully, then to a huge piece of what looked to be plain, white paper. Then he sat down at a counter, turning his back on the whole thing.

"Well, at least he's not in the way. Did you realize she was that far along?" Bully asked.

"No, I did not. No wonder she was a little off her grub and drinking gallons of water, it seemed like." Silk felt a flicker of guilt.

Rye, Pat, and Tom walked to the bar, noting there was more than one drinking hole in Topeka. Maybe they had time to visit the saloon later. Yes, they had a bit of bacon at the cookhouse, but if the weather and the birthing had anything to do with it, there wasn't going to be any shooting practice. With nothing better to do or look forward to they found a crowded bar where they could have a smoke, swear if they felt like it, find a woman if they wanted one, and imbibe a whiskey or two. Not a bottle or two, of course, because too much drink leads to too much talk, and talking could be real dangerous. There was cash in the buckboard currently resting outside the livery, and snow collecting on top of a stolen church organ. They settled in for a gambling session, achieving their idea of perfection, after all their travels, in Topeka, Kansas.

They heard screaming outside. The bar emptied quickly.

"Rebs?"

"No, saloon roof collapsed in the back. People trapped. Probably rotten wood and heavy snow."

"Have to get some horses rigged to pull away the debris. Hurry, please."

"Well, that's the end of that I guess," Rye said. "C'mon, better see how we can help, but I'll bet we don't need horses. Oh my God, look. The front is falling into the street."

"Get back, everyone. You'll be trapped. Get back, quick." A woman with her head in her bonnet was fighting against the wind with a dark parasol. Rye grabbed her out of the way and knocked her hat to the snow. She was a wiry little man.

"Look what I've got here," Rye called. Pat noticed but no one else was paying attention. "What you doing, all dressed up and staring at what's happened?"

There were people running back and forth and even in circles, but no one was organizing anything at all. They heard screams from behind the saloon. Someone was calling for help. Someone else was calling for his mother. Others were shouting they were coming, just hold on. It was chaos, and Rye and the boys thought they had the instigator. Otherwise why would a man be dressed as a woman in the middle of the day?

Bully charged into the crowd and began giving orders, and things began to settle. When the front of the saloon did eventually collapse later in the afternoon, no one was hurt. When Bully saw the man Rye had caught, he pulled his arm right up behind his back and marched him to the jailhouse.

"We never use it unless it's some kind of drunk and very disorderly," Bully said to Rye "and of course there's no real law, so we'll have to keep an eye on this varmint all by ourselves until someone can come to take him to Leavenworth or the justice can come here. He's wanted for all sorts of unusual things, everything from thieving to drawing naked woman on walls and even setting fire to things. He's got some kind of religious thing going on, I think. Name is Jacob Crabb, in case you see him on any wanted posters. You can get a hundred dollars for him. But you'll get more for Silk, I'll warrant."

Bully had been away from the livery most of the day and returned quickly. Tara was weak but had survived the delivery of her foal, a male. "Silk was so proud you'd think he'd sired him himself," Bully told Tom. "You'd better come for a look, but don't make too much of a fuss, for Tara's sake. With any luck Silk will leave them here where I can care for them until he's a yearling. Try and tell him what's best. He might just listen to his friends."

"Got a name for him yet?" Tom laughed a little. "I suppose we're all like kids around a new horse."

"Well, Duncan had a horse that died. He wants to call him Thunder. What do you think?"

CHAPTER TWENTY

Killing his cousin would take planning. It wasn't the kind of thing that should be talked about. Buck would have to keep his intentions to himself. If he did it right, if he waited his chance, if he could stay patient, he would succeed. Moon Feather looked at him the way she always did. She never interfered unless he asked her to help, like he did that night in the cave. His soul had cried out for help, and she had come to him. She had also brought a man of this world who had vanished after he had helped him back to town. Moon Feather knew what she was about.

In his head he asked her about his future. Never once had she answered except to say it was in his own hands. His future was his to make for good or evil; it was his alone. His choices were his own, and accepting what came of them was also his own. *Well,* he'd said, while he was recovering from frostbite, *I suppose I'll know if it's evil when I stop seeing you.*

No, she'd said. *I'll always be there, even on the day you die in this world, but you might forget to look for me and I'll just have to wait. I will always be there, no matter what. You might get extra help if you need it, but I'll always be with you. Even if you decide to murder Duncan.*

So I shouldn't murder Duncan?

It is up to you, she'd said.

The conversation was turning in circles.

"Wake up, Buck." Poppy was gently shaking his shoulder. "Mary's downstairs. She's managed to leave the store for a bit. She wants to see how you're doing."

"I'll have to get dressed again, then?"

"It's not like you're naked, Buck. I'll get Ben to help and then he can help you back down to the bar. How does that sound?"

"Why do you sound so excited?"

"Just real nice to have something to do with my day that isn't purely business, is all."

She turned, went to the gallery above the floor of the Diamond—now filled with more smoke, people, and noise than there had been in the early morning—and raucously bellowed for Benjamin Walter MacLaren. There was a round of applause, but Buck wasn't sure if it was for the bellow or the scraping chair and running footfalls of a heavy man coming up the stairs.

Ben looked shocked. "Lord, woman, where'd you find a voice like that?"

"My pa was an auctioneer out east. When my mother wanted him to come home for something she used to send me to get him. I had to make myself heard over the slavers."

"There's a long story behind that, I think." He eased his way past her into the small room.

"Not so much. Auctions stopped, if you recall. Give Buck a help to get down, please. Can't let a young woman of good repute come to visit a young man in his bedroom, can I?" She left, her skirts swishing, to announce she was back downstairs and back in charge. Pete remained behind the bar. Now that the snow had started again and looked to be a good dump of the stuff, he was concerned about his stock levels. He might even have to organize a trip to Lawrence sometime before Christmas. It would depend on weather and judgment.

Buck used the handrail on the wide staircase to hold on with his right hand, and Ben's steadying arm on his left to get down the stairs. His foot was throbbing, so he winced a bit, but he got there. Mary was sitting in the back corner, near the second heater. She was sipping something from a china cup, her glorious red hair pulled up under a winter bonnet. Tendrils did manage to escape, though, so Buck felt she was probably a little less formal than she was making out. It was worrying that she wasn't smiling.

He managed to get to her without much assistance from Ben, but he was glad to see that the doc and Ian were joining them as well. He needed some of the pain stuff.

"How are you then, Mr. Ross?"

"That's very formal, Miss Grant. Apart from feeling like a horse has just stepped on my foot I'm just hunky-dory. How are you?"

"Peachy."

"Mary. What's got into you?" Ian was horrified at her attitude. "That was rude, girl."

"Yes, I suppose it was. My apologies."

No one at the table believed her. She continued to sip her tea.

Poppy, who was of necessity sensitive to changes in atmosphere in the saloon, came sliding over to see if anyone needed anything. "I could do with a whiskey, Poppy, thanks."

"Yes, I'm sure you could, Buck. That be all right for your patient, Doc, or do you think he should build up his strength a bit more before he has a drink?"

"One won't hurt, Poppy." The doc didn't want to get involved in something he knew nothing about.

"I'll let you have one then. Mary, I'd be grateful for some girl advice in the laundry if you wouldn't mind coming for a quick look." She inclined her head to the kitchen and laundry area at the back of the building. "I'll ask Pete to get your drink, Buck." The two women left the table, and the men breathed more easily.

"Are you all right, Mary?" asked Poppy, once they were alone in the kitchen.

"I'm just tired and I wish people would stop putting pressure on me. I think Buck is odd and I'm not sure I want to have anything to do with him."

"Well you'd better tell him straight then, girl."

Pete came over with Buck's drink and sat down to speak to the men. "I've done my best with her since her mother died, and the Lord knows she's been a good, strong girl," Ian said. "I couldn't have got through the loss of the twins without her, but I wish she'd understand she has to consider her future." Ian actually had tears of frustration in his eyes. "Buck, I know you have a fondness for her, and I really believe she has a fondness for you. I'm sorry she misspoke to you."

"She's maybe tired or worried about something, but I'm not concerned, don't worry. She'll turn good again when she's ready." Buck smiled. "If she's ready." They all laughed, but Pete put the problem in a bite that could be easily swallowed.

"Well, I'm not a father, but we all know how the world works," he said. "These days especially, young women have to have a protector."

"That's exactly right. Exactly right. A father is happier to think that if anything happens to him, his children will be safe even if there is a war on, and especially as it appears that very war is getting closer and is dragging on longer than people were saying." Ian sounded a little mollified.

"Looks like it'll keep on until into the spring of '62 at this rate."

"Well, Doc, are you too old to be volunteering?"

"Partly that, and partly too damn sensible. There'll be plenty of doctoring needed afterward, I'll be bound."

"I think I should at least volunteer," Buck said. "If they don't accept me because of my foot at least I can't be called a shirker. I'll talk to you later, Doc, if you wouldn't mind."

The men sipped their own thoughts and feelings for a few minutes.

"Occurs to me that womenfolk aren't good at keeping to their own thoughts," Buck said.

"Oh, yes, they are, young man." Pete glanced through to the kitchen and scanned the movements of his staff as they went about their business on the saloon floor. "They store it all up, what they're really thinking, and then they tell you all at once as if you should have known. Usually on the way to bed, when you're too tired to defend yourself."

Doc and Ian nodded in agreement. Ben just shrugged and sighed as he finished his rum. The saloon door opened as two locals left. Pete rose to say thanks and good night to them. They were trying to make their way home before the snow and dark set in. The good Reverend Parker came in with Ryan from across the street. Poppy and Mary returned from the kitchen at the same time. Poppy pointed, only pointed, at their boots. Both men returned to the boardwalk to stamp off the snow.

"That's another way women can make their feelings known," Ben said. "Sign language, or just the way they look at you. It can be scary sometimes. More scary than a loaded gun, Buck, trust me." Well, Buck thought, Ben was most likely to know what he was talking about.

Mary rejoined the table. Pete lifted another chair closer so all present could sit together. The reverend always sat at the bar for his first whiskey, then mucked in with any assorted company after it. He wasn't the type to preach God in another man's church, as Pete believed his Diamond to be, but then Pete never smelled of whiskey in the reverend's little white building at the other end of the street. It meant the respect was mutual. Pete was generous, too, with the Sunday collection, being fully aware he'd get most of it back over the bar.

"Good to see you up and about, Buck. How are you?" The reverend actually sounded like one sometimes.

Buck had learned not to tell people the truth, thanks to his little spat with the glorious Mary. "Fighting fit, I hope. Just saying I should volunteer soon." He heard Mary gasp.

"You'll have to be able to ride first, surely."

"Well, yes, but that doesn't mean I can't put my name down. If they want to wait for me to heal, that's fine, but I should volunteer in the first place. If they don't want me at all that's fine, too, but as I was saying, at least I can't be called a coward." He lapsed into silence, not hearing what the others said. He was watching a battle in his mind. There were flags of both sides falling into mud. He could make no sense of it. He came back into the room. Doc was hovering over him. "You left us for a minute there, Buck."

"Sorry. It happens sometimes."

"Maybe get you back upstairs, I think."

"No, I'm just fine, Doctor Fraser. Every once in a while I see things that aren't here, but nothing bad ever happens. I'm fine, really. I don't want to be rude, Miss Poppy, but I'm hungry again. Maybe that's why I leave and come back like I do. Aunt Jenny used to think so."

"That's good. If your feelings for food are coming back, you'll get all better quicker." She called Clara over. "Mr. Buck would be grateful if you could go to the kitchen for some eggs and bacon, I think." She wasn't sure if Buck was ready for that much.

"Just bacon if you don't mind, and maybe a slice of bread with it. I don't like eggs, really, and to be honest I don't think they like me very much. I make rude noises after I eat them." Poppy laughed out loud. "You are getting better, Buck. You sound more like your young self. Don't you think, Mary? Doesn't Buck sound better?"

"Yes, I think so." She still wasn't happy about something, but Buck chose to leave it alone.

Ryan had taken his time talking to other people at the other tables before he wandered over to see Buck. Like everyone else he asked how he was. Buck asked him to sit. Poppy felt the atmosphere change again and was, for all her years of experience, taken aback by Buck's sudden change in personality.

"Relax, Mr. O'Neill," Buck said. "I'll pay you for the wood you've cut, and once I find someone who needs it, I'll sell it on or even build them a privy if I have to. Neither of us will be out of pocket." Buck appeared to Poppy to have grown, if that was at all possible. He was definitely sounding older than he had not five minutes before. He extended his hand. The men shook on it, but Ryan only because he felt outgunned. Yes, outgunned was exactly right. He was going to volunteer to build the privy while Buck was laid up.

The saloon door opened in time to let the tension out of the room. A woman dressed in unusual clothes stood at the door.

"Do you serve my kind?"

"What kind?" Pete called.

"My husband and I are from the far eastern part of Europe. We're called Gypsies, even though we're not, really. We're Romany. Do you serve Romany? We are cold and hungry. We have money."

"This is the Black Diamond, woman. If you have money, we have whiskey and food. You are very welcome."

Mary grabbed Buck's arm. "Do you think she's a witch?"

"What's a witch?" He patted her hand and grinned at her.

CHAPTER TWENTY-ONE

The new Thunder was shaky on his legs, but he was standing, and that was what mattered. He was weak and maybe born a bit tired after being hauled from his mother by the rigging Rye had constructed. His hind legs were scratched but not broken, as they might have been by the stress of it all. Bully had seen and done it all before, so a better birthing Thunder could not possibly have had, as far as Silk was concerned. Tara was a tough old girl and would recover, given time. Bully was right, though. It was time she had her own green pasture. As long as Bully could find one where she'd be safe Silk was happy, and for once he didn't look for payment. Tara had always been good to him. He needed to return the favor. The only problem was where to find another lead horse.

Bully and Silk didn't have any time for each other, but they did agree on horses and their needs.

"Be better to let them both go to the same home. Not likely the other one would get along with a different lead. Got a team for you if you want them."

Silk agreed to go to the other livery to have a look.

"See what your boy drew?"

"What you talking about?"

Duncan was just finishing the big bit of paper as the light started to go. Bully took it to the doorway to get a better look. He ruffled it a bit to make it catch the light more.

"You're out of your time, laddie. If you were born a hundred years from now, you'd probably be able to go to art school or something. As it is, in wartime anything pretty is important as it stands, but pretty doesn't stand all that long unless it's genius stuff."

He looked at it a bit longer. "Your ma was right. It shows who I am but not what I perfectly look like. What you think, Silk?"

Silk was coughing a bit. "Better keep it away from me in case I bleed on it."

"You always were a heathen, Mr. Silken." Bully took it back in and pinned it to the wall over the counter.

"If you're around this time next year, Duncan, I'll let you have Thunder in payment for this as long as you can prove to me that he wants to be with you. Deal?"

"I thought Thunder was Silk's."

"I just traded his old team plus Thunder for a new team of mine that I keep at the other livery. Now, after all the excitement of the day it might be time for dinner, another bed and then—because I think the snow is stopping—I'll set up a shooting range for you in the morning. Silk wants to leave tomorrow afternoon if he can."

Sulking, Duncan cleaned the charcoal from his hands and went back to the bunkhouse for chow. He wasn't happy about losing his horse, the new Thunder. The idea of waiting another year for a horse was an impossible one. He would have to do something about it. No man, no real man, would ride a buckboard all the way to Texas.

Silk came in, coughing again. "Doc says it's the weather and the strain of everything. He wants me to stay put till the spring, but I said I've promised to get the new organ to Validation in time for Christmas. He says I have to keep my neck warm with scarves, my nose and mouth covered all the time I'm outside, and he's given me this chest medication that tastes awful. Makes me a mite dizzy sometimes, so you may have to drive a bit, one of you." He showed the brown glass bottle to Pat.

"Heard of this stuff before. Special thing in it is called cocaine. 'Member Lizzie the cook, in Leavenworth Hotel? She swears by it, only problem being that when the chest is gone she's used to the taste of it." He showed his indifference in the way he handed it back.

"I'm going to see our new team, if anyone wants to come."

Duncan hadn't taken his boots off, but Tom was relaxing with some book he'd found lying around, so he said he'd stay.

"That's heavy. Looks more like a doorstop," Silk commented.

"Well maybe you'd take to it better than me," Tom said. "It's about some guy trying to catch a white whale."

"Probably written by someone who's never seen the big water. Even if the sailor catches the whale, I'll bet it takes him to the bottom of the ocean." Silk laughed through another coughing fit. "Any sailor worth the name will tell you that whales can be right canny, right canny indeed. They can plan a revenge."

All but Tom went to meet the new team. The snow was tailing off. Once again Silk tested the air with his finger. "More from the south this time. With any luck, and if this team is any good at all, we'll be near Validation by this time tomorrow. Maybe at your old house, Duncan, or at least what's left of it."

Rye saw the team first. They weren't a bit like Tara and the rest of them, but they looked healthy and strong enough. He patted their sides and drew his hands over their haunches. "Mouth and teeth sound enough Mr. Silk."

"New shoes?" Silk coughed again.

"Looks like it." Rye picked up each hoof to check.

"Good temperament. The previous owner knew what he was doing." Pat sounded impressed. "This one will look like she's walking on an angle what with two white socks on the same side and no markings at all anywhere else." He stroked her nose.

"What you think then? Worth the trade?"

"They're younger and fresher that's for sure." Rye nodded.

"They'll do us fine, I think," Silk said. He looked at Duncan. "You keep your distance from them. I don't trust you near anything living, especially horses. I am sure you're one of them that would have tortured kittens for the fun of it."

Duncan stood with his mouth open and, without thinking, he told him it was puppies, actually.

"What have you landed us, with Silk?" Pat felt revulsion.

"Oh, come off it, we all knew he was crazy when he offered us money to do his parents." Rye spat at the floor while he glared at the kid.

The horses in the livery weren't used to loud voices in the confines of a building. They started to stamp and snort.

"Outside. Now," Silk ordered, and began to cough again.

The men cleared out of the warm wooden building. The sun was very nearly all the way down.

"You're not really going to teach this creature how to shoot straight, are you?" Pat asked.

"I'd rather he shot straight than missed and blinded something by accident, don't you think?" Silk said.

"Personally, I'd plug him right here and now." Rye stated a fact.

Duncan started to move away. Pat caught his fat arm, digging his fingers in hard enough to make him squeak.

"Don't be so shortsighted, Rye. We need him as part of us. Hell, if it'll make you feel any better you teach him to shoot sometime. It doesn't have to be in the morning. He's got uses. He managed to sweeten Bully so much we're getting a new team for an old team plus a drawing. That on its own is good enough to give Duncan a place," Silk said.

Duncan began to relax and Pat felt it. "Don't you ever think I'm not watching you," he told Duncan. "Don't you ever think I won't shoot you where you stand if I catch you harming a horse or for that matter a woman, should you ever find one stupid enough to put up with you."

He turned the boy around to face the bunkhouse, giving him a hard kick in the backside as he did. Duncan turned in fury to see Pat standing with his gun drawn.

"That's how fast I am, kid. I'm so fast I can make three decisions at the same time. I can draw, I can shoot, or I can decide not to shoot. Today's your lucky day. You won't get two. Go cannie, as Mr. Silken would say. Wouldn't you, boss? Wouldn't you tell Duncan to go cannie?"

"I've been telling him that since the very first day, but I'm starting to think on whether he knows what it means," Silk said. "Watch your step, Duncan. Think on it. You've paid us, you've gained us some goods, and now you're going to take us back to Validation starting tomorrow where we are going to have us a fair old time. And you, my lad, are going to look like a hero if I can figure out a way to blow up that little church of yours."

Pat, Tom, and Rye began to walk ahead. "Cold and hungry, boss. You coming or going back to the hotel for the night?" Tom liked to know the details.

"I'll take this little piggy with me tonight. I'll keep him safer, I think."

"Probably right, boss. See you at the first light."

Duncan followed Silk at his heels to the big hotel. It was different than the one in Leavenworth. It was busier, for a start. Men were wandering in and out of huge rooms that had large, round, polished tables in them, most covered with cloths and holding their own lamps and bottles and glasses. There was more than one bar and an assortment of women; some dressed like real ladies and others dressed like they wanted to be real ladies. There wasn't the usual raucous laughter Duncan had heard in public establishments, most likely because it had a different purpose than most venues. The hotel in Topeka, or at least this particular one, was a place where commerce was carried out and trades entered into. It did not exist purely as a bed for the night, let alone for a woman to share that very bed. The beds in this hotel were usually booked for a week or even longer while businessmen entered into contracts and special deals. Sometimes even wives and families joined them.

"Either to put a deal into perspective or so the wives can keep an eye on their men," said Silk.

Duncan was amazed by all the colors and fashions the men were wearing. "I just want to sit at a bar table somewhere and watch everyone."

"You're lacking in the head, boy. We'll have to get you some decent clothes first. You look like one of those people who've been thrown off their land in the old country."

Silk dragged him to the tall, polished desk, where a man in a black frock coat defended it by his attitude. He was bareheaded. Duncan wasn't used to seeing a man behind a counter without a hat on. Mr. Grant at home never took off his. Ma used to think he slept with it on, but Pa said Mr. Grant slept with a white nightcap on so his bald head didn't get cold. When Silk introduced him to the man behind this specific desk as his nephew who had just arrived from the east, he looked the part. He was grinning at the thought of Ian in a nightcap.

"Any chance of a bed?"

"I'm sorry, Mr. Silken, the only thing I can do for you is to put another single bed in your room." The concierge—as Duncan was later to find out, this was his title—remained unimpressed.

"That is a very good idea, young man," Silk replied. "May have to keep an eye on him, you know. Lost his parents before a good

Christian soul sent him to me." He leaned forward and crooked his finger at the man. "Not right in the head, I don't think." He leaned back, giving his newly adopted nephew a squeeze on his shoulder. "Be fine with me for the night, then. Get you something decent to wear before we take you to dinner or other socializing, but meanwhile I'll get Robert here to organize steak and potatoes. How does that sound? Maybe even a cake for dessert."

Duncan got the gist that he was being monitored for good but stunned behavior so he played into it. His mind was racing ahead, and he needed time. Was Silk crazy? Why would he want to blow up Reverend Parker's church? What was he going to blow it up with? Did he have a stash of dynamite or something? That was easy to come by, what with the railroads using so much of it. Thieves of the high caliber of Silk and his gang would have no trouble, as long as they weren't greedy about it. Pa had used a stick once to blow a huge stone out of the way, to turn the course of the river just a little down and to the left so the trees would get more water. It worked, and made the trees easier to take care of. Duncan didn't think that Silk's plan was going to turn out for the best. He felt doubly anxious when Silk said he'd be considered a hero. That wasn't a hat he wanted to wear. He wanted to be rich, that was all. He didn't care about how he got money; he just wanted lots and lots of it.

The bed arrived just before the steak. Duncan excused himself to go out to the privy. Silk laughed at him. "No outside privy, just a flush toilet down the end of this hall. Ever seen one?"

"Heard of them."

"Come on, I'll show you. Try to avoid doing what most folks do. Don't play with the flush mechanics. It makes things difficult for the person needing to use it after you." He took him down the end of the hall. "That is what is called toilet paper. It's what you use instead of the *Weekly*."

Duncan touched the paper without print on it. "Too soft to draw on, though." He was disappointed.

Duncan, like everyone who used a toilet for the first time, was distrusting of it. What happened when the hole was full? How would they dig another one? It would be a genuine problem for Buck. He smiled as he sprayed the bottom of the ceramic round and round in circles. He even gave a bit extra to the blue painted flower just under the rim. The noise from the flush was louder than he reckoned with, making him jump back, grateful he'd buttoned up first. He watched the waste swirl down into the hole, trying to picture where it would go. He hoped he'd need to go again before he left in the morning. He'd like to own one someday.

"You're finished?" Silk rapped a couple of times on the door.

"Yup." Duncan needed a bit of alone time. He needed to think. He followed Silk back to the room while he cogitated. He had to talk to the others. He would hang around with this gang for the next few days, but he could vanish if he wanted. He still had money and could buy another horse if he needed to. He needed to get a feel for the other men. Did they follow what Silk was up to? Maybe his mind was going the same way as his chest. As young as he was, Duncan had seen people do things when they were fevered, say even more, plan huge deals. Perhaps Silk was real sick. Maybe he had chosen the wrong time to be with Silk's gang. One thing for sure, if Silk was intending to blow up a church, it wasn't that his conscience was bothering him.

CHAPTER TWENTY-TWO

"Have you seen Piddlin since you got better?" Mary asked.
"I haven't forgotten about her. Joss says she's just sad without me. Maybe someone could help me over to the stable, you think?"

"Pete's getting busy now. How about you, Mister MacLaren, do you think you could get him there? I'll stay and come to get you when he's checked her over."

"Sure thing, Miss Mary. I've got a piece of wool we can put under your foot so it doesn't touch the snow or get cold. Be right back." He vanished up the stairs two at a time, leaving them alone at the table.

Buck looked at her. "Things are changing Mary, aren't they?"
"In what way?" It wasn't like her to be coy.
"I won't be working a farm, and I won't be going into the army."
"Well, not for a while. That's just a waiting game, surely, Buck."
"I think that's what Jenny would have called being patronized."
"What's with you, Buck?"
"I've been making decisions."

"What kind of thoughts have you been having? Anything to do with your daydreaming?" Mary was starting to sound angry.

"I've been reading lots of stuff. There's a world out there. I want to see it with no encumbrances."

Mary leaned in to him. "Well, let me tell you, Buck Ross, I have no intention of being, as you say, encumbered, with you, either." She was as close to growling as a coyote. Buck shrugged at her, pushing himself back out of the danger he sensed—but not this time, from the top of his head. This time it felt purely like self-preservation.

"That's good, then. No hard feelings." They pushed back into a respectable distance.

They heard Ben return downstairs just as the Gypsy girl and her husband came in. Pete seated them at a table a little way from the door. If he'd wanted to get rid of them he'd have put them right in front of it, smack in the middle of a draft from underneath it and a tiny hole in the floor beneath. It was where he used to put Silk's boys when they visited. They never knew why they felt so cold, just thought the whole place was as bad.

Mary was fascinated by the way the woman walked, so sure, so confident in herself. The clothes were obviously handmade. It didn't look like there was a single stitch by a machine. Each square of fabric was different, but all seemed to mesh in perfect harmony. That was it—this lady moved in time to her own music. She sparkled and sang and danced, all at the same time. Why did she look so sad and tired, though?

Even Pete stopped still behind his bar. He had a huge tankard of something in his hand. The Gypsy husband came in looking like he was dressed from top to toe in bearskin and wolf. His hands were covered in what looked like beaver mitts. When he took them off there was a huge diamond ring on his left hand. The conversation stopped in the whole bar when he snapped off what appeared to be a curved cutlass, sat down and placed it, handle side out, under his chair. He acknowledged Pete. Pete brought him the tankard and asked what he would like to eat. The husband looked at his woman.

"Do you have peas and cornbread?" He spoke in a language that sounded like American except he chopped into each word, one at a time.

"Of course, but what kind of meat?"

"A chicken would be good, *da*. A chicken."

Pete nodded, hoping to hell that there was a fairly young one. Poppy could quickly wring its neck, gut it, and fry it. He looked behind him to the kitchen. He raised his eyebrows to Poppy who, like everyone else, had stopped what she was doing. She nodded and vanished.

Pete pulled the chair out for the lady Gypsy to sit down. "Are you warm enough?"

"Yes, but before we eat, and now that my husband has his drink of vodka, I would like to be of help to a young man named Buck. Could you—oh, no, there he is." She spotted Buck near the back of the room. "I would like a large whiskey."

She floated toward Buck's table. Pete followed, his instincts telling him he should, although he wasn't sensing anything untoward. A chicken screeched from the kitchen. There was a loud chop. The Romany nodded his approval and crossed his arms over his chest.

"My name is Rebecca. My husband is Froika. We mean no harm and are just going west like so many others as you might do very soon, Mr. Buck. May I touch your chest, please?" There was something about her that made the company want to hear what she had to say. Moon Feather stood behind her, so Buck nodded. She leaned forward, bent her head for a minute, and then gazed into his eyes.

"You are one of us. You see things you don't yet understand. You started your life wounded. You are surrounded by women, though. You will be protected if you listen to your head and heart at the same time. You must always pause before you act. You are not one of those that can afford to make an excuse for an action you have already done. Your job in this life is to learn to control your abilities. You weren't successful at it the last time your soul was here, so you have been slowed down. Do you have trouble walking, Mr. Buck? Yes, I see you do. It's to slow you down, to make you think." She stood up and left him as suddenly as she came over to him, then turned to Mary and told her she was right, she could afford to wait. Mary nearly jumped out of her chair.

"What does that mean, Mary?" Buck asked.

"I don't want to marry just yet, and I was talking to Poppy about it earlier when you were still laid up." Now we've had that very conversation, she thought. I feel much relieved.

Buck was now absolutely sure of what he wanted to do, with no encumbrances, as he told her.

Pete was about to move back to the bar. Everyone could smell the chicken frying. No one was watching it. Poppy and her girls stood in the kitchen doorway as if Rebecca were a sideshow.

"Let's go to see Piddlin, will we?" Ben was grateful for the genuine excuse to leave.

He tied a loose knot around Buck's foot to hold the sheepskin in place. Buck picked up his stick, taking Ben's arm and Mary's shoulder. They nodded at Froika and left.

"That was spooky. Was she right though, Buck? Is that why your mind goes for a walk? Do you see things you don't understand?" Ben was fascinated.

"I'll tell you later, if that's all right. I really want to see Piddlin all of a sudden. I've got an itch at the top of my head, and I need to see if her ears are twitching. It would mean there's either really bad weather or a real bad man coming for a visit." He hopped to Piddlin on his own and promptly burst into tears. Ben and Mary left him to it for a spell, understanding the relief he must feel. Piddlin decided it was worth being alive and started to give him a playful time of it. She twitched her ears, stomped her feet, and threw her head in what felt like four directions at the same time. It took Joss and Buck a while to get her settled, but she had made everyone laugh. Buck asked Joss to take her for a walk tomorrow if he could. "Nowhere near the farm, of course, maybe east or north."

Joss was more than happy to do it. Seeing Piddlin come back to her true self also did him the power of good. Buck was staring at him over the top of Piddlin's withers. "Whatcha doing, Buck?"

"Don't rush to the war, Joss. If you want to join the army, do it when you're eighteen and it's all over for a while. This country will always have wars to fight. If it comes to it, and you need to go anywhere at all, you should go to a place called Kentucky. The grass is so green it's nearly blue, and the horses are handled as if they're on a par with the Lord himself—or so I've been told. Sounds like a paradise made specially for you, you think?" He stopped staring, shook himself, and smiled weakly before he settled his head on Piddlin's neck. "I've been told I have to say good things when I hear them. I don't know where the words come from." Buck lifted his head to look at the lad. "I didn't mean to scare you. Sorry, Joss."

Joss felt queasy, changed the subject and turned to Mary. "You see the Gypsy horses? They look normal without all the fancy harnesses on. Never seen their like before, though. Very big and proud. Look at the massive necks and hooves." Mary spoke to them and petted them. It was good to see they were cared for.

"They must be worth a fortune, don't you think?"

"What, Miss Mary? The harnesses or the horses?" Joss had never considered it.

"Both of course, child." She giggled at him.

Ben spent most of his time with Black Satin and was content that his horse was getting excellent care. He said as much to Joss, who blushed and tried to be all man when he said he was just doing his job, sir.

When they got back to the saloon Buck's head had stopped itching. That meant to him that the trouble on the way wasn't weather, it was human, but no human in this place. Ben was looking at him in a different way as he made his way back to his table. Poppy said she'd killed another chicken while he was gone. She knew he didn't like eggs, but how about a chuck? He'd have to share it, of course.

"Well that's really good of you, and thank you kindly." Buck felt himself getting stronger. Just seeing that Piddlin was fine and they would be back together real soon brought him back to earth in a solid way.

Poppy had noticed Rebecca with her hand on Pete's chest. She knew there was nothing to be jealous of, but still, men don't listen very well to things that are said. Rather than wait for Pete to say he wasn't listening, he didn't hear the woman, or he didn't believe her, she sidled up beside him to put away a tray and listen to the conversation. Clara would have to keep an eye out for the chuck.

"That young man, Buck, has murder on his mind," Rebecca quickly whispered. "Don't let it sneak into his heart and stick to his soul. You have never wasted a single bullet; don't waste this one, for the boy's sake. Don't hesitate. Aim true."

She gave him a tired smile and then gazed at Poppy. "You are a wonderful woman. Don't let this tough old fellow forget it." She'd just made a friend for life in a madam who had once been a fallen dove and who now cared for three of her own.

Pete started on the piano. Froika went to his wagon and returned with a fiddle and another instrument no one had ever seen. Rebecca played the fiddle, but the music was sad. There were many people in the saloon now because word had spread about the Gypsies. They sat drinking—which continued to worry Pete because of his low stock—and crying for the loneliness of the sound she made. Froika changed the tempo and Rebecca danced. She caught the good reverend tapping his foot and grabbed him to whirl with her. In the middle of the short dance, she gazed at him very briefly and somehow made him feel she'd seen right through him.

"You will be given a church organ," she told him. "It's stolen. Offer it back. Don't worry, you won't get into trouble for it, and you will be allowed to keep it simply because of your honesty. Honesty is not all that foreign to you, is it?" No one had ever heard the reverend laugh like that. The Gypsies had been sent from God, the people in the saloon felt. Validation had never had so much enjoyment.

CHAPTER TWENTY-THREE

"I seen a bunch of men coming from the east." Joss was coming full tilt into the town and hadn't dismounted from Piddlin, whose ears were twitching very nearly in circles. "I think Duncan's with them."

Ben had been seeing to Black Satin's early-morning feed and mucking out. "Were they coming to town?" He held the reins while little Joss jumped off Buck's horse.

"I think they were going the back way to the MacGregor place."

"That would figure. Must be Silk. It sounds like something he would do—try to sneak in and out without being noticed until it was too late. Did he see you?"

"Don't think so, sir. What do you think Mr. Silk wants to do?"

"It'll be thievery and killing if he thinks it'll pay him to do it. Don't you worry about anything, though. I'll get Pete and Buck. We'll cut them off before they get here. Stay put and get the horses ready. Buck will need the special stirrup he carved for himself."

As he ran back to the Diamond, Ben heard the young lad say he was sorry to Piddlin. He'd have to change his rig out and the horse wasn't all that used to the new get-up. Ben hoped the kid's dream of owning a horse ranch would one day come true for him.

Pete saw Ben clomping through the heavy drifts of snow that had fallen over the last week. Some businesses had given up shoveling until the weather settled, but he had dug himself out so people could congregate and complain about things. It felt better to bellyache in a warm place. He was out of most of his stock now, relying on watered-down whiskey. He hoped his patrons wouldn't notice after the first decent shot. No one had said anything yet. There was plenty of rum for Ben, and it wasn't popular with the locals, so Ben thought everything was just fine. Pete would have to ask him to go to Leavenworth with him once the weather looked like he would be able to get away for the three or four days it would take to get there, buy the stock, and return. Poppy was never short of food, somehow. Perhaps he should take advice from her on how to manage his seemingly endless problem. Obviously, keeping a well-stocked pantry of any kind was women's work. Idly, he wondered how she would feel about starting a still—just over the winter months, of course.

Ben stopped at the door, motioning for Pete to come to him. Pete joined him on the cold boardwalk, closing the heavy door behind him.

"Joss saw Silk, and most likely Duncan, with another bunch of men heading toward the back way to the farm."

"I'll get ready."

"We'd better get Buck and go to meet the trouble that'll come to us unless we get hold of it first."

"I'll get my rifle, but do you really think Buck is able?"

"He has revenge in his heart. I don't think we should try to stop him. I'll go back to the stables. Meet you there."

When Pete walked back inside his manner had changed. "Is there something wrong, Pete?"

He ignored the reverend's question, going directly to Buck.

"It looks like Duncan's back on the farm, probably with that Silk fellow that Ben wants to capture. You coming?"

Buck had made a moccasin shoe with a special lift in it where his toe used to be. It wasn't the most comfortable thing in the world, but he would refine it. He stood up, still leaning a bit on his stick. Pete had forgotten how tall he was. "I carry a gun on my left hip. Duncan won't know that."

"Might not come to that, Buck. We don't know if Duncan's with them because he wants to be or because they made him join them. Take your time. We'll find out the truth before we have at it. Deal?"

Those newly black eyes of Buck, those eyes that reminded Pete of the name of his Black Diamond Saloon—hard, cold, and unseeing of what was in front of him but not what was beyond him—actually frightened the older man. Somehow Buck had aged well beyond his years in the last month. Now Pete understood what the Gypsy woman had said. Murder was on Buck's heart and mind. If the doing of it ever got into his soul, it would affect him forever, so much that he might enjoy it. Pete would have to lift the burden from the shoulders of this young man if that was at all possible.

"We'll find out first. Deal." Buck shook his head and smiled, but not the smile of the innocent, gentle lad they had grown to know and love. This smile came across as deliberate and ingratiating—like it was stuck onto his face for effect.

"Pray for us, Reverend Parker." Reverend Parker didn't think Pete meant it. He'd been wearing his collar as a shield for a very long time. He remembered the day of his first killings and could smell more killing coming.

Poppy had Pete's two Sharps rifles ready. They gleamed with the care that had been lavished on them, but still Pete had a good look inside and out, making sure that they were well-oiled and ready to go. He held one in each hand as he slogged through the drifts to the livery. Buck got in the saddle, warm in his long, fur-lined coat,

The Mindwalker

the one with the wolf-skin collar Mary had sewn for him with help from the other women of the church. He wore his one new boot that he'd made from the old boots he'd been cut out of that night. Joss, who had helped Buck up, gently placed his foot into a wide, tough, cowhide contraption that fit around his heel and kept his toes up at the same time.

Ben made sure of his own guns. For the first time since he had arrived he hauled his dragoon from his saddlebag and tied it twice around his leg, once at his thigh and once at his knee.

The lad looked so unusual that he impressed people as threatening. It was probably a good thing to look that way today. It might put someone off trying to kill him. His revolver rested easily on his left thigh. Buck had never understood why a right-handed man would draw from his right hip. To him it made more sense to take your right hand down across your body, whip your pistol or revolver out of a holster on your left side, and turn it to spray whoever got in the way. Buck had been practicing this way for a long time, in the woods while Duncan was having one of his never-ending naps. Today it was time, today he was ready. Duncan would die.

"You're quiet today." Mary had come rushing to the stable.

"Duncan's back. Got things to do. See you when we get back." Mary took a step back, partly to get out of the way of three horses and partly out of shock. Buck sounded bigger somehow, like a commander.

"Buck Ross, I'm not sure I like you. I'm not sure I've ever liked you," she whispered to herself as she pulled her pretty, blue knitted shawl over her mouth and readjusted her buffalo hide.

Joss straightened the stalls and cleaned them out—he had never been so scared, even when the ferry crashed into the wrong side of the river last year, killing a team of horses, sinking the stagecoach, and drowning some ten or so women and children.

"As long as no one gets hurt that shouldn't get hurt, eh, Miss Mary?"

"That's true, Joss. That's true." She stomped through the drifts and was grateful there was nothing more coming from the heavens.

It was one of those gray days that was spending its time thinking about where it was going to go. Mary thought it would clear by lunchtime and maybe bring some custom to the store, so she returned to see how her father was. He'd been fretting some about things happening that he didn't want to happen.

He had left the east with all his family—his wife, daughter, and two sons—because he didn't like the way people were starting to think. It had cost him everyone, apart from his daughter. Mary. She would leave very soon, probably to go off with that Buck boy. He might be sweet on her, but Ian wasn't sure Buck would be able to provide for her, so when Mary came back from the stables he was pleased that he wasn't the one that had to broach the conversation.

"Buck just said he'd see me later."

There was a little gasp from the needle-and-thread end of the store—the haberdashery, as Mary liked to call it because it sounded more Boston. Shona let herself be known to them so she couldn't be accused of eavesdropping. Mary acknowledged her. Shona returned her polite nod. Miss Mary had aged. It was unlucky for a woman to age. Buck looked wonderful even through his injury. Age suited men better, it seemed—especially the farther west they got.

"You should hear this too," Mary said, "especially now you suspect he might be a relation, after seeing the family tree in that Bible."

"What did you tell him?" Ian's hands were shaking, so he held on to the counter. "Stop shaking, Pa. Let go of the counter. I said nothing, but do you know what? I'm not sure I even like him anymore, so no, I won't marry him, and as a matter of fact, Pa, I think I'd like to go back east for a spell. In the spring, of course. Why don't both of us go? We could have a vacation."

"You sure? It's not like you've spent any time thinking about it."

"There's a few months to get ready for a trip and we don't have to tell anyone, do we? It's not like anyone would care."

"Buck might."

Mary cogitated. "He's going west, I think. I hope he finds what he's looking for, but I'm afraid it won't be me." She flounced off into the back to see if they really were as low on paraffin as she thought they were.

"Oh, dear. She's in love," Shona said.

"Not as much as we thought, though. Things seem to have taken a turn, Mrs. Haggerty."

"I would be flattered if you would call me by my name, Mr. Grant. Now everyone's seen the Bible and knows my Christian name is Shona. I would like to hear it from the right people."

"We'll shake hands on that, Shona. My name is Ian."

Mary stuck her head around the corner at the end of the aisle when she heard the sound of laughter.

"What are you two plotting?"

"We have just decided to be less formal with each other. Your father has my permission to call me Shona. So do you. That makes sense, don't you think, especially as we helped to save the life of a young man who happens to be my nephew."

Mary took the dozen steps to the front where the daylight helped her see what was really happening. There was a flutter in her belly and an ache in her head, but her heart was as cold as the snow in the mountains.

"Don't be so hard on him, Mary," Ian said. "He's had a bad time of it, even for this part of the world. Things could change by spring. Swallow your words before you're forced to swallow your regrets, daughter."

"I would still like to go home in the spring. I can think there. Maybe visit with old friends. Mrs. McIver and Allison would make me welcome. They send letters inviting us anytime, Papa. You know that."

"You've got your dander up, girl. Settle your red head down. We won't be able to stay open for much longer today so check the paraffin as you were doing and just keep thinking—that's what you're good at." He slapped his hand on the wooden counter. Mary stared him down. Shona placed the darning wool she wanted on the counter and asked the price. The two older people rolled eyes at each other and the moment was gone.

"I think we'll donate the wool, Shona. It's for the church, isn't it?"

The clatter of hooves and the whoops of men leaving on a mission brought all to the front door. Mary stifled the tears, but Shona didn't.

Ian put an arm around his daughter. "No one dies today except those that the Good Lord needs to take back around his own campfire."

CHAPTER TWENTY-FOUR

Buck rode quietly between Pete and Ben. He wasn't used to the weight of his dragoon on his leg. It felt tightened securely enough. The snow wasn't as deep as it could have been—maybe it had something to do with the unusually dry summer—so they made steady progress toward the Kansas River. The farm was situated on a tiny tributary, but if they'd been trying to do this trip at the beginning of spring it could be running too high and fast to cross. No, high summer by skiff and low winter by land were the best times to take this trip.

"Foot all right, Buck?"

"I'm managing fine, Ben. Just fine."

"Doc let me have some poppy juice to carry, in case you were needing."

"Maybe after we've done the work we're coming to do. Not right now, though. Thanks." Buck knew the juice could make him want to sleep. He sounded like he was speaking through gritted teeth and then he stopped riding. He just stopped—either that, or Piddlin plain wouldn't move. The other men, used to Buck taking his mind for a walk, sighed against the rising cold and waited, turning to watch.

Piddlin's ears twitched. Buck took off his hat and scratched his head. Piddlin started to move forward past Pete and Ben. No one said anything as Buck encouraged his horse, and the group picked up speed. Buck knew the way better than anyone, so when he turned a sharp left to go over the ice-edged river, the others followed. They found themselves hidden in the middle of fifty or so massive pecan trees, facing where the small house had been.

Ben straightened. "Silk."

"Duncan's lost weight," Pete observed.

"How do you want to do this?"

"Follow me." It was Buck's prerogative to lead.

The other two men trailed at a distance that made them look like they were followers, but they knew they would have their own jobs to do. They stayed far enough back to get a clear shot if they needed to.

"Do you think he'll talk or shoot first?"

"I hope he talks to Duncan first. Maybe he'll see sense." Pete eased his rifle from its saddle holster but didn't cock it.

Ben withdrew his Springfield, resting it gently across Black Satin's saddle.

"Nice rifle, Ben. Old friend?" The men were quiet about complimenting each other on their choice of weapon. Neither of them took his eyes from the gathering coming together between the trough and the old privy. They controlled their breathing, as professionals were used to doing.

Buck edged Piddlin within clear sight and earshot of the gang. Duncan was bending forward into the back of a buckboard, one of the other three men was fussing over the horses, another was threatening to draw his gun, and the last had a rifle trained on Buck. Silk was looking past Buck in the direction of the men behind him. He coughed and spat onto the ground, wiping his bloody chin with the back of his ruffled sleeve.

"You've been looking for me a long time, Benjamin Walter MacLaren." Silk had teeth that looked like they'd just eaten a raw steak. He'd had to open his mouth wide to shout into the trees.

"Will I take you in with or without a struggle over it?" Ben had brought Black Satin closer, ten feet behind Buck.

Duncan straightened from the buckboard holding his Pa's Colt, his new one, the one he had taken with him to meet Silk. He knew that by virtue of owning the Colt he had proved he would be a good member, a valuable member of the gang. Now he was aiming it directly at his cousin Buck as he moved around behind Silk.

Buck was speaking in the low, controlled voice that had brought a chill into the air of the saloon.

"Are you the man that shot my pa all those years ago?" He stopped Piddlin in front of Silk.

"Yes."

"Tell your men to drop their guns, Mr. Silken. Please." Buck's voice was even quieter as he looked Silk in the eye.

Silk motioned to the boys to disarm.

"Kick your guns away, where Pete and I can see them." Ben was businesslike about things.

After a time when all orders were followed Buck moved again, circling slowly.

"Did you see my ma die?"

"I thought you'd die, too." Buck moved behind a bit. Silk tried to follow him.

"Don't move, you son of a bitch." Buck released his dragoon from its holster. Ben and Pete cocked their rifles, the sound carrying in the sharp winter air. Silk stopped.

"Did you kill my aunt and uncle last month?" He moved Piddlin forward to Silk's left.

"Well, no. That was Everly did that. And Pat, I think. Everly's not riding with us now."

Buck was in front of Silk again. He continued to circle him. Ben and Pete remained in control, their rifles following every twitch of the gang members.

"I'm going to think on this for a bit."

Buck rode past Silk to where Duncan was standing. "You got my back, Mr. Tait?"

"Count on it, Mr. Ross. You can count on it."

"You too, MacLaren?"

"You can bet on it, sir."

"You going to shoot me, Duncan?"

"Might just do that."

"I haven't got a gun aimed at you. I'm not even off this horse."

"So I'll have you dead right now." Duncan fired. The shot went wild into the sky and he wound up flat on his back. Pete had caught him with a shot in the neck. Duncan gurgled and gasped his last few breaths. Buck sat to watch until it was all over, his blue eyes dispassionate, the dragoon loose in his right hand, crossed over the wrist of his left and resting on the saddle horn. Piddlin danced and nickered.

Rye fired at Pete, but Ben was well ahead of him, and when Pat sought cover behind the trough where Jenny had died, he found Buck pointing his gun straight at his head from only a few feet away.

"Which of you raped my aunt?" He had a full view of the fear in Pat's eyes.

"His name was Everly Plastow. Rye killed him for it. Didn't want to ride with scum." There was no confidence in the man's voice.

"He use the knife on her, too?"

"Must have. Liked to scar womenfolk."

"Empty your gun and give it to me." Buck reholstered his own, knowing that Ben and Pete had Silk and his gang in their sights.

The Mindwalker

He bent down to get the pistol as Pat handed it to him butt first. "Pick up my cousin's gun for me." They took their time moving closer to the men forming around Ben and Silk.

"Follow me." There was an attitude about Buck's voice and manner that meant the situation was now finally under his control and only his control, so men much older and more experienced obeyed without asking any questions. He returned to Silk. Pete had demanded Rye's gun, and things were starting to come clearer. The man that had been fussing the horses but had never drawn his gun decided to come over as well.

"The watch if you please, Mr. Silken." Ben extended a bare hand.

"Lost it years ago."

"Horse hockey. Watch. Now."

Ben hadn't moved one inch.

Silk took a while to get past all his coats, waistcoats, and shirts. When he finally found the watch he parted with it smoothly.

"Use all that time planning an escape? It took quite a while to find something you use all the time. Excuse the pun.

Ben rode up to Silk. "I wasn't going to use steel bracelets but I don't think you've a mind to admit you've seen the last of your wandering days? You won't come easily Mr. Silken." He snapped one heavy handcuff on each wrist. The bar between them was big enough so Silk could hang on to his pommel if he needed to. He'd have to be desperate to make a run for it now. Ben shrugged at Buck. "Your turn."

Buck gave Pat's gun to Pete, who also had Rye's. He kept Duncan's Colt loose in his hands and tucked his old dragoon safely away in its holster.

"Why did you kill my parents?"

"Your Pa owed me money—a gambling debt."

Buck stopped and grinned at Silk. "That's a lie. What he did have was the title to a piece of land in Boston. That is worth following someone halfway across a country for, not pieces of coin or bits of paper."

Silk's shoulders took a fighting stance. "You got it?"

"I do, Mr. Silken, I most surely do. Duncan had it for a bit, but he was too busy drawing his pictures on the pages of the Old Testament and wiping his arse with the Book of Revelations to notice the papers had been glued into the dust cover." Buck was allowing Piddlin—whose ears were now fully poised forward and absolutely still—to prance. It was good to feel her coming back to herself, so he gave her her head. She distracted Silk, at any rate. "Did you wonder why Duncan didn't burn the privy?"

"Not one bit. He was a fussy, lazy, little grunt. I was surprised to hear he had taken out his anger on a house, though." Silk pointed at the body, empty of all its fluids. It stank already. "Better bury him before we go. Want me to ask my boys to do it?" Pat and Rye shouted they wouldn't do it. Tom nodded and said Duncan should be buried with his folks. He turned toward the cemetery that was filling up too fast to be natural.

"What's your name, Mister?" Ben spoke up.

"Tom Wilson."

"You wanted for anything, Tom Wilson?"

"Probably, but not in this state." He continued his walk to the boneyard.

"Wants to retire to Missouri after we deliver the organ to your little church," Silk said.

Everyone was smiling of a sudden.

"So, when I escort you to Fort Leavenworth," Ben said, "I can put in a good word for you because you found God, are fully repentant of all your sins, and to prove it, you've just donated an organ to a church?"

The gang stopped grinning. Ben and the others were laughing out loud.

"Now, let's get this over with." Ben was back in charge.

"You two men help Tom to bury Duncan." Ben pointed his pistol at Rye and Pat. "We'll have coffee brewing just as you finish, and I will let you go then, to Missouri or California or even Texas, as long as I never see you again after this, the Lord's day of the twentieth of December 1861. If you decide to run for it, well, I'm sure you're all wanted somewhere, so my friend here—who has never missed a shot in his life, according to a Gypsy called Rebecca—will shoot to kill you, and we will collect the bounty. Now, is that fair or is that fair?"

The men, who knew this was very fair, skedaddled to the cemetery.

"Come see the organ if you want."

"I'll search the buckboard first, if it's all the same. Never know what's lurking under the seating of these things. Here's my Sharps, Buck. It's loaded. Can't go far wrong, even if you miss. Keep it leveled at him, though." Silk coughed again. "Don't let that pity-me hack distract you, Buck. It's an old ploy, isn't it, Silk? Miner's lung, was it? You weren't down those dank caves long enough."

Ben ran his hand under the passenger side of the buckboard.

"Ah, now that's an impressive haul. Cash and a deed book. Would take the right sort of con man to pull this off. Maybe with time, the father and son—being Duncan, of course—down on their luck and Pa dying of the flux, could've worked a real deal selling land they didn't own. At least they could say exactly where it was and get a man with a good steady artist's hand to draw up some false documents. Yes, that could be some good money."

"So, is that why you grabbed hold of Duncan?" Buck asked. "'Cause he could draw?"

"Your cousin missed his calling, or at least nobody noticed it. If you ever want to see how good he could have been, go visit Bully Carlson in Topeka. He's got a fine piece of art in his shed."

"Why don't you give the pity-me thing a rest, Silk?" Ben said. "This the organ?"

"Don't take it out the box. It's been hard enough getting it here in one piece."

"I can see you must have opened it to check the contents or something, so if it's all the same, I'll do the likewise."

Silk moved forward quickly, but Ben was wise to him. He tripped him up and managed to take the knife from his boot. In one flowing, smooth movement, the knife was at Silk's Adam's apple. Pete grabbed Silk and threw him onto his back on the ground, squeezing his foot onto his chest. He used his other rifle to keep him in his place.

"Dynamite? Sounds real old to me Mr. Silk—even maybe a bit dangerous. What's this?" Ben put his hand right into the guts of the organ and came out with a glass container nearly full of ice. He shook it. "No, definitely not an explosive of any kind. Even if it does say Nitroglycerine. Sorry Silk—a complete waste of money and why would you want to blow up an organ, anyway?"

Silk was showing his fury. Pete let him sit up so the blustering would sound better. It didn't. All the sounds of how he didn't know it was there just made him appear the weak man he'd always been.

The legend that was Ben MacLaren was performing as the Lord had intended him to do. Silk knew he was done for. His days of wandering were over, his days of prison cells about to begin, unless he could do something. He'd always got out of jail before—this would be the last time.

"Do you think we can get back before it gets pitch dark, Mr. Ross?"

"There should be just enough moonlight to get us there, Mr. Tait."

"Want to give Piddlin a rest? You can sit on the board for a bit. Rest your foot and let Piddlin get her balance back in order before we go back to town."

"We're going to Validation?" Silk asked.

The Mindwalker

"Yep. Lots of reasons for it," Ben said. "First of all, I'm going to wire the fort to tell them to expect you and to get a rope ready. Second, I'm going to wire the captain's family to see if they want to come for the hanging. Third, I want to see the look on Shona's face when you return the watch. That, Mr. Silken, is the real reason I've given a damn about you at all. Not the money I'll be paid, not to extend the legend that appears to be developing around me, but purely and simply so that Shona can be reunited with a watch that is engraved 'Always Faithful, Jamie.' Slip off Piddlin and lead us home, Buck."

"Mr. Tom Wilson, you can follow if you're going north." Ben and Pete looked askance at Buck. "He just wants out of all of it," Buck said. He handed Pete's rifle back to him. "Didn't need it, thank God."

"Probably won't get too far until spring, but it be good and thankee." Tom couldn't recall when he'd seen a kid with so much nonce about him.

A screech and a loud warning whistle came from the direction of the family plot. Pat McBride was waving his arms, and Rye was frantically pointing into the pecan grove.

"Indians." Pete stated the fact while he raised his rifle. Ben followed. Silk saw a chance and asked for something to defend himself.

"Nope." Ben raised his Springfield to his shoulder.

"Put your gear away," Buck said. "It's Mark and a few of his friends."

Moon Feather smiled at her father, and Buck softened at her presence.

CHAPTER TWENTY-FIVE

"They're Indians, kid. Indians!" Silk couldn't credit it.
"You never seen one, Silk? Never had any dealings with them?"
"I've heard plenty and didn't like any of it."
"Certain sure they've heard plenty about us and thought the same."

Buck moved Piddlin forward, tapping his fist on his breastbone as he did so. "Stay back, everyone. I'll see what's to do." He turned in his saddle. "Put your guns all the way down." Ben cleared his throat.

"You sure?"

Buck looked at him. "Why wouldn't I be?" He met with Mark and the other five Natives at the edge of the orchard.

"Spirit has blessed you with good friends."

"And you." Young and old acknowledged common ground.

"We hunt."

"I thought that. What are you hunting?"

"Wild turkey, as you say, but I see you hunt wild men. Look, they come down from the graveyard."

"Join with us awhile."

Mark spoke to his hunting party who, in single file, silently rode past. The sky was beginning to darken quickly now and the stars to show themselves. The only sounds were the hooves on the ground and the chink-a-clink of the leather harnesses on the buckboard's horses. Once the hunting party had disappeared again into the forest, Mark came alongside Buck. The two of them rode toward the anxious bunch of men.

Mark looked at each in turn and nodded his head like he was being introduced to them. Moon Feather did her job well.

"This is the man who killed your family?"

Silk was sitting on his horse, the edgy Vengeance. Ben held the reins.

"You can't kill him because of your laws."

Ben straightened his back as he sensed a threat. "Mr. Silken has to go to Fort Leavenworth, to be hung by the neck until he stops kicking."

Mark shook his head. "Want me to kill him for you?"

"Don't waste your energy, Mark. The white man will kill his own."

"Fine. You do it then, Buck."

Silk started to hack again, coughing and spitting up great gobs of blood.

Mark began to head off to join his men. "That one will die long before he gets to your jail and it won't be a good death, not the death of a brave man. Will see you again, little brother, but not most likely in this world. My daughter will not be with you much longer either." He flicked his reins on the pinto's neck and left, neither looking behind nor acknowledging the others.

Buck raised his hand in a salute just as his head began to itch and Piddlin's ears began a jig.

"What's to be doing?" Ben was still watching Mark.

"We have to leave. Now. There's either bad men or bad weather coming, and I tend to the very bad weather."

Buck slid into the seat of the buckboard, leaving Piddlin to follow behind. "Came in to this farm on one of these, might as well leave on one. It's what gave me my name."

He led them across the wider part of the river because the wagon was too large to take the shortcut. It was a good thing the water wasn't running fast or deep. The horses were rattled and scatty because of their long wait in harness and the smell of death and blood. It could have been so much worse. Buck's head was still giving him bother.

Ben and Pete, as men of the natural world, also had their instincts open to any suggestion of trouble, especially as there was no chance now of getting back in any light but starlight. They were warned by the wind and the taste of the cold that more snow was coming. Each of them began to pray to himself.

"Halfway there, I think." Pete had to raise his voice over the noise of the rising wind. He tucked his head back into the buffalo skin he'd so sensibly brought.

Tom, Pat, and Rye took up the rear of this company. Neither Ben nor Pete objected. There was nowhere else for them to go. They'd laid stones on top of Duncan, as they couldn't bury him deep enough.

Silk bent over his saddle, trying to stay clear of as much wind as he could. Every few minutes he'd cough and spit. Vengeance pulled the reins from Ben's hands and charged into a stand of last year's sunflowers. Silk sat up, grabbed the reins and made a show of escaping, pulling his horse left against the buckboard's team, causing them to start and snort. Silk was heading for anywhere except jail.

Pete stood in Buchanan's stirrups, aimed his rifle and missed. Ben gasped in shock. He tried his Springfield. Maybe it was the cold that caused its inaccuracy. They all heard what they thought was Silk shout a victory whoop and then, from behind, Buck used his uncle's new Colt. At least Duncan had kept it clean. Silk rose

The Mindwalker

up in his saddle, falling backward, arms out, pinwheeling. Then he slid from the rump of his horse. Vengeance danced and shook. Rye shouted for him. Pat whistled. Tom trotted to fetch him back.

"Where do you think you're heading?" Pete tried to save his pride.

"Good horse, Vengeance. Take him along—maybe trade him."

"Quite possibly, but I don't generally trust a volunteer unless I've told him what to do." Pete turned to assess Pat and Rye.

"You, in the wool hat. Go fetch back that horse. I'm volunteering you. At this range I won't miss again." He aimed his rifle. Rye followed the horse, feeling the rifle aimed at him.

"Take my knife, Mr. Carp. I need a remembrance of my first kill."

"Dear God, boy. You can't expect a finger!" Ben was horrified.

"That's not a thought I had. Silk is about to lose the loose part of his hair—his sailor's pigtail, if you wouldn't mind, Mr. Carp?" He unfolded his jackknife and handed it to Rye, who showed a certain glee in his acceptance of it.

"This will be my most profound pleasure, Mr. Ross. A profound pleasure indeed."

He whistled and called softly to the big stallion.

He dismounted, removed himself to Mr. Silk, the outlaw, con man, and killer, and took a fair chunk of the man's hair. He thought about his Meerschaum pipe and tobacco while he was at it. The spurs would fetch some good money. He removed them from the nearly rotten boots, had a thought about the coat and hat, but realized he had no use for them, and stood up. Silk was breathing his last. Weakly, he pointed to his boot.

"Gold. For you." Blood trickled from the old sailor's mouth onto the fresh snow.

Rye bent down. "Silk, if there's gold in that boot, it'll still be there in the spring. You'll still be here, too. Nice knowing you."

"Bastard," Silk growled at him. Rye gathered Vengeance and struggled back through the snowdrifts, determined to keep his own counsel, spurs tinkling in his hands.

He led Silk's horse to the others, who had been able to see movement but weren't sure what he'd been up to. He returned directly to Buck, cleaned and folded his jackknife, handed it back, and passed him Silk's pigtail with a small piece of scalp attached. Buck tucked it into his belt near his holster. He patted it as he settled deeper into his saddle.

"My hand slipped in the cold. Sorry. Got a gift for someone, though." He showed everyone the pipe and then shoved it into his coat. "Any takers?"

"Am I hearing spurs?" Pat always had good hearing.

"Yup, and I'm keeping them. I got 'em, I own 'em." He remounted his horse.

"That mean the horse is yours as well?" Tom didn't mean to stir more trouble.

Pete pulled up short. "This is how it goes. We survive this. We get food in our bellies, warmth in our bones, and a night of sleep out of this damn snow. Then we divide the spoils over coffee the next day." He slipped his rifle back into its long saddle holster. What was left of Silk's gang remained mum and exchanged dark looks.

"Well done," murmured Ben. "Now, can we get going?" He rode alongside Buck for a while and wondered if the Gypsy woman had been right. The kid looked fine, perhaps too fine for a first kill. Pete was thinking the same. "Let's hurry along. You're right, we'll settle things when we're warm."

The wind dropped, the road began to look familiar to everyone and then, blessing of blessings, they saw that someone had set fiery torches along the path. As they traveled they doused them and put them in the back of the buckboard. When Ben saw Poppy standing outside the livery he knew he hadn't been the only one who'd found God in the last four hours.

Joss and Ryan near as flew out of the stables to catch the horses. Shona came for Buck, she said. Ben thanked Mary for her kindnesses as she held a lamp for him to feed and water Black Silk. She had to leave shortly, she explained, because Ian had come down with something. Pat, Tom, and Rye hovered around the buckboard. Tom took care of the team. Doc Fraser arrived to see his patient. The townsfolk worked like a team. They said very little, none of it loudly. All of them having spent their lives around horses, they understood that a calm approach was essential to keep things settled and get the work done in short order. Buck sat on a rise of hay with a bucket of water and bits and harness to clean. All commenced to warming, feeding, and watering the horses. Someone threw a blanket on each of them. When they had done all they could, Joss straightened and said a quiet and well-meant "Amen."

"Is that the Gypsy wagon?" Buck finally took time to look around him.

"They couldn't get through. Told them it was the wrong time of year to travel." Ryan was matter of fact about it. "Most likely have to wait until late January if they're lucky. Horses likely to eat us out of all the hay we've got. Have to see what they intend to do or make some arrangements elsewhere." He kicked the toe of his boot against the stable floor, talking half to himself.

Everyone struggled through the snow to the saloon for warmth and food. Pete and the doc helped Buck hop there, relief spurring them on. "That has got to be the longest day of my life," Tom said, "and on the shortest day of the year."

Poppy had been busy, her girls helping and Shona and Mary fixing rooms, stoking fires, cooking, and heating plates. She hadn't used the good china, as she called it, because Christmas was still to come, but she was flushed with excitement and fighting back tears as she held on to Pete like she wouldn't be able to breathe without him. She made him sit near the bigger wood-burning stove, helped him with his boots and jacket, further embarrassed him by telling him off for scaring her by being away too long, and then burst into full tears before running to hide in the kitchens.

"As if I wanted to be out in that snow." Pete rested his bare head on his hands, breathing in the warm air of his home.

"The day will turn into a hard night my friend." Froika presented him with a large whiskey and an even larger hand on his shoulder. "I drink my own vodka, so am considered safe to stand in behind your bar, *da*?"

Pete's laugh, his astounding belly laugh, silenced everything. The music started. Rebecca danced. Everyone talked, of mostly good company, but the presence of Pat, Rye, and Tom in a corner of the bar cast a pall on the evening.

Buck sat with Pete, Ben, and Doc at a table near the fire. He pushed himself up suddenly. Doc, taken by surprise at his patient's unexpected movement, steadied him.

"You three can sleep in the stables tonight after you've had a bite to eat. Tom, see me tomorrow before you leave. Pat and Rye, make yourselves scarce as soon as the weather lets you." He sat down hard. Everyone stared at the new Buck Ross. Shona brought her hand to her mouth and thought what a good thing Mary and her father weren't here.

"You missed, Mr. Pete. Mr. Ross has taken his first scalp, as they say." Rebecca stood beside her husband, hands on hips.

"Better than you know, lady." Pete was mortified at having to admit his mistake.

She threw back her head. "Ha! It is how it is and now has to be cleared and cleaned, but only over time and good work. Is that agreeable to you, young Mr. Buck? Are you going to go Silk's way and join them in the stables tonight, or do you have the courage to continue on the path you were on this very early morning?"

"You're supposed to stay at my house, Buck." Doc's voice sounded tenuous. "Mine or the stables?"

"Don't understand the fuss here," Buck said. "Like she says, it is how it is. Nothing can be changed but all can be cleaned and cleared. I'm coming with you, Doc, if you've still a mind to teach me to doctor."

Doc Fraser shoved his welcoming hand under Buck's nose. "Starting tomorrow then, Buck Ross." In front of everyone they shook hands. "Starting tomorrow, Doctor Fraser."

A huge cheer went up. Poppy wasn't sure if was because of her arrival with a platter of roast pig (followed by the girls bringing taters and greens, such as they were at this time of year) or because the strange Indian girl standing behind Buck was actually glowing.

"Where'd you find a pig at this time of year, you genius lady?" Pete reached around her waist.

"Ryan found him. Wild one, I think, but I didn't ask questions. I just cooked it." Poppy was still in a mood about something.

Doc turned from the window. "Think I'll visit Ian before I can't actually get there."

"Hey, now. You've got to eat something first. Dedication is fine, but if you're not strong enough, you'll be no good to him," Pete said. A murmur of agreement passed around the room.

"That's a good idea I suppose. Just hope Ian eats something." Doc sounded distracted.

"Come back to us in this room, please, Doctor Fraser. You're starting to look like our Mindwalker." Ben grabbed and shook his shoulder.

"Yep, don't let anything come of things. You don't need to be poorly until you've taught Buck some medicine." Shona was solicitous.

Poppy put a plate of pork in front of Doc and then piled it with greens and many, many potatoes because she knew he adored them. "Put that in your belly, Doc." He nodded—blissfully.

"You strong enough to chew, Buck?" He was nearly eighteen. He was ravenous. He nodded like a vulture coming across a fresh kill. Poppy giggled. "Thought you might be."

"So, the rest of you. I'll leave the food on the bar, and you'll start at one end and work to the other like they do in some swanky New York restaurants, I hear."

"It's called a bread line in Chicago," shouted Ben over the hubbub. "Either way, it's grub."

The girls had placed plates, forks, and food in order on the bar. Ben lined up behind Shona to help her with the taters. "I have something for you." He was quiet when he said it. She looked up into his soft, brown eyes. "I'll give it to you tomorrow, if you're available." She agreed and managed a tiny curtsy.

Rebecca appeared in front of Shona as she was about to take her seat at the smaller table near the fire. "Jamie is pleased with Ben. He feels he would be a suitable protector for you. He says he will still be faithful, but he needs you to let him go." She spoke so quietly Shona wondered if she even heard her.

CHAPTER TWENTY-SIX

Doc sidled out after his dinner and another whisky. He was right. The wind was whipping snow into the doors and windows of the saloon, causing drifts that might soon reach the height of the first window sash. He knew he wasn't being sensible about things, but Ian concerned him. Doc hadn't said it, but he feared cholera.

He took some of Poppy's food for Mary and Ian, not so much because he was worried that Mary wouldn't eat properly, but because it had been his experience that the better a person with diarrhea and vomiting could keep food down, the better their chance of living. He plodded against the vicious wind that carried ice crystals sharp enough to pierce his eyes if he'd been able to keep them open. He was moving forward out of a sense of self-preservation. He could spend the night with Ian if need be. It was very difficult for him to trudge past his own abode, but he managed and entered the general store, its single light flickering in the window.

Mary rushed out from the living quarters in the rear, shotgun in hand. "For God's sake, lass, it's only me. I didn't think you'd hear me knock over the sound of the wind." Doc had been scared enough for one day. He was a born worrier—when he worked in New York his colleagues had warned him he cared too much.

Mary broke the barrel from the butt and carried the Winchester over her forearm as she led him to her father's bed. "Sorry, Doctor. Just the wolves from a while back. I'm still feeling edgy."

Doc could smell the problem before he laid eyes on Ian. He really did wear a nightcap. Doc took a split second to control a fond smile. "I brought food from the Black Diamond, Mary. You need it. So does your pa, but let's look at him. Can you bring me a light, please?" She replaced the shotgun beside the till and fetched the lamp from the window.

The wind was rising and sneaking its way around the bed. Doc felt the draught come up through the floorboards as well. Mary had placed pots around him on the floor so he wouldn't have to go far if he was sick or opened his bowels. She was exhausted with it all, especially because the only place she could get rid of the waste was out the back door, which was becoming more difficult to open as the snow built up. At least the mortuary had no incumbents for the moment.

"I know this will sound insane, Mary, but do you have any warm, fresh water?"

"Probably near the sink. Why?"

"I need you to take these pots outside and dump the contents. Then I need you to clean them and bring them back here. Then, and only then, I need you to wash your hands in that warm water. Do you have any lye soap?"

"Yes, but how will all this fix my pa?"

He showed her. Ian was sleepy and confused. Doc pointed to the man's sunken eyes and asked her to touch him. She took a firm grip of his forearm.

"I'd tell you that he shouldn't be cold in this weather, but it's a cold almost like the cold of a corpse. Is he dying?" Mary was whispering.

"Not now that I've seen him. We have to get him to eat something every couple of hours or so."

She vanished. Doc straightened the bed, lifted a few of the pots, helped Ian be sick, and actually hummed an old jig under his breath while he was doing so. It reminded him of happier times working in the big city—job satisfaction, some wag had called it. "Doing God's work" was what his late wife had called it. At this time he couldn't deny that what he was doing brought him joy. He knew that the eventual outcome was in the hands of the Creator. That's what doctors in the hospitals couldn't accept—they could be second-guessed.

Just wait, he thought to himself, until Pete finds out he's going to be a father. Doc was sure Poppy was in the family way, and born worrier that he was, he was concerned about her age and her possible well-being, let alone the well-being of the babe.

"Does he have the influenza?"

"No, Mary, but would you know if he's eaten anything or had a drink of something odd?"

Doc helped her replace the bucket and pot, one to receive vomit and the other for the other fluids. He stood to stretch, managing to further observe his patient. Ian's condition had come on suddenly. Hopefully it would leave quickly. His worries were unfounded. Ian didn't have the right tinge of cholera.

"Now please go wash your hands and then I'll do the same. All right, Mary?"

He heard her pouring water and the scrubbing she gave her hands. Perhaps she was using the extra time to think—he certainly hoped so, because he was going to need her.

"Your turn, Doc." She returned while drying her hands on a new towel she obviously had removed from the stock the store normally held for special occasions like christenings or birthdays. "Can't get cleaner than brand new, Doctor Fraser." She handed it to him.

When he came back Mary was sitting on the bed, a large blanket around her shoulders and her feet resting on a doubled-up buffalo hide. The girl was nothing if not practical.

"No more sickness, then?"

"Doesn't have anything to be sick with."

"Any soup in the house?"

"In the bottom of the pot. I'd get some well water from near the livery, but I'd be stuck in snowbanks by now. What do you think to melting some snow to add to it?"

"You go right ahead and melt the snow, Mary, but don't add it to the pot. The problem may have started in that very pot. Let's see what Polly has sent over. Maybe we can make a loose mash of something."

"Are you saying I cooked the wrong way?"

"No, Mary. I'm saying that at this time of year there may be something wrong with the well water—just as Doctor Snow discovered in London when he traced the cholera."

A tremendous frozen breeze arrived with a rush from the front of the building.

Mary extricated herself from her warmth and repeated her earlier dash to the front door—shotgun and all. Doc hovered behind her.

"Who the hell are you?" Mary had the gun at her shoulder, her red hair loose around her shoulders, her stance one of someone who meant all business.

"I'm Tom Wilson, ma'am." His hands were straight above his head, although he had no obvious weapon. "Mr. Buck sent me here."

"Put up your gun, Mary," Doc said. She hesitated. "I met this man earlier in the saloon."

She relaxed but not, this time, enough to break the gun. She held the muzzle down across her body.

"Is there something you want?"

"Mr. Wilson was one of Silk's gang, but the only one who saw the sense of knowing when it was all over." Doc moved forward.

"Can I put my hands down, ma'am?"

Mary nodded.

"Pat and Rye are going to bunk down in the stables. Mr. Buck and Pete said I should make myself scarce to the general store in case they killed me in my sleep if I joined them with the horses. I can pay my keep, miss, if you'll accept a set of silver spurs and a white-colored pipe."

"Mary? You there? Mary?" Ian's voice sounded raw.

"Right with you, Papa."

Ian was sitting up, stretching his hands out in front as if searching for something.

"I'm right here, Papa." She reached for his hands, almost flinching away when she felt the cold emanating from them. She sat on the narrow bunk, helping him to lie back on his pillows.

"Thirsty." His eyes closed again.

Mary scooted to the sink.

"Is that fresh water, Mary?" Doc called.

"Got it from the pump just yesterday."

"Nah, lass. Get some fresh snow for him. Let it melt in his mouth. I'll bet there's a dead animal or something that's turning the water foul."

"I'll fetch it for you, miss. I'm still dressed for the outside." Tom appeared to be a useful scoundrel.

Mary passed him a new bucket from the storeroom floor. "Be quick." She reorganized her shotgun, which had been lying beside the bed, and sat down with Ian again.

"I'll stay here and make sure he doesn't get lost." Doc could hear movement outside, and voices just outside the window. He recognized none of them, and there seemed to be about four plus Tom's.

Tom pushed through the door with the bucket full of snow. The other voices left in the direction of the saloon.

"Could be trouble," Tom said. "Tall Indian looking for Buck has gone to the saloon with another four of his kind. We met up with him as we were leaving his farm." Tom was visibly shivering. It wasn't every night a man went out a door and came across a small band of Indians. "Getting real cold in here. Stoke the fire a bit while I tend to Mr. Grant, will you?"

"Did I hear Tom say something about Indians?"

"They seem to be friendly with Buck, so I shouldn't be too concerned. Look, the snow is here. Why don't you put a drop on his lips to see if he'll lick any? If he can keep anything down at all overnight you'll have a pa on Christmas Day."

A gun exploded outside—at least it sounded like a gun, but then the sky lit up like the fireworks on the Fourth of July. Looking for safety, Tom jumped right into the bedroom to stare at everyone already there. "It's the dynamite, I think. It was starting to feel scratchy. Bet that's what the noise is."

"Where did you have it, man?"

"That MacLaren fellow said it'd be fine in the corral while it was still snowing."

Ian was licking frantically at his lips. Mary gave him more snow. Doc stood to place his buffalo hide over Ian's shoulders and asked Tom if he'd like to join him to see if the livery was still standing. He was no veterinarian, but there were far too many horses in those stables to be kept safe and sound. Beyond patching up one or two it would be down to Joss and Ryan to sort things—kind of an old-fashioned triage system he guessed, but it had worked with Napoleon (so he'd read), so it would work here: those in most need would come first.

"Keep on dripping snow into him, Mary." Doc hoisted his skin over his shoulders and jammed his well-worn, wool-lined fur hat on his head.

The two men braced themselves to open the low door. They stood still while they looked toward the livery and past the Black Diamond.

"Mary, come real quick, girl. Your pa will be fine for a moment or two. Come see all this." Another explosion shook the air. This time the fire of it went whizzing right past them toward the church.

"It's fireworks. It's bloody fireworks!"

Mary grabbed her skins, wrapping them around her head. Customers were pouring out of the saloon. With a quick glance at her pa to reassure herself, Mary joined the crowd standing in the middle of the snowdrifts and acting like children at a Sunday school picnic. Reverend Parker showed up, happy that the wild firecracker had whizzed past his church to land in the boneyard, right on top of the headstone of Miss Wright, who had most certainly not been right—for anyone.

"Silk would have been furious," Tom said. "He should have known better than to buy explosives from a man in a skirt."

"Say what?" Doc was grinning.

"Tell you sometime when it's not so cold." Tom was wrapped up in a warm memory.

Mark and his band of men were amazed by the colors and excitement, and caught up in it, too.

"We don't get the blame this time then," Mark said. The crowd tittered, surprised by Indians using English.

The wind dropped to nothing. Snow still fell, in large flakes and straight down. The fireworks stopped with the wind. The horses were kicking and screaming in the stables.

"Oh, my Lord." Joss and Pete ran to their charges. Ben told Buck he'd come to get him when they'd settled everything. Buck's head had completely stopped tingling. Rebecca and Froika guided him back inside.

"Can you see her, Mr. Buck?" Buck felt like he had when Duncan's puppies had to be shot, small and defenseless again.

Moon Feather was caring for Piddlin now. Her ears weren't twitching anymore, either. "It's a good thing we are not privy to our very own future isn't it?" Rebecca handed Buck off to Poppy, a woman who knew her business very well.

CHAPTER TWENTY-SEVEN

He sat with his right leg up on a chair and played with a bullet from his old Colt. The gun was now his only connection to his old life, and he had decisions to make.

It had been pleasant to get a glimpse of Mary, but he didn't envy her position of yet again having to nurse a dying relative. Doc said Ian could make it. He probably would, then. He shifted a bit in his seat.

"Should maybe get up to bed, lad." Ben had told him the news. Piddlin just collapsed, he'd told him. She'd been a brave old mare. Her saddle and accouterments would be kept in the stable until he needed them again. Ben had sat opposite him with one hand on the table and another resting on his massive knee, with tears in his eyes. Shona had come to stand behind him while he gave Buck the news. The scene could have been taken as one of domestic bliss if no one knew the conversation.

Poppy arrived with Pete. "C'mon, Buck. Toe will never heal if you don't let it. Bed. Ben and I'll steady you."

"You're going to your usual room nearest the facilities and the heat, but I'll put a pot and a basin in there for you." She pointed at Clara who, for once did what she was told without an argument. "Tell me, though, is it true you'll vouch for those Indians?"

Halfway up the stairs Buck stopped to reveal more of the new Mr. Ross: "As long as you can vouch for your men, I feel safe in vouching for mine." He hopped up another step.

"Well, Buck Ross, don't you start getting uppity with me or you'll get one heck of a cold breakfast."

He hopped up the last three stairs, stood on the landing, and grinned at her the way he would have last month. She tut-tutted, put her hands on her hips, and sashayed to her kitchen with a smile on her face. Now if she only felt a bit better in herself, she'd be happy.

Pete and Ben, duty done, returned to the main floor. They were bone-tired. Froika and Rebecca could share the double room overlooking the street. The Natives were happy to stay in the stables with their horses. If it hadn't been for the snow, their mounts would have made a better attempt to escape the fireworks, but now that they had settled in well the Indians were grateful for the shelter. They weren't concerned. They could pay with three wild turkeys, if that was agreeable. They were well informed of the history of Pat and Rye, who were busy on burial detail, transferring Piddlin and another horse that had died from the fright to the coral until they could be seen to in the daylight. The second was one of Silk's team. As the two remaining gang members had their own mounts they weren't willing to take responsibility for it. The buckboard could be left behind in case anyone wanted to chop it for firewood. The harnesses were very old and would be better buried with the horse or used for something else.

"That will make an astounding good Christmas dinner, don't you think Poppy?" Pete said of the turkeys. "If you clean 'em in the morning, hang 'em during the day, and cook 'em the next on the open fire outside, after Ben and I ready it, we could have a feast for everybody." Poppy nodded and then promptly fainted, falling straight back into Mark's arms.

"Better fetch the doc."

Tom volunteered. This was a solid town—a surviving kind of town. Validation was well named, he thought. He'd like to find a use for himself here, so he jumped the many drifts on the way to the store. This time he knocked before he entered, announcing himself as "Tom with the silver spurs." Doc thought it was a great nickname.

"What can we do for you, Tom Silver Spurs?" He was sitting in a chair beside Mary who was managing to tempt Ian into a bit of tatters and pork gravy, one tiny lick at a time. So far, things were staying where she put them, and she was gratified at her efforts.

"Poppy fell down asleep, kinda."

"That's not surprising." Doc turned back to Mary.

Doc rose slowly. You be fine for a bit, Mary?"

"Your day will never end, will it, Doctor Fraser." It was a statement of pure fact.

"With any luck I'll get back to my own house sometime tomorrow. At least the wind has dropped."

Tom and the doc were beginning to tramp down a path between the two buildings.

"Good thing Buck sent you to us."

"Better thing that Miss Mary didn't shoot me."

"Very true. That would have been an awful mess to clean up."

"You're a worrier, Doc. Just like me."

"Doesn't get us anywhere."

"Nope. Solves squat all."

They were silent until Tom held the swinging door open for Doctor Fraser. Poppy was sitting while Rebecca fanned her.

"Better have a look at you then, Poppy. No, in case anyone is worried"—he glanced at Tom—"Poppy doesn't have the symptoms of cholera. Now, I think I'd better have a look at you, if you think you can get upstairs."

She began to cry again. "There's nothing wrong with me except Pete's going to be a pa…"

The room sent up a massive cheer. Froika loudly announced a shot of whiskey for everyone who wanted it, and Pete (still thinking of his short stock) shouted, "No, please, no." He nearly fainted himself when he finally slowed down long enough to look at Poppy, as if he'd never seen her before.

"When?" He sounded like he'd been on the receiving end of a hanging rope that snapped before it finished its job.

"When what?"

"When you going to pop?"

Poppy howled this time.

"How do I know?"

Pete grabbed Doc's arm. "When?"

"I have to examine her first, Pete." He forced Pete's clutching fingers from his arm.

Froika passed the barkeep some of his own stock as he slapped him hard once on his back. Pete narrowed his eyes. "How did you know?" he asked, after taking a good slug.

"Rebecca is woman. She knows these things."

Pete guided him toward the bar as the doc helped a sniffling Poppy up the stairs. Rebecca, the only woman available to help, joined them.

"Not the condition of my woman, the condition of my bar. How did you know to cut it?" Pete was keeping his voice down.

"I cut nothing. See? No blood."

Pete showed him, from behind the counter, the good bottle and the homemade leftovers from last year's Leavenworth stock. He raised an eyebrow.

"Don't be fretting, Pete. Everybody has to cut their bar stock at this time of year." MacLaren rose from the table, joining them at the bar. Pete suddenly began to polish the wood.

"Hope you don't mind, fellas, but I'm going to turn in. Totally bushwhacked, I am, if that's not a bad turn of phrase for this part of the country."

Doc tried to come downstairs without making a scene, but with the news he had to share he had no chance at all. Poppy, probably for the only time ever in her life tagged along behind a man, and managed to look shy.

"It's going to be a summer babe." She blushed as she said it, looking hopefully at Pete, who kept polishing the same part of the bar.

"That's a good thing," Pete said. "Have some strength in him before the snow comes back next year."

No one fell for the bluster. People shook hands as if everyone had something to do with the event. Poppy went back to work in the kitchen to give herself something to do while she forced down her terror. Doc had warned her things could be awkward because of her age. It amazed her that he hadn't given her the credit for knowing her life and the life of her baby were already under threat. She'd always known somehow. It was like some kind of deep instinct. Was seeing the glimpse of the Native woman behind Buck a special kind of bonding? She began to pluck the first of the three turkeys Mark had left, grateful for solitude as she did it.

The noise out front was settling down. Pete damped the stove. Doc and Tom left for the store, the men and the Natives for the stables, and Froika and Rebecca for their wagon, which was parked just between the livery and the wood yard. They declined the offer of the bedroom. Poppy came forward, Pete put his strong arm around her, and they went to bed to make long, slow, silent love.

"It could be a girl, you know." She was lying on her side, Pete tucked in behind her, skins underneath and above to keep out the draft.

He puffed at that comment. "I bet this talk between a man and his wife…"

Poppy's eyes opened. "You'll marry me?"

He buried his head deeper into her back. "Be proud to."

This time she didn't let him see her tears, but she went to sleep quickly, her fingers locked into those cupping her breast. She got a shock when she woke up to see the sun shining. He'd let her sleep in.

Clara knocked gently. "Mr. Pete asked me to bring you some breakfast. Just coffee and a bit of bacon. I hope it's all right. Congratulations, by the way."

"You can be such a good girl when you've a mind to be. Did you give Buck a good time?"

"More than once." Clara was coy.

"Don't get used to him, girl. You've still got a job to do. Did you wash yourself?"

"Yes, ma'am. Didn't know a nearly eighteen-year-old couldn't find his way around a girl's body."

Poppy pulled her bodice down and adjusted her shawl. "Don't want you getting too cold, now. Doesn't surprise me Buck was new. Jenny kept both the boys from the fires of hell, as she called it." She began to brush Clara's long, dark hair. "No, they weren't like you, girl—fending for themselves at fourteen." Clara winced as Poppy pulled and dragged the tangles out. "When you going to be sixteen, then? January?"

"The first day in February, I think. That's what I'm claiming, anyway."

"Sounds and looks about right. Now, let me look at you." Poppy sat on the edge of her bed to prod and inspect her fallen dove. This new word, hooker, didn't have any class attached to it. It sounded dirty for some reason, so Poppy maintained three fallen doves during the high season. The rest of the time they'd come in if needed or get work for themselves—plenty of work in the stables at the moment, if they could stand the company.

"Right, you'll do just fine, now run along and turf Buck from his bed without getting back into it with him."

She heard bedroom doors opening and closing and the creak of snow on the roof. At mid-morning she came downstairs to air her room and check on the others, including Buck's. He was just coming out the door, so the madam asked him—as she escorted him back inside—if Clara had asked him to leave while she aired his room. He actually blushed, which would have been charming to anyone else, but not to the businesswoman in Poppy.

"Clara didn't come to you last night because she was fond of you, she came because I paid her to. Now, you can pay for the one she gave you this morning and you can give her a good tip. Another thing—I won't let you use her again tonight. All I need this winter is for my best girl to fall in love with a customer or worse, the customer to think that all he has to do is name the time and place. Been in this business too long to let a young affection develop, Buck. Now, downstairs, if you don't mind."

Buck asked himself why women all sounded alike when they put their foot down. Well, as long as they weren't shouting or crying. Feeling like he'd had a whupping, he hopped downstairs as fast as he could.

"Nothing as worrying as a female's cold anger, is there, lad?" Pete smiled up at the landing to cover his comment.

CHAPTER TWENTY-EIGHT

All the turkeys were hanging in the back pantry. Poppy opened the wooden boxes she had been guarding since the summer. Everyone was thrilled to see canned peaches and chocolate-covered almonds. This was going to be a good Christmas. Reverend Parker had called to ask for Clara's help in sweeping the church before the women of the parish came to decorate it. Poppy hadn't released her.

"If you need my girl to clean your church you'll pay her," she said, "unless you can open your heart enough to let her help in the decorations." If it was possible for Poppy to become more strident due to her pregnancy, she had, and the reverend took her point. Both she and Clara, and Shona as well, would join with the good women of Validation to dress the church for the Lord's birthday. Reverend Parker knew he was beaten. If any of the outlying parishioners managed to attend church tomorrow he would have to ask them to remember the story about who should cast the first stone.

"I was glad to hear of your summertime addition."

"Pete wants to jump the broom with me before then."

"I can announce it before the Christmas sermon, then?" The reverend knew people would count the months on their fingers when the babe was born three months earlier than expected, but the older ladies of the parish, such as Mrs. Pelowski and Mrs. McMenemy, most likely would be satisfied at the child's legitimacy as long as the intention was there.

"I think you'd better do that just as soon as those old busybodies get in the door," Pete said as he came upon them huddled near the big stove.

"Many felicitations, Mr. Tait. Well done!"

Pete let his belly laugh rumble again as he watched Poppy scoot for the kitchen.

"Do you think we'll get a decent amount of folk for the service?"

"We're preparing here for the whole McMenemy clan. Mrs. Haggerty has space and so does the general store if people aren't superstitious of the mortuary."

"Is Ian repairing to himself, then?"

"Give me a hand with this keg of good whiskey, will you, Reverend?" The two men rolled it to the end of the bar, enjoying the sound of the sloshing, knowing that after the New Year celebrations of 1862, there would be very little left to make that sound of wealth and prosperity—until next Christmas, anyway, when the war would have been over for a long time.

"Doc says," said Pete, "he may have made the wrong diagnosis. Could have been something he ate, he says. Better not say that too loud because Poppy and Mary would both be in a lather."

"Who the hell—sorry Rev—is making that noise?"

Voices were working themselves into a fine pitch outside on the snow-covered boardwalk.

"That's all Indians are good for: working with shovels. Who do you think you are MacLaren, bullying us?" Pat looked small trying to stand up to Ben. "They're warm and in the livery playing with the horses while we white men are out here freezing our nuts off shoveling the snow."

Ben folded his arms across his chest. "Apart from the color of your skin, there is another difference between you." He sounded bored. "You're alive because I let you stay that way in spite of breaking the law into more than one piece. They are alive because they should be. Never done anyone any harm, and as far as I can make out, don't intend to. I know if I returned your guns before I saw you out of town you'd most likely shoot me in the back." Readjusting his gray hat and feather, he placed his gloved hands on his hip and gun. "Now, digging snow will at least give your hands something to do before I give you your guns back in time to leave on the New Year if the weather continues to hold." He sighed. Ben grinned at them when he watched their faces fall all the way down to the hell that Pete had inquired about. He swung open the front door of the saloon.

"Morning, Reverend Parker. Good to see a man of the cloth actively looking for his flock."

"You'll be joining us tomorrow, then?"

"Wouldn't think so, sir. Not one of those that only goes on the high holidays. I'll keep well out of it if it's all the same." Ben threw a leg over a stool at the bar, near to Buck but with a good view of the door. "At least at Christmas and Easter I know where all the crooks and marauders are. All I've got to do is wait at the back door if there is one and the front if there isn't." Pete slid a glass of the good stuff toward him. "You wouldn't believe how many men want to be with their ma for Christmas; good time of year for a man in my profession." He slugged back his drink, not expecting it to be as powerful as it was. He gasped, looked at Pete, and asked him where a man in the back of nowhere got a malt whiskey as good as that.

"You can have another after church tomorrow." Pete had his hands stretched out from each other and leaned over the bar toward him.

"You threatening me, Pete Tait?"

"No. I'm bribing you."

Ben stared him down. Buck tried not to laugh.

"I'll think about it." Ben turned to face Buck. "How you doing today? Good sleep?"

Buck was so embarrassed about blushing he blushed some more. "Thought so, kid. Good for you. After everything you've been through there's nothing a man needs more than a good night's rest."

Ben stood up. "Mrs. Haggerty. How are you this fine day?"

Shona shook the snow from her coat and wrap before hanging it on the coat hook near the door. "Come to see if Poppy needs any extra help, and I need to have a word with Mr. Ross here, if he wouldn't mind."

Buck wasn't really used to being called mister just yet, let alone by a government official. He asked her if she wanted him to come to the office because she sounded so proper.

"That would be suitable, Buck. Just before dark if it's all right, please." She headed toward the kitchen.

"Could I have a word with you too, Mrs. Haggerty?"

"I'm run ragged at the moment, Mr. MacLaren. Can it wait till after church tomorrow?"

"That would be perfect timing, ma'am." He tipped his head, forgetting his hat was on the stool beside him.

"Women."

"I hope you don't include me in the tone of that word, Buck Ross." Mary looked tired.

"How's your pa, Mary?" Pete was genuinely concerned.

"Doc is outside checking the water troughs to see if an animal has crawled in to die. He thinks Pa's sickness may have come from there because he filled his flask from it. He's not really sure if he's got the cholera, which would be a blessing."

"Sit down girl, you look all in." Poppy had arrived from nowhere. "Yes, I'll get bean soup to you. Warm and fill you at the same time. Got to have you ready to eat a full turkey spread after church tomorrow."

Shona sat to join her. "You've heard that Poppy is to be a mother in the summer?" She said it quietly, but the men at the bar heard, nudged Pete again, nodding.

"The poor thing." Mary was quiet too. The men looked at each other again, this time like the little boys they could be sometimes. Poppy returned and Mary congratulated her as she squeezed her hand. Many words were said in the gesture—words only a woman could hear.

"I feel we should have an entry fee to this place today." Pete announced.

Froika and Rebecca piled in, carrying a huge tea urn. Silver it was, ornate with amazing designs of crowns and unicorns. They set it on a table nearest the kitchen so people could enjoy hot water for whatever reason at any time. Froika was the man in charge of the machine, but Rebecca's hand was the one small enough to light the tiny flame. Pete poured more vodka for the big man, more doctored whiskey for the rest. Poppy stirred the pot and served soup. Once again the music began, this time with Pete on the piano.

Everyone was beginning to look forward to the dinner tomorrow night.

Doc was the last to join the early Christmas Eve spontaneous shindig. He sat beside Mary, then left nearly as quickly as he'd come in. She got up to join him.

"Doc found a rotten white raven in the bottom of the trough near the horses. He thinks it was an accident. He's sure that's what's wrong with Pa." Ben helped her on with her wraps and coat. "Can you escort Mary a little way, Buck?"

Buck acquiesced because he needed to talk to her and take the opportunity to meet with Mrs. Haggerty. "I'll get my crutch. Just a minute."

"I'll join you," Shona said. "Help me with my things please, Ben?"

Ben adjusted Shona's coat onto her shoulders as she adjusted her scarf. As in the many sweet little stories Shona had read in her childhood—stories of girls falling in love with just one look—Ben's eyes took on a look. Her life would never be the same. She could hear nothing but the music playing in her heart. He tucked her into her coat and walked away.

Pete gave a low whistle as Ben came back to his seat. He could tell MacLaren may, just may, have met his match.

The small group struggled through the snow, but Buck really felt it, so Shona let him into the land office. Mary managed the last few yards on her own.

"Stoke the fire a bit, will you, Buck? I've got to dig out some papers." Shona let herself into her office as Buck, familiar with the peculiarities of her potbellied stove, got a good heat rising from it very quickly. She came back to sit in the big stuffed chair he had seen her spend so much time in last month. Was it only last month?

"Here you are, Buck." She moved some official-looking papers toward him and turned up her lamp. "I don't want to leave things lying as loose as they are. Things could fall into the wrong hands in this world of "it doesn't look like it belongs to anybody I'll have it." When the weather lifts enough I'll send a wire from Leavenworth to put through your claim to the farm. I also have to notify them that you are now the sole survivor and owner of the land in Boston." She watched the fire for a minute in the hope that this would affect him in the way she wanted. "You could be a very wealthy young man, Buck. Wealthy enough for even Ian Grant to give you his blessing with his daughter."

Shona had underestimated him. "I have had a conversation or two with Doctor Fraser. He agrees that I don't have enough learning to go to a proper school to be a doctor, but he says that young men these days can be taught the rudiments by another doctor and then go west, for instance, to set themselves up in a practice. I don't think Mary would like that idea—matter of fact, I know she'd prefer it if I asked her to go to Boston for me. I won't do that, either." Buck settled back. "This is a time where I wished I could smoke. It'd most likely be a good thing to be doing while I had a think about things"

Shona harrumphed. "Better go live with your friend Mark if you want to sit and smoke to think."

"Yes. I intend to. Just after Christmas, if he's agreeable. He said something interesting to me: men can't cure a great deal but we can heal just about anything."

"I'll have to think about that one." Shona said.

"When I was in the cave he told me I'd been called to be a healer. That I would be given the words to speak. I would have to learn to trust my inner voice, whatever that means."

"You've always trusted the voice in your mind, Buck. Why change?" Shona spoke softly.

"I have something for you." Buck changed the subject abruptly. He trickled the gold and silver bits that his parents had left with J. T. onto her side table. "I was going to ask you to try to straighten out the land for me. I'm going to ask Tom Wilson to work it for me. He's got a sister somewhere, but maybe she'd like to come here instead. If you could set up something that says he has to pay me a yearly cut of the crop for his trouble, I think that would be fair."

Shona had thought she'd have to walk him through everything stage by stage. Now she felt she was dealing with a high roller.

He stood up to shake her hand. "Moon Feather, remember her? She says to tell you that Jamie will always be faithful, but it is time for you to move on. He approves of your new beau because he knows you'll be kept safe. I guess he means Ben. That right?"

"Keep it to yourself, Buck," she whispered with her tiny hand over her lips.

"I will. Must go now. Ben's coming. Thank you, though—for everything. Maybe you and Ben could use the land in Boston. Let's see how things go." For the first time in days she noticed him scratch at his head.

"Bad weather again, Buck?" she called after him. He turned to her.

"Feels worse than that, Mrs. Haggerty. Stay warm." He pushed his walking stick into the snow ahead of him, and hobbled toward the stables.

Shona stood still. Someone had told her once that every cripple found his own way of walking. Buck proved it. She took his advice and returned inside. Unaccountably, she began to giggle. When Ben opened the door, knocking as he did, she looked shocked. "He told me you were on the way."

"Who did?"

"Buck. I thought you and I were going to meet after church tomorrow."

"Changed my mind. Have something to give you."

He'd folded the watch around and around in the red handkerchief he kept for good days. It looked small in his big hands as he delicately offered it.

"Is he dead, then?"

"Buck did it for me, after I demanded it back."

Shona stroked it while it was still in Ben's hand, eventually cradling it in hers after. She used her tears and a corner of his kerchief to dust off the back. She could read "Always Faithful" as if it had been etched in yesterday. The "J" in "Jamie" was fading into an "I." Ben gave her an arm to lean on, lowering her tenderly into her large, padded fireside chair.

"I can make a coffee if you want."

She looked up at him, his face just as she had pictured it. "How are you at making tea?"

CHAPTER TWENTY-NINE

Some people lit the torches again to welcome any Christmas revelers. Last year Pa McMenemy had created two sleighs and used two teams of his mules to bring all the family to church. The good folk of Validation had marked the way for them this year purely out of hope that they would try again. They lit another, shorter path in case the Pelowski family, in spite of their patriarch's queerly bent leg, managed to arrive again.

The town's few children, including the one who had taken exception to Ben, were playing happily in the shadows the torches cast, pretending the movements made by the flames were old Nick the Devil. It didn't matter about the snow or the war because Christmas was a constant. Everything faded away into bad memory once the season, short as it was, started. The day brought many of the outlying families together.

Ian was decidedly stronger. Mary was setting the shop to rights to make it clear that if the visitors needed anything, she would be able to supply it. The church was decorated and a corner appropriated for the box containing the organ. Reverend Parker, having seen the stamp that said "Property of the U.S. Government," decided it should be covered with an old bedspread and dressed with fruits of the season. In the event, Poppy designed a garland of turkey feathers combined with pine boughs. It prevented the congregation from feeling they had committed a mass act of breaking the commandment Thou Shalt Not Steal.

After closing the large wooden door of the Validation Church of God, the workers adjourned to the saloon. Joss—poor, hard-working, young Joss—returned to the stables to finish up before joining everyone else. He opened the side door and was thrilled to see the mules had arrived. That meant girls he could talk to, boys his own age, and someone sensible to talk about the war. Once again the sleighs were tucked tightly inside Ryan's wood shop.

"I will join with you at your celebration of your Jesus's birthday." Mark's language sounded stilted. He left the livery in a hurry and Joss thought no more about it.

Vengeance was kicking up—unusual, but maybe he wasn't used to sharing with mules. The stables were full to overflowing. Joss, looking around, decided that the accommodation was becoming dangerous to the well-being of his charges and made up his mind to see if Mr. Grant could house one or two of the horses donated, so to speak, to the town by the late Mr. Silk. Even that would make it less frightening for the big horses such as Vengeance and Black Silk. Buchanan appeared to be upset only if he didn't get his feed on time. Cantankerous old horse he was, but Joss was fond of him. He wandered slowly to the back, checking to make sure all had water and a mouthful or two of hay.

He heard the side door open.

"Needing a hand, Joss?"

"Thanks, Buck, but should be fine." Joss looked hard at him, almost desperate, when he deliberately took off his hat to give his head a thorough scratch.

"You're not, though, kid. Is he, Mr. Ross?" Vengeance snorted when he heard Silk's voice.

Buck dropped his hat to draw his dragoon. Joss felt a hand lift him backward and hold him around his neck—choking him.

"I shot you. You're dead."

"England breeds 'em tough in Yorkshire, lad."

"How'd you get here?"

"Nice family, the McMenemys. Told them I was desperate to see my brother Ben before I left this world for good. Especially as it was Christmas an' all."

"Brother?" Joss was choking, but Silk's grip was loosening.

"Thank the Lord, no, wee man." Silk smirked at the innocence of young Joss. "The McMenemys believed it, though. Felt right sorry for me they did, when I told them my horse and silver spurs were stolen along with my gun during the holdup. Asked them to drop me in here so I could sneak up on him later. Nice surprise for him like, after my little friend Joss helped me to clean up a bit first. "

"But Rye cut your pigtail—right to the scalp."

"Rye's a good man. Always does as he's asked. Helped me to sit against a tree before he left. Stuck a cloth of mine to my shoulder—high up you winged me, you little ferret."

Silk touched behind his head to confirm the tender area. Buck fired. The horses started to kick and scream in panic. Joss ran out the side door. Silk was still standing up on his toes, looking like the drawing of the plague devil in Doc's books. The only thing missing was the fire coming from his mouth. His eyes rolled back in his head. He found the handle of a scythe as he staggered under Buck's bullet.

The main livery door swished open as the curtain would move in a theater. Silk took on the appearance of the Angel of Death—big, dark, red mouth and skin. Mary screamed and ran back to the saloon. The sound of gunfire had brought most of the customers to the boardwalk. Froika and Rebecca were the only two that ran

The Mindwalker

toward the trouble to see if they could help. Mark and his fellows lurked in the background, willing to do as instructed if someone asked.

Silk hoisted the scythe over his head to bring it down on Buck. Pete stood on the boardwalk in front of the saloon—this time he didn't miss. The Angel of Death received the gift of an extra eye, a small red one, right between the two natural eyes God had granted him.

Moon Feather was standing at Vengeance's shoulder. She patted him and stroked his nose, settling him immediately. She told Buck he would be a good horse to replace Piddlin, whose head showed just over the other side of Vengeance's neck. Her ears were twitching, still in harmony with her longest, dearest friend. Buck's mind returned to the present moment.

"My head is still scratchy. Where's Pat and Rye?" He watched Silk sideslip down the support pillar, leaving a slim trail of blood behind him until he settled into the sawdust, one of his now badly ripped boots nearly falling off. Buck gave him a swat with his crutch, just to make sure. Bootmaker that he was, he absentmindedly tugged at Silk's toe. A gold coin fell out. He re-holstered his pistol and bent over to retrieve it. "Pete?"

"He's well and truly dead this time?"

"Yep, but he's left something behind on his way to judgment. Look at this."

"That's gold. I've never seen real gold money. I've only ever heard of it. Look in the light. There's a head on it." Buck let him examine it. "That looks like an eagle, or maybe two on the other side. Looks like a twenty-dollar gold piece to me, but maybe Ben will know or even Ian or maybe even Froika for that matter. Could be more." Pete handed the money back to Buck. "I'll pull off the other boot before his body goes stiff."

That was all there was, which disappointed Pete. They did find maps of all kinds in Silk's pockets—mostly of the sea, though. Maybe they showed where he had traveled. There was one, wrapped in a leather folder, which read, "San Francisco, South America, the Cape, and Cuba into New York." It was stamped "S.S. Central America," but it meant nothing to anyone, especially since it looked like it had been left in the rain. Buck wrapped the coin in it and returned it to the brown folder. Silk had kept a copy of his wanted flyer.

"Probably real proud of it," Buck commented. "Good thing I listened to my itch. Wouldn't have been dressed for this party otherwise—how did you know to come in here?" He and Pete rolled Silk onto an old tarpaulin and proceeded to drag him from the stables.

"Mark came to get us. He'd seen the bastard slinking into the building, couldn't believe his eyes, thought as Indians tend to do that the ghost of Silk had come to haunt you and came to tell us. Poor man couldn't even talk right."

"I thought the same when I saw him." Joss's small voice surfaced from just outside the livery door.

"You tell Poppy I've sent you to have a small good, and don't forget the word, *good*, whiskey. Tell her I think you've aged a couple of years."

Pleased at the compliment, Joss helped Buck close the door and then scooted for shelter.

"You're taking all this in your stride, aren't you, Buck? Maybe Ryan's right about you being born old."

Ben was standing at the livery door, trying to calm the ladies especially. "Not fit for women's eyes, just go back to your toddies, ladies. The menfolk will see to this mess." He was trying to sound calm, but even Ben couldn't prevent the shake in his voice.

"Look, Pete." Mary finally showed up again. "Is that the other two, that Pat and Rye?" She pointed toward the church, where two obviously male shadows were silhouetted by the torches. Their intent was clear—fire the church. People started running toward them, preventing Pete from getting a clear shot. He shouted his frustration, but no one listened, so he joined the melee. Rye had lifted two of the torches and begun to dance with apparent joy as he tried to set the door on fire. Pete was close enough but still couldn't fire with any safety. Ryan, of all people, was directly in his sights as he tackled the little bastard. Others came to help by piling on top. As all gangs are, once one was gone the other followed—this time the nearest, quickest to land Pat was Tom Wilson.

"Not a good idea, idiot." Tom had his forearm across the freebooter's throat as he was struggling to escape. He wasn't particularly interested in his old accomplice's opinion of him—being called a cretin didn't affect him one way or another.

The fire hadn't taken any kind of a hold. Now the biggest problem for the restless town of Validation was what to do with these two morons. Lynching was bandied about—but not on Christmas Eve, surely. It fell to Ben, who people felt would know about these things. He put on his large, gray hat with the eagle feather in it and tied each of the recalcitrants across the back of one of Silk's old team horses. He prevailed once again on Pete and Buck, who asked Joss to help him saddle Vengeance—his well-named replacement for Piddlin.

They took Pat and Rye deep into the woods and behind a strong wall of last year's sunflower stalks. Slapping the rumps of the horses to keep them out of the way, they forced each man to his knees, first one and then the other, and wasted, as Pete referred to it later, a bullet on each of them. At this time of year, all sorts of animals would enjoy clearing the mess.

People in Validation heard the shots and stopped on their way back from the church, then nodded and kept going, justified in their decision to let McBride and Carp go to the Lord on his birthday. The men rode into town three abreast. The loose horses, creatures of habit, trailed along behind them without any fuss so all returned to the overcrowded stable within minutes of each other. Doc was waiting.

"Good time for you to start your training, Buck. Might mean I can join everyone at service."

"You definitely decided on being a sawbones, Buck?" Pete sounded fascinated.

"We can never get enough real ones where I come from. They're mostly quacks." Ben was most definitely impressed.

Buck dismounted from Vengeance, using an overturned bucket as a step down to the floor.

"Not going back to the farm," Buck said. "Hope to volunteer for the medical side in the war if it's still happening and once my six months is up with the doc. Kansas men are volunteering like the war won't be won unless they're accepted, and at once. I said before, I'm no shirker. I can't march, but I can do my bit."

"Come on then, Mr. Ross, let's get you started. First help me make sure Ian is as able for church in the morning as he says he is. Come with me then, lad. Your killing career is officially done, your healing one is about to start."

"Leave you to it then, Doc." Ben, hearing about medical matters in such a clinical way felt his stomach lurch, which reminded him he needed something to eat. God, it was dark.

Pete wheeled in behind him, catching Joss's collar. "You too, laddie. Enough for one day. Thought you were having a drink of whiskey? Come with me to get some real grub into your belly. Where's Ryan got himself to?"

"I'll find Ryan and get him to bed down the horses again."

"Just thinking that maybe Mr. Grant could take the two you had with you in the woods earlier. There'd be more room here."

"You're a real forward thinker, aren't you, Joss?" Ben, although he would never admit it, had taken a fondness toward the boy. "As I said, I'll find Ryan and see if we can tuck these two in behind the general store. Go with Pete and have that drink."

"We're going that way," Doc said, "so I'll tell Ian that his stable has guests over Christmas. If Tom's there, maybe he can set things up."

Tom certainly was there, and was more than happy to be put to use. He wanted to make a good impression on the young lady with the beautiful red hair. He was only ten years older, well nearly fifteen really, but he knew he was capable of cleaning himself up to standard if he needed to, and for Mary he'd buck up his ideas.

Ian was relaxing in one of his wicker chairs, pillows padded around him, a blanket over his legs, and a fire going well in the stove. Mary was resting in the chair opposite.

"You're tired to extremes, young lady," Doc said. "Get to your bed, please. I'll leave Tom here all night if you want. The tackle he placed on his old mate was enough to convince me you'd be in safe hands. What do you think, Ian? You happy for that?" Doc had pulled up a stool to sit at eye level with his patient. "Buck has started his Doctor training tonight. He is here to listen and learn."

Buck was mesmerized by the effect Doc was having on the atmosphere of the room. Even Moon Feather stood absolutely still, watching his work, nodding very occasionally.

He asked a number of questions, seemed pleased with the answers, took Ian's pulse, listened to his heart with a cone thing, patted his patient's knee, and proclaimed him fit for church in the morning. He would have to wait to see if he'd be able to partake of a full Christmas meal. Doc always looked so worried; it was the only time Buck had noticed it. Maybe being older, having to pay more attention to detail made him more observant.

Doc turned to Mary. "All you need, and very badly, my girl, is a good night's sleep. I would leave Buck, but he needs sleep too, and he'll be at my house for the next few months while I teach him.

We'll have to get a hurry on because the war will most likely be long over before he gets a chance to fix a wound."

Tom returned to say the two horses were warm and comfortable. He wasn't all that sure if Annie was happy to share, but they'd cope. He was smiling down into his boots.

"Tom, you're on duty here tonight, if you wouldn't mind. I need both of them to have a good night of solid sleep. Could you see to that? Just keep the fire going enough to take the edge off the cold. Now, Buck and I are going to check on Poppy and maybe even see if the Pelowski family has managed to get here so I don't have to go there to check on Pa Pelowski's leg."

He busied himself putting his instruments back in his bag, put his coat on, and signaled to Buck that he was to follow him to the saloon.

"I'll see Poppy on her own until you've got some experience, apart from the carnal variety, with women. You'll be staying with me, as I said, so I can go into Ian's case with you and explain why I got his diagnosis wrong. I can't tell you how glad I was, how glad I am. We don't ever need an epidemic."

The bar was heaving with heat and people but not as much laughter as there should have been. Even the McMenemy clan was subdued. Fear generally drained people once it passed. Buck found himself a seat at the bar, trying to make it apparent he didn't need or want to speak to anyone just yet. He took off his slouch hat and accepted a tankard of something warm.

"Is good Russian tea. Make you, as you say here, virile, I think. Give a woman a good time." Froika hugged him around the shoulders long enough to make Buck feel like he'd been adopted by a wild man from the far western mountains—the ones he'd heard of from the many guides taking migrants to the west. During the season he'd wondered if any of the guides had been there—ever.

Mary sidled up to him, trying to make her usually soft voice heard over the music and tumult that was beginning.

"What are you doing here? Doc told you to stay warm and sleep."

"So, you've decided to quit the farm and take up medicine, then." She got right to her point.

He looked at her, most especially her eyes. They were calculating and hard.

"Yep." He turned to face her, one hand on his good knee.

"Pa says I can marry you if I like."

"Really?"

She nodded gently, as a girl was supposed to.

"Well now, Miss Mary, that would be mighty fine except for one thing." Pete was clearing the bar now that he'd replaced his rifles above it. He was hovering over the conversation.

"What would that one thing be, Mr. Ross?"

"I'd have to trust you, and I don't. Did you hear about the land in Boston, the farm land, and the gold coin I found in Silk's boot?"

"What gold coin?"

"The one I'm going to give to Tom Wilson if he agrees to manage the farm for me. Maybe you should take a fondness to him." She slapped him, and not playfully.

"We've known each other nearly all our lives, Buck Ross. You should know me better than to think of me as one of those women." Her quiet voice was no longer as quiet.

"All I know is that before you nursed my foot, and I thank you for that from the bottom of my heart, you thought of me as strange and you told people you wanted nothing to do with me. Well, now I want nothing to do with you. My day hasn't been easy, please have the decorum to leave me in peace." He took a large sip of his tankard, staring right into her eyes over the lip of it. Moon Feather was as excited as he ever saw her get. Poppy came up behind him and whispered something in his ear. He hopped off the stool, turned his back on Mary, and returned to the table he always sat at when he was in the saloon. Ben and Ian were sitting there with the doc, who showed consternation when he noticed Mary leaving the establishment.

"What was she doing here?"

"Fixing to marry me. I told her she'd be better off with Tom."

"Thought you were sweet on her."

"She wasn't sweet on me, so I changed my mind."

"My, how things can turn." Pete was actually looking at his intended while he said it, but his words applied equally.

"That was your Indian guide again, wasn't it?" Poppy was still whispering in his ear. "I wonder why I can see her."

Without letting go of his tankard, Buck stood, bowed to his companions, and escorted her deeper into the saloon to get her away from as many people as he could. "You can see her because you are going to be a mother. Moon Feather will be with you when you need her. She will be at the birth of your daughter, so please do not worry overmuch, she tells me." Poppy nearly fainted again.

"I've got a girl?"

"Yes, and for my sake would you do me the honor of including the name Jenny in her name?"

Poppy had all sorts of thoughts racing through her.

"I'll call her Jenny Rose, if that sounds right."

Buck nodded and began to walk away, but it was as if he'd heard one of her musings.

"No. By the time she gets to that age she'll become a farmer's wife. She won't make her living as you have had to. Moon Feather says not to worry, so don't."

He slugged back the remnants of his drink, which made him feel stronger, and returned to the men. Rebecca was waiting for him.

"You will be good at this. You will never give information to anyone unless it is to help, but as for the real world? Learn to keep your feelings to yourself more. You're young. You have a healing journey to take. You will learn." She patted his chest. "May see you in church, may not."

CHAPTER THIRTY

The wind was rising, but Christmas Day did arrive just as God planned it. People rose from their beds or blankets. Children cried as if in competition. People brought food out from hampers and bags. The aroma of fresh coffee announced that Poppy and her girls were on duty in the kitchen. No one rushed to anything. People smiled on Christmas Day. Even if they suffered during the year, Christmas made them forget for a few hours. Christmas gave them memories to keep them strong for what was to come, and hours in which they didn't have to be mindful of the past.

Buck spent his night comfortably with Doc, talking about the form of his new life. Mark knocked on the door in the morning light. Moon Feather stood behind him. He brought a gift of a piece of ash wood. It was, he said, for Buck to carve his new pipe—the one he would need to be a healer. Buck gave Mark Silk's white pipe. It intrigued the Native, who was pleased. "You finish this learning with the doctor, then you are welcome to come to learn from us. Like your own wise man has said, your time of killing is past."

"How do you know I said that?" Doc was always wary of the inexplicable.

"One day you incomers will learn how to listen to the wind."

Doc cleared his throat. Mark bowed and took his leave. Moon Feather clapped her hands for some reason not obvious to Buck.

"We'd better get going up to the church, don't you think?"

"See what Reverend Parker and his harem have been up to."

"What's a harem?"

"A group of women, usually wives."

"More than one wife?"

"The Arabs can have more than one, they tell me." Doc put away his small plate of bacon.

"The reverend isn't married, though."

"Dear Lord, no, but I assure you if any of the women living close to Validation town could talk him into it he would be married before Easter 1862, let me tell you."

"This marriage thing sounds like a gamble."

"Pick the right girl for the right reasons and you'll win the gamble, boy. If not you'll lose every day for the rest of your natural life." Doc opened the door thinking that Buck still needed someone to give him a special chat. After everything—losing his parents, his aunt and uncle, nearly killing his cousin, losing his best horse, and then definitely seeing an end to a killer—he remained an innocent. A boy couldn't stay innocent in this land, not these days, anyway.

The door of the church was ajar, sweet smoke emanating from inside. The Natives lit sage and sweetgrass as people filled the pews. Reverend Parker was at the front, Bible in hand, scarf with embroidered crosses on each end of it. "His harem has been busy this year." Doc nudged Buck as they sat down near the back, as far away from the single or widowed ladies at the front as they possibly could. Mary, Ian, and Tom sat behind them.

"What?"

"Keep your voice down, I'll tell you later."

Pete, Poppy, and her three girls joined the congregation, setting off a rustle of skirts in the front seats. Buck stood and motioned to Doc. He joined his friends and sat so close to Clara a hair couldn't get between them. He held her hand, thus turning Poppy's head. He smiled, she glared, he grinned, and Clara just blushed and looked at her boots.

The McMenemys arrived, even the oldest member. They were made very welcome, especially by the reverend.

Froika and Rebecca entered quietly.

"I would ring the bell, but as we all know, it snapped under last year's ice, so Ben—you're last in with Mrs. Haggerty there—will you check the street to see if there are any latecomers? No? Right, well, let us pray." Ben closed the chapel door, locking in the heat from the tiny wood burner and the press of bodies.

The service proceeded wonderfully well, even though the children, not being used to church, made a noise during the reading and praying bit. Most of them got their Bible studies from their parents and then the good reverend himself when he dropped in during the summer season—mostly.

"Now, before we leave to feast at the Black Diamond I have an announcement or two. The large box at the front is indeed an organ. It is, as most of you suspected, stolen property of the U.S. government. Mrs. Haggerty has agreed to handle the problem, so will send a wire as soon as the snow lifts and someone can be sent to Lawrence."

"I think the government may be too busy to be worried about an organ, Reverend," someone said. "Let's hope so." Several people nodded, and someone muttered something about it not being stolen guns, thank the Lord.

The good reverend rustled about and cleared his throat.

"Would Miss Poppy Diamond and Mr. Pete Tait please stand to be recognized? These two are to jump the broom or the rope whatever they prefer or is to hand at the time, at the grand party we will have on the first anniversary of this Great State of ours." A great cheer went up. No one knew if it was for Kansas or the happy couple, and no one really cared.

A buzz started as the congregation began to leave. "Before you go," the reverend raised his voice, "if anyone is contemplating marriage, please let me know in time for the service on New Year's Day." Buck did not meet Mary's eyes. Chuckles were heard. A buzz of gossip would follow the group as they headed to the saloon for Christmas dinner.

Buck, Ben, and Shona stopped at the land agent's office before they continued to the festivities.

"I have something for you, Buck." Ben presented him with Silk's gun, holster, and knife.

"You keep that evil gun, Ben. If I were you I'd just melt it down to nothing. Let the holster rot with its owner, but the church needs a good cross and Piddlin needs a memorial of some kind, so I'm grateful for the knife even if using it to carve something may be regarded as a sacrilege by some." Buck sounded sad. He left to catch up with Tom and there, in the middle of Validation, in front of Ryan's wood yard, Buck made arrangements with him to take over the farm. There were two conditions. First a yearly rent—not a cut of the profits—and second that he never change the farm's name. Buck passed him the folder with the coin in it.

"This will help rebuild the house and stable." They shook hands on it as Buck asked him to clear the titles with Mrs. Haggerty. Mary and her father were coming up the still snowy road with the good reverend so Buck touched the brim of his hat, and gave them a nod of respect before he left for the festivities.

The joyful noise coming from the Black Diamond was bound to attract everyone whether they were of good cheer or not. Two of the ladies from the front pew, a Mrs. Christianson and a Mrs. Dawson, were trying hard to keep the hems of their long dresses out of the snow without showing an ankle, but weren't succeeding very well. Buck and Ben made a show of averting their eyes to enable the ladies to maintain their dignity. Someone held the swinging doors open in order to prevent them getting caught. The men continued behind to help them out of their wraps. Not a single word was exchanged, not even a "thank you" from the two grand dames. They looked for the two seats near the fire they had demanded of Poppy.

"Over here please, ladies." Poppy seated them at the bottom end of the door, exactly where Silk sat. There was no obvious draught from the doors, but Poppy was hoping that the cold would sneak up through their feet so they wouldn't stay long enough to make others any more uncomfortable than they already were.

Mrs. Dawson started the inquisition by asking when Poppy was expecting her child. Poppy answered honestly but was rescued from further probing by Shona, who politely asked if she needed any help serving the dinner. "Yes, now that you're in the family way you should get some extra help, shouldn't you?" Mrs. Dawson blustered and shook. Shona dragged Poppy from the table, both of them giggling like children.

"If this wasn't Christmas Day..."

Pete banged his boot on the bar. "Sshh, everyone. Reverend Parker will say a grace and then we'll eat. Sshh."

Reverend Parker had done this many times. He always waited for silence to settle. Aware that the food might be getting chilled, he kept his grace short and to the point. Sometimes he was even humorous, so the diners actually looked forward to his words on the chance they were granted another reason to feel warm about this day.

"Forgive us sinners while we eat our dinners, thanks be to you, oh Lord, and may your birthday be as happy as our Christmas. Amen."

The roomful of people roared in appreciation, then went quiet when the door opened and let in another blast of cold air.

Persephone McMenemy was pointing outside. Her mother moved to catch her but stood up, looking outside. She turned. "Come and see. Quick."

"I've been all over this country and at different times of the year, but I didn't know you could have a rainbow in Kansas in winter." Ben was awestruck. The others came outside without their coats and drank in the beauty for as long as it lasted.

"They say a rainbow is a promise that a bad thing will only happen once, Mr. Buck." Persephone put her tiny cold hand in Buck's. Buck had never seen Moon Feather from the back, but she was standing right beside the child. She turned to him. "Your luck will turn to the good now, Mr. Buck the Mindwalker."

He stayed on after the others returned inside, sharing his space with Moon Feather and Piddlin for a few more minutes. He felt himself physically expand into his new life. He turned to go back in, seeking an extended discussion about pipes and carving ash with Mark and his friends.

Printed in Great Britain
by Amazon